In It For
The Long Run

The Mike Snow Trilogy

A V TURNER

In It For The Long Run

The Mike Snow Trilogy

First published in 2017
A V Turner

ISBN No. 978-1978130722

Snow on the Road and *Snow's Angels* previously published as
E-books in 2017.

DEDICATION

To Dad and Bessie, with love always.

And to Trentham Gardens, in your beauty I found inspiration.

PROLOGUE

When male nurse Mike Snow learns that the woman of his dreams is soon to be single, he sets out to win her affections in the most extraordinary way.

Through running.

With only his cat, Sidney Greenstreet, to confide in, he plans an elaborate plot to win her heart, but the path of true love seldom runs smoothly.

Set against the backdrop of Trentham Gardens, this unusual love story charters Mike's journey through life, love, friendship and distance running.

* * *

Snow on the Road and *Snow's Angels* were the first two novellas in the trilogy. These have been published separately as E-books and available to download from Amazon. *Snow on the Summit* is the final in the series and all three stories follow in this book.

Snow on the Road

A V Turner

Book 1 of "In It for the Long Run" - the Mike Snow trilogy

CHAPTER ONE

If there was any time in his life, that Mike Snow had to show a completely calm exterior, whilst jumping for joy inside, it was most certainly today. He was sitting in his local pub with best friend of ten years, Jim, who suddenly announced that he and his wife were no longer an item.

Trying really hard to show concern rather than a big beaming smile took every ounce of acting skill he could muster.

"Oh mate! Seriously? You never said anything about you guys having problems," he said, sympathetically.

"Er, well, we haven't been having any, Mike to be honest. It's me. I've sort of been seeing someone else, you see. Laura found out by accident." Jim stared guiltily into his pint glass and his face coloured slightly.

"Bloody hell, Jim. How long?"

"Erm, about a year."

An awkward silence fell between them, and Jim played nervously with his beer mat.

After what seemed like an awfully long time, Mike was the first to speak.

"How's Laura taken it?"

"Not brilliant, has to be said. Especially as it's Gracie's teacher," he replied, flushing again.

"Jesus, Jim. What a mess! I just don't know what to say."

They sat in silence again, until Jim made the excuse of going to the Gents', leaving Mike alone in the busy pub to reflect on their conversation.

At no point in their ten-year friendship had Jim ever given Mike reason to believe that he was anything other than totally loyal to his wife and 9-year-old daughter. They had seemed a very happy family, the perfect couple.

Mike himself was no stranger to divorce. Now 51, he had been single for the past 9 years, and apart from the odd girlfriend here and there, was happy to be so. At the age of 42, he had taken up running as a hobby, and it had pretty much taken over his life. Apart from his job as a nurse in the local hospital, he lived a pretty simple existence: work and running. He'd even set up his own club, The Trentham Trotters. He liked to call it a club, but it was quite simply a group of people he knew from either work or socially, who met once a week for a run 'round the streets. They usually did between 3 and 5 kilometres each time, and it was always a relaxed social affair.

But the thing was, Mike had a secret. One he had kept for a very long time, and not ever mentioned to another living soul, apart from his cat. Mike had been in love with Jim's wife Laura for 5 years. Never once had he told her, or given her any reason to suspect it. Quite the contrary in fact, he had pretended *not* to like her very much, to put everyone completely off the scent. So you see, the news that their marriage was now over, and even better news that Jim had another woman, was music to Mike's ears. He just had to hope that Laura felt the same way, but convincing her that he actually *did* like her, was going to prove tricky. He had a long journey ahead of him.

He allowed himself a few thoughts about her whilst Jim was in the Gents'. Whenever he did think about her, he felt warm and happy inside. A smile appeared on his lips. Mike's love for Laura had grown over time, and was not the lustful type that you would expect. No, he was most definitely a hopeless romantic, not a macho male. More of a Mr Darcy than a James Bond.

Suddenly, Jim was back at the little table they had shared in the corner of the pub by the fire, and he resumed the conversation.

"Look mate, I know you are probably thinking I'm a real shit for doing what I've done, and I'm not proud of myself. I will quite understand if it makes things awkward as far as our friendship goes. I'd hate to lose you as my best mate, but it's your call."

"Jim, you've been very good to me over the years, both of you, but it's come as a bit of shock really. Let's just say it might change the dynamics a bit for a while. I'm sure things will settle down in time."

"Ok, good, yeah, yeah, I appreciate that. Another pint?"

"No, I'm good thanks. Running at 7 tonight," Mike replied.

Jim strolled off in the direction of the bar, leaving Mike's head buzzing with quiet excitement.

Mike left the pub an hour later and walked the half mile back to his house. He shared his home these days with a very large tabby and white cat, called Sidney Greenstreet. An unusual name for a fat, lazy moggie you might think, but Mike loved the old films from the 1940's, and so when he had rescued Sidney from the RSPCA it seemed appropriate to change his name from Whiskers to something a little more original, and it suited him very well.

Mike quickly checked his watch, fed an eager Sid, rubbed his ears for a few moments, and then ran upstairs to change into his running gear. He had exactly half an hour before his running club, the Trentham Trotters met up for their weekly run.

As it was an unusually mild evening for the middle of April, he opted for his favourite running top and his usual shorts. Checking his fitness watch, he went back downstairs.

It suddenly occurred to him that he hadn't looked at his phone all day, so he checked that as well. A lump rose in his throat.

A text from Laura.

'Ok, let's take this nice and steady, don't bugger it up before you've even started,' he thought to himself. Slowly, slowly catch ye monkey.

He took a deep breath and opened the text.

"Hi Mike, I guess by now you will have heard the news. Just wanted to say, that it would be sad if we couldn't keep in touch. I don't want you to feel awkward about staying friends with both of us. I know your loyalties lie with Jim rather than me, but I wanted you to know you are always welcome here. Grace would miss you."

"Oh Sidney, if only she knew how very wrong that was. My loyalty will always be with her." Mike sighed and contemplated his next move. He caught sight of himself in the hall mirror.

At 51, he wasn't in bad shape. A trim physique, but not very tall, he barely reached 5' 9". He was greying at the temples a little more these days, and his sandy hair was receding rapidly. His heart sank. Jim was quite the opposite. Tall, dark and muscular, handsome in a rugged sort of way.

"She ain't never going to be interested in me Sid, no way," he said out loud, sucking in his tummy. Sidney Greenstreet purred, churped and rubbed affectionately around his master's legs.

Mike checked his watch, ten to seven. Bugger, time to go. He would think about how he would reply to Laura's text on the run.

* * *

"Evening all!" Mike shouted cheerfully as he ran up to the crowd of waiting runners.

"Sorry I'm a few minutes late," he apologised, rubbed his hands together and smiled.

The Trentham Trotters were an eclectic bunch of people. They ranged in age, size and ability. Ten strong, and consisting mainly of women, the male content reached only 3. But Mike was grateful for anyone to join them. A strong runner himself, he generally ran with a guy called Keith, who at 64, was the oldest member. Around the same height as Mike, but slimmer and more athletic. Nice enough bloke Mike thought, but fancied himself a bit with the ladies, particularly the younger ones in the group.

"Got your legs out tonight girls, and very nice they are too, if I may be so bold," Keith remarked as some of the female runners had decided on shorts. He rubbed his hands together and smacked his lips, as if he were about to tuck into a large roast dinner.

A couple of the younger girls giggled.

"A lot nicer than yours, it has to be said Keith, and less hairy," exclaimed Pam. She was the mother of the group, 60 years of age, built like a tank, and strong as an ox. She stood, hands on hips with a 'don't mess with me' expression on her rugged, weather-worn face.

"Right then people, everyone ready? Three or 5k tonight?" asked Mike, desperately trying to diffuse a possible sticky situation.

A general rumble of positivity rippled through the group, and they decided on a 5k. Mike and Keith generally paced in the middle, the younger girls ahead with the young guy Matt, chatting and giggling, and Pam bringing up the rear. Mike was always mindful never to leave anyone too far behind. Regardless of their ability, he was nothing if not supportive.

"All ok back there, Pam?" he shouted, slightly out of breath. "If you need to walk a bit, just tap me on the shoulder."

They were already 2 kilometres in and he could hear Pam's rasping breath behind him.

"A-ok boss, happy to keep going," she replied brusquely.

At 3k, Mike felt a tap on his shoulder. "Need a wee," Pam declared. "Shan't be a tick, just popping behind this hedge here." Mike slowed right down and asked Keith if he wouldn't mind catching the others up to let them know. Keith was happy to inform the girls in shorts of the situation and ran off with a renewed vigour.

"I'll keep watch for you Pam, make sure no one's coming," Mike reassured her.

"Right oh!" exclaimed Pam and she disappeared behind a hedge. After what seemed like an awfully long time, and a lot of huffing and grunting, Pam reappeared.

"Thanks boss, all done. Ready to soldier on?" she asked, giving him a playful but hefty punch on the shoulder.

Mike winced a bit because Pam gave a strong punch. He dreaded to think what would happen if they were in a bear hug situation.

"Absolutely, let's go. I think the others are at the top of the hill waiting for us to catch up. Not far to go now," he smiled.

"Righty ho!" she replied cheerfully and set off at top speed leaving Mike a little way behind, with a great view of Pam's knickers hanging out the top of her running tights.

CHAPTER TWO

After a brief chat, and a pep talk by Mike, the group bade a breathless and sweaty farewell, promising to meet up the following week. The attendance had always been pretty good, and only two or three had dropped out in the beginning. Mike decided to have a warm-down, gentle jog home. On the way, he thought about what he would put in his text to Laura. He had left a suitably cool gap between her texting him and his reply, so he pondered thoughtfully on what he would say.

Once home, he showered and changed, gave Sidney Greenstreet a treat or two, and sat down in his lounge with a glass of wine.

He took out his phone and looked at it blankly. Sidney sat staring at Mike from the middle of the lounge, and churped, '*Go on Dad, text her. Go on!*'

'Right then, here goes," Mike said out loud.

"Hi there Laura, (*too familiar? No, no pretty good so far*) Thanks for your text, sorry for late reply, been running with the Trotters this evening. Be great (*no, no too eager*) be good to keep in touch. If you need a chat any time just ask." Mike pressed send.

Within two minutes he had a reply.

"Thanks Mike, means a lot."

Ah. Ok. That had been a very short conversation, and he felt a little crest-fallen. A long distance silence hung in the air between them. Laura and Grace lived only half a mile away, easy walking distance, but he felt like they were a hundred miles apart at this moment in time.

His phone suddenly lit up again, and his heart leapt. Laura again.

"Not free for a chat now by any chance, are you? Just wondered if you fancied popping 'round for an hour before Grace goes to bed. Be really nice to see you."

What Mike really wanted to say was. "I'll be 'round in five." But he held back a few minutes.

He looked at Sidney, and Sidney returned the stare.

'Oh bugger it,' Mike said under his breath. Would it seem too eager to be going 'round there after only hours of discovering Laura was now, in essence a free agent? Probably. He thought for a moment, then replied.

"Sorry, not available tonight, but I'm free Friday, if that's any good?" *Send.*

Ten very long minutes later, came her reply. "Ok, no problem. Seven-thirty at mine Friday?"

"Yep, that's fine," he replied.

Well, it was a start. A slow one, but a start nevertheless.

The next three days saw Mike at work. He loved aspects of it, but the hours were long, and sometimes, it seemed a thankless job. He had worked for the NHS for 20 years and would probably continue to do so until he retired. Working on a colo-rectal ward, there was seldom a bed unoccupied.

By happy coincidence though, one of his colleagues was Pam, from the running group. Despite her brusque and tough exterior, she actually had a heart of gold, and Mike was immensely fond of her.

"Top 5k last night boss," Pam whispered as she came back to the main desk after doing a set of obs on a new patient.

"Not a bad one, Pam, I think everyone really enjoyed it," he smiled.

"Are we going to enter the Trentham 5k again this year? Jolly well love doing that. Raise a bit of money for the Stroke Association," she said.

"Funny you should say that actually Pam, I was only thinking it'll soon be time to register. I'll check with the club on Monday night, make sure everyone's up for it."

"Righty ho then," she said and went off to check on her new patient.

It was then that Mike thought of a totally brilliant plan.

* * *

When Mike returned from his shift that evening, he mulled over his next move, not only with Laura, but with his running group, and hatched a very clever plot to combine the two.

He changed out of his uniform into his running kit, fed Sidney and set off for his one lone run of the week. It was time he had to himself to think about things. It was dark, but the street lights gave him enough to see by. It was peaceful and quiet, no one around. He loved this route. It calmed him after a stressful shift at work, and so aided a really restful sleep.

His plan was a fairly simple one, if it went in the right direction. Go to see Laura and Grace tomorrow night, drop into the conversation that it would be good for Laura to start running, help her mentally cope with the stress of the divorce. Start her on a couch-to-5k regime, enter her into the Trentham Gardens 5k, spend lots of time with her, coaching etc. She gets addicted to running, she eventually falls for his charms, and *Bingo, she's his forever. Sorted.*

Friday came all too soon, and by 3pm Mike was already nervous. He had only seen Laura briefly the previous month, and then things had been different. It was only in the last week that Jim had turned everything on its head. Quite how he was going to be on the excitement score by 7.30 pm that night was anyone's guess. He had already chosen what outfit to wear, light on the aftershave, play it cool and casual, don't make too much eye contact, be nonchalant. What time was it now? Three-twenty pm.

It was going to be an awfully long afternoon.

After one glass of wine, another change of clothes, mouthwash, and just a little bit more aftershave, he was ready and it was 7.10 pm. Time to go. Best not take flowers, that would look odd, so instead he had opted to call for something to give to Grace instead. Poor thing must be going through it, especially as her dad was now living with her teacher; very awkward.

Mike put on his jacket, checked himself in the hall mirror, said goodbye to Sidney and opened the front door.

"Hey mate, how you doing?" There on the threshold stood Jim.

Shit. Seriously, shit timing.

Mike stood completely transfixed, and his gentle, kind heart sank to his boots.

"You all right mate? What's up?" Jim laughed and they both stared at each other.

"Jim! Right. Yeah, I'm erm, yeah I'm ok. Just going out actually," he replied nervously. *'You complete bastard James Eddison,'* he thought to himself. *'You complete and utter bastard.'*

"Where you off to? Thought we could catch a pint, maybe something to eat?" he said.

"Well, I've got plans to be honest Jim, promised someone ages ago about tonight. You should have texted me earlier." Mike stood his ground.

"Right, yeah sorry mate. It's just that Julia is out tonight with her friend so I thought I'd call on the off chance see if you were free." Jim looked very disappointed, and Mike suddenly felt a bit sorry for him.

But something made Mike think. *'Hang on a moment. This is the guy who left his wife and daughter because he's been knocking off Grace's teacher. Now he's at a loose end one night, he suddenly comes crawling 'round looking for a mate to hang around with. Hmmm, don't think so. Stand up for yourself, Michael.'*

"Look, how about next week? I'm free then if you want a lad's night," he said.

"Ok, I'll see what Julia's got on. Maybe you could come 'round and meet her, have a meal." Jim was desperately trying to make normality out of chaos.

"Yeah, maybe," Mike replied fumbling with his keys, and locking the front door. "Gotta go Jim, I'll text you over the weekend."

Jim muttered an 'Ok' and walked to his car. "Have a good night, whatever you're doing." He threw the last sentence into the air for Mike to catch it, but Mike was already off down the road, in the direction of his local supermarket.

CHAPTER THREE

Mike was already fifteen minutes late by the time he turned up at Laura's house. He had virtually run 'round the supermarket looking for something to take Grace, and had come away with a Minecraft Annual, which he hoped would suffice. He knew she liked playing it with her friends, and was fairly sure she would like it. He also grabbed a bottle of wine for him and Laura to share.

Laura opened the door, and in Mike's eyes, light shone from behind her like sunshine.

'Breathe, Mike, breathe.'

She smiled, and Mike's legs turned to jelly.

'Play it cool, just act normal, not too much eye contact, remember.'

An awkward moment of *'Hi, how are you'* later, and Mike was inside their home. Grace was watching a DVD, freshly bathed and ready for bed. She leapt up off the sofa and ran into the hall to give Mike a hug. She was young for her years, and threw her arms round him playfully, but Mike detected an air of sadness about them both.

"Hey Gracie, look what dropped into my bag." He produced the book from the plastic carrier and she squealed with delight.

"Ah, wow, thanks Uncle Mike!" she said excitedly and disappeared off back to the sofa to have a look at it.

"So. How are you both," he said, looking at Laura with an expression of seriousness on his face. He didn't have to hide any emotions at this point, because his concern was real. They had been abandoned.

"Come on into the kitchen Mike, we can have a better chat in there. There's things I don't really want Gracie to hear."

Laura's kitchen was the real hub of the house, and Mike loved this room. Open plan, it combined working kitchen with a large sofa and a TV at the other end. So designed that Laura could cook and chat to her guests or family at the same time.

"Glass of wine? You walked I'm guessing?" she asked.

"Love one, thanks. Yes, left the car at home, nice evening so I walked it," he replied.

Whilst she was busy getting them both a drink, he allowed himself a few moments to study her.

She was certainly beautiful, there was no doubt. Blonde, with just a hint of auburn in her shoulder length hair, the pale blue eyes that he regularly dreamed of. He didn't even mind that she was slightly overweight, it only added to the whole package of the Laura that he loved. If only she knew how one smile from her made his day, and kept him going until the next time he saw her, which he hoped was going to be a lot more often. She reminded him so much of Shirley MacLaine, the film star from the old movies he loved.

There was so much love emanating from Mike's side of the room, that birds almost sang, and light shone from up above. Such was his pure, old fashioned genuine adoration for the lovely Laura.

She poured them both a glass of wine, and joined him over on the sofa. They sat at either end, a suitable distance apart.

"Before, you say anything Mike, I just wanted to say, thanks so much for coming over tonight, it really does mean a lot to the both of us. We so wanted to keep in touch with you, but I know it's awkward at the moment," Laura said.

"Well, it came as a bit of a shock to be honest, when Jim told me last week, but I'd like to remain neutral, because, as I said to him, you've both been good to me," he replied.

"That's such a relief, it really is. Shall we make a promise, not to talk about the split, just concentrate on good stuff? That way, you won't feel like piggy in the middle. There's plenty of things to talk about apart from that, and it could get boring and difficult for you." She stared at Mike with those pale blue eyes.

"That's a great idea," Mike said. "But, if you ever need anything, I want you to promise you will always come to me."

"Promise," she replied.

They both smiled at each other, and Mike's heart grew just that tiny bit bigger.

* * *

The evening had gone very well, and Mike had not

left Laura's house until just after ten-thirty. As promised, they had chatted about things other than the split, and he had found both Laura and Grace relaxed and happy, if a little empty and sad.

The best bit was that she had spoken at length about how she wanted to make a fresh start for herself and Grace, possibly move house, but stay in the same area. Laura had a very nice job in a florist, which suited her personality, Mike thought, being around flowers all day. Also, Laura had her parents living close by, which was handy. They were both 70, and very fit and active. They enjoyed a close relationship with Grace, and regularly helped out with childminding when Laura was at work. But Ron, Laura's dad had never been a big fan of Jim, and made absolutely no secret of it either. The news of their split had him virtually jumping for joy.

At the end of the evening though, Mike had put a proposition to Laura, and it hadn't gone down as well as he had liked.

"Listen, it's just an idea, but why don't you come along to the running club Monday? Give it a go, see if you like it. It's so good for you mentally, running. Helped me loads when I split up with Diane," he said.

"Oh, honestly Mike, I'm no runner. Really, I'd be absolutely crap at it. Wouldn't know where to start," she replied.

"Well, just give it a go, come the once and if you don't like it, doesn't matter, you haven't lost anything. We either opt for a 3k or a 5k depending on how we feel. You can do as little or as much as you like." He shrugged in a nonchalant sort of way.

'Come on Laura...'

"Maybe in a couple of weeks' time. I might. Just

let things settle down Mike, and maybe I'll give it a go," she said.

'Bugger.'

"Okay," he said light-heartedly. "They're a great bunch of people, you'd like them. We're training for the Trentham Stroke Association run in October, so you could maybe join us on that if you like." Instantly he regretted that last sentence, as the look on Laura's face was one of complete horror. He had been getting ahead of himself.

"Jesus, absolutely not!" she laughed. "I can't even run to the bottom of the garden, Mike let alone 5 kilometres round the Gardens. I do love it there though, as you know."

Mike did know. Laura's parents had bought her and Grace annual passes for Christmas, which meant they could go as many times as they liked for free. It was their favourite place in the world. Peaceful, serene and breathtakingly beautiful. Laura's favourite thing to do was go up there on a sunny day, have a short walk, coffee from the kiosk next to the café and sit on a bench, overlooking the lake, watching the world go by. Sheer bliss.

"Well, have a think about it, no pressure. If you wanted to do the Stroke run we could start you off on a couch-to-5k plan," he said.

When Mike left, Laura had hugged him for the first time ever. She wrapped her arms around his neck and he felt the warmth of her body against his, the faint scent of her perfume surrounded him, and he felt a lump like a brick fill his stomach.

"Thanks so much Mike, for everything. You are such a good friend."

'*I love you, Laura. Always will,*' he whispered in his head.

"Oh hey, no problem! That's what friends are for," he replied in a very jolly fashion and bade his farewell.

He got 'round the corner, out of sight and clutched his head with both hands in sheer frustration, letting out a stifled whimper. Then he walked home, thinking what to do next.

CHAPTER FOUR

Mike busied himself that weekend with the usual stuff, shopping, a couple of short runs, and on the Sunday he dropped Jim a text.

"Sorry about Friday, Jim. Are we still on for next week?"

A reply was an hour coming.

"No worries, matey. I think we might be going away Friday night until the Sunday. Fancy a pint mid-week?" Jim replied.

Mike texted to say that he could probably make the following week instead, as he had extra shifts, so they left it at that. Clearly, Jim was rather busy with Julia, and vice versa, because Grace had said she turned up to school late a couple of mornings, looking rather dishevelled, with a 'vampire bite on her neck'. When Laura told Mike over the phone, he flinched at that little snippet of information, but rather than sound annoyed, Laura laughed and didn't seem phased at all.

Monday came 'round, and it was Mike's last day off, and also that evening was running club. All the usual runners turned up, apart from one of the younger girls, and Mike gathered them all round, because he wanted to ask a group question.

"So, everyone, as we know, it's now April, nearly May, and getting to that time again, when we register for the Stroke Run at the Gardens. I've checked online and it's October 9th this year. Can you all make it? Guessing you all want to do it again?"

There was a general positive murmur from the group, nods all round. "Yep, Mike we're all up for it again," piped up Keith. He was someone Mike could always rely on to turn up on time, never let you down; game for whatever. He was dressed that evening entirely in beige, apart from sporting some very new running shoes in lime green. Keith would always jog on the spot when Mike was talking, Rocky Balboa style, throwing in some fake air punches just for good measure.

"Excellent. That's great news then. Registration normally opens 3 months before, so I'll remind you all nearer the time so you can enter by phone or online." He smiled. "Erm, Pam, you don't need the er..." he said quietly.

"No boss, thanks. Good to go," she replied.

"Three or 5k tonight?" he shouted.

"A few of us thought just a quick 3 tonight Mike, is that ok with you?" asked Matt.

"Absolutely, no problem at all. Three it is," confirmed Mike with a thumbs-up, and off they went.

Mike and 'Beige Keith' as he was affectionately known, stayed midway between the faster younger runners, and as usual Pam, bringing up the rear.

It occurred to Mike that despite the fact that Pam always sounded like she was going to collapse any minute, she kept up pretty well, and never missed a week. When asked, she said how much she looked forward to her 'weekly jog'. She loved the outdoors, and her rugged complexion confirmed this. Pam also loved brandy, but had never been known to combine the two.

Their weekly run over, Mike said the usual farewells, some words of encouragement and off they went, in different directions, full of feel-good endorphins.

He returned home approximately 15 minutes later, and followed his usual routine, change, shower, light tea. Feed cat. Chat to cat.

He had work in the morning, so an early night was called for, but he had a hankering to watch one of his old films, and 'Casablanca' was a favourite. He searched his vast DVD collection, picked out the relevant film, and took it upstairs with him and Mr Greenstreet to watch in bed.

Barely half an hour in, and Mike was fast asleep, leaving Sidney glued to the screen watching Humphrey Bogart and Ingrid Bergman saying, 'Play it again, Sam'.

* * *

Mike had a busy week at work, and as usual the time flew. Pam had a few days off, so no quick chats in the staff room about running this week.

By Thursday, Mike was tired. He was in the middle of his third 12-hour shift, and about to embark on another final one, before taking three blissful days off. A quick ten-minute break in the staff room, and he just had chance to check his phone for messages.

Not expecting any, he was surprised to see a total of 7 missed calls from Laura.

Not texts, *calls*.

Immediately, Mike was worried. This was unusual. Laura had been texting him more frequently since their meeting that night, which he was thrilled about, but *7 missed calls?*

Either she had a sudden urgent need to profess her undying love for him, she'd simply been leaning on her phone by mistake, or it was something more serious.

'Best find out Mike, and don't mess about, do it now.'

He hit the dial button on his phone, but Laura's was engaged and went instantly to answer phone.

"Bugger," he said under his breath. He tried again, and the same thing happened.

He was expected any minute back on the ward, and was going to take a patient down to X-Ray for 2.30 pm.

One more try.

This time, he was lucky, it started ringing. Laura answered within a couple of rings.

"Hey, Laura, it's Mike, everything ok? I've got a load of missed calls from you," he asked quickly.

There was no answer from the other end of the phone, only the sound of someone crying.

"Mike, I'm so sorry to bother you. I've been trying to get hold of Jim, but his phone's off. It's Dad, he's had a stroke," her voice faltered at the end, and she began crying again. "Sorry to bother you, Mike, I know you're at work," she added, tearfully.

His heart sank. Hearing Laura so upset tugged at him, and all he wanted to do was hug her and tell her everything was going to be all right.

"Oh my God, Laura, when did this happen? I'm so sorry. Is he in A&E now?"

"He had it about 10 o'clock this morning at home. He'd dropped Gracie off at school for me because I had an early start at the shop. Mum said he went home, sat down with his coffee, and said he didn't feel very well. Next thing, he's on the floor. He's been in A&E for ages; they're doing a scan and stuff. I'm down here now, but I've got to go get Gracie at 3," she said.

"Oh Laura, I'm so sorry, love. Listen, I'm heading down to X-Ray in about ten minutes. I'll pop along and find you as soon as I can," he replied. "Don't worry, everything's going to be fine, ok?" He tried to reassure her.

"Ok," she said but dissolved into a melting mass of tears again as Mike rang off.

Never let it be said that Mike wasn't good in a crisis. He instantly leapt into action, and flew out of the staff room to find one of his colleagues. After explaining to two of them the situation, he agreed to take his patient down to X-Ray as promised, and would then nip into A&E to find Laura and her mum and dad. Sue, the other Charge Nurse said she would collect the patient after his X-Ray so Mike could have a little time. He thanked her, and said he owed her one, over his shoulder, and disappeared down the corridor pushing his patient in the wheelchair.

The fact that Mike was a seasoned runner now went very much in his favour. He ran into the lift, pushing a somewhat startled patient, pressed the down button, and appeared in the reception of the X-Ray department faster than Mo Farrah ever could. He quickly booked the patient in, told him that Sue would take him back to the ward afterwards, and set off in search of Laura.

A&E was surprisingly quiet for a Thursday afternoon. The receptionist called after Mike.

"You ok, Mike? Who're you looking for?" she enquired.

"Ah, Barbara, hi, yes erm, Ron Beresford?" he asked. "Either TIA or stroke, came in about 10, half 10 this morning."

"Oh yes, he's having a CT scan at the moment, but the family are sitting in the cubicle waiting for him to come back. Go ahead, it's number 3."

Mike thanked her and hurried off.

Before he pulled back the curtain, he composed himself a little, and took some deep breaths. He could feel his heart racing, and didn't want to have a flushed face when he saw Laura, and her mother again. He had only met Carol twice over the years, and both times she had seemed a bit scary. Today, though was a tense situation, and he wanted to make the right impression.

Pulling down his tunic and straightening the pens in his pocket, he put his head 'round the curtain. Laura and her mum were sitting on the plastic chairs looking worried. Laura jumped up straight away, and looked very relieved to see him.

"Oh Mike, thanks so much for coming, I'm so grateful," she said, and gave him another of those hugs he was growing quickly to yearn for.

Carol, on the other hand, stared blankly at him, and then offered a very weak smile when she realised who it was.

They passed pleasantries, and Mike assured Laura her dad was in the best place possible.

"What have they told you so far?" he asked.

"He's had a small bleed on the brain, and his speech is slurred, can't move his left arm or leg. Keeping him in obviously. They seem to think he's had something called a TIA. Just in the process of getting all the information together Mike, then they'll be able to tell us more."

Carol stood up and stretched. She looked tired and drawn. "Still can't get hold of Jim, though," she said, and her expression changed.

CHAPTER FIVE

Laura had been to pick an emotional Gracie up from school, and Mike had finally managed to get hold of Jim.

"Sorry, I've had my phone off all day mate. What's up?" Jim sounded sheepish.

Mike was fast losing his patience with Jim. Not only had he left his family high and dry for another woman, but he was now playing silly buggers. He hadn't seen Gracie in two weeks, and he was impossible to get hold of.

"Look Jim, I thought you ought to know, Ron's had a stroke. Laura asked me to phone you again; she's tried I don't know how many times today. Could you come and take Gracie back with you, because it might be a long night." The tone in Mike's voice was steering towards terse now and Jim could hear it.

"Erm, well I don't know if that's gonna be possible really, Julia and I are..." Jim was cut short.

"Right! Ok. We'll sort it out this end." Mike's tone became even sharper and he ended the call without even a goodbye.

'Tosser', Mike said under his breath. He was cross now and marched off to inform Carol and Laura that Jim was yet again letting them down. He had a feeling that he and Jim were going to catastrophically fall out at some point, and what's more, it could be permanent.

In the small meeting room on the Stroke Unit, Gracie was sitting on Laura's knee, and Carol was pacing up and down, as much as she could do in a confined space.

Mike delivered the news, and Laura could tell he wasn't happy. Gracie's face was red from crying and she was tired and hungry.

"Bloody typical!" Carol spat.

"Mum," Laura threw her mother a look. It said, *'He's still Gracie's dad, don't forget'.*

Mike broke the tension with his plan of action.

"Look, I've finished my shift for today, would you like me to take Gracie home with me, while you girls stay a bit longer? I can give her some tea, settle her down on the sofa with Sidney and they can watch a film or something. Just an idea," he said.

Laura sighed. "I'm going to keep her off tomorrow Mike, so it doesn't matter really what time she goes to bed. It's Friday, one day won't hurt and I'm not at work. What do you want to do Grace?"

"Stay with Mummy," was all she would say. The child was shattered and upset.

After a lengthy conversation, it was decided that Laura and Grace would go home, and Carol would remain for another hour or so. Mike offered to stay with her until Ron was ready to see them.

"Thanks again, Mike," Laura whispered and gave him one of those lovely hugs.

Gracie hugged him and said, "It's not that I didn't want to go to your house, because I really want to see Sidney Peelstreet."

Mike smiled. "Don't worry, we'll do it very soon, ok? You and your mum come over for tea, and you can have a chat with Sidney, watch a film together," he reassured her.

She gave him a very tired smile, and after saying goodbye to Carol, they left, leaving them together alone in the meeting room.

"I'm just going back to my ward, Carol, to get my coat and things. I'll be back in about five minutes," Mike said leaving Carol sitting with tears in her eyes, nursing a very bad coffee from the vending machine.

When he returned, she was still sitting in the same position as when he had left. She gave a big sigh.

"They said anything?" he asked.

She shook her head. "No," she said after a few moments.

"I'm sorry Mike, I'm just really pissed off," she broke the slightly awkward silence.

'Oh God, what's coming now,' he thought.

She put her coffee down on the table at the side of her, and had her elbows resting on her knees, facing him. She stared at him for what seemed like forever, and Mike could feel little beads of sweat popping up on his brow.

"Warm in here, isn't it? Just going to take my coat off," he said, clearing his throat nervously.

Carol could be a formidable woman. Seventy years of age, and she was still in amazing shape. At nearly six feet tall, slim with the same blonde hair as Laura, she was statuesque, beautiful and stylish. Mike thought that she could possibly wear a bin liner and still look marvellous.

She moved a lock of hair away from her face with a perfectly manicured hand, and fixed him with an icy stare.

"Now, I know he's your best friend, Mike. But right now I could quite happily throttle that bastard," she whispered through gritted teeth.

Mike breathed again for the first time in what seemed like forever, and felt his body temperature return to normal. He had been convinced that Carol was going to tear a very large verbal chunk out of him for moving in on her daughter so fast after the split. He allowed himself to relax a little.

"Not only has he been dipping his wick elsewhere, and with Gracie's *teacher*, for Christ sakes, but he hasn't seen his daughter for two entire weeks, because he's been too busy bloody shagging. *Now,* he can't even pull his dammed trousers up to come and help when we really need it. *BASTARD!*"

Mike could tell by now that Carol was, in fact rather pissed off. He thought carefully before he spoke.

"The coffee's bloody shit here too, Jesus." Carol interrupted him before he had the chance to speak.

"He's been a huge disappointment to me too," was all Mike said.

It was true. Jim had only been thinking of himself, and as a result had let everyone down around him. Even now, he was getting deeper and deeper into trouble, and would eventually ostracise a large portion of people that had once been important in his life.

A nurse suddenly came bustling into the room, wearing a plastic apron. She quickly took it off and put it in the appropriate bin.

"Oh, hi Mike! How are you?" She seemed surprised to see him and smiled cheerfully.

After they had passed pleasantries, she introduced herself to Carol, and announced that Ron had been booked into the ward, obs done, had got some paracetamol, and was comfortable.

"Can we see him?" Carol asked.

"Yes of course, only for a few minutes though, he's very tired and needs to get some sleep now. Been a long day for him." The nurse smiled again and showed them through.

"I won't come in, Carol, I'll let you carry on" Mike said quietly.

"You bloody well will, Michael," she replied. "He'll want to say hello before you go home."

Mike relented and went to say a few words to Ron, who looked tired and pale under the bed light, which shone dimly on his face.

After five minutes, Mike said his farewell, and Carol stood up and hugged him. *'My God, she's strong,'* he thought. *'I definitely don't want to be in Jim's shoes when she gets hold of him.'* She had the hug of a wrestler, did Carol.

He went home, tired and hungry. But just managed to text Laura quickly before he went to sleep.

Up at 6 am for his final shift, then three blissful days off. Sidney Greenstreet snuggled up in the crook of Mike's arm and purred.

'Good job today Dad, well done,' Sidney thought. And they both drifted off to sleep.

* * *

The following morning, Mike woke at 5.45 am

feeling dreadful. He was tired beyond belief, and for the first time in years, felt the strong urge to throw a sickie.

Sidney Greenstreet was sitting on his chest, staring at him with those beautiful big green eyes, which said, 'feed me, or there's gonna be trouble'.

Mike groaned. To get himself out of bed this morning was going to take throwing himself at the wall to stir into action. He staggered slowly to the shower, and ran the water with his eyes shut until it ran hot. He clambered inside, leaving Sidney sitting on the other side of the shower curtain, eagerly awaiting his breakfast.

Once he was suitably awake and dressed in fresh uniform, he texted Laura to see how things were.

She replied within minutes and said that she and Gracie were still in bed, having a lie in and would go see Ron at 2.30 that afternoon for visiting.

"I'll pop along to see your dad this morning on my break," he texted back.

"Thanks Mike, you are such a star," she replied.

He smiled to himself and sighed. Sidney looked up at him from his food bowl, and meowed. "She is pretty special, isn't she, eh Sidders? Her mother's got a hug like a bear, though."

Sidney meowed again.

Mike headed out the door, and before he could unlock his car, his phone beeped again.

It was Laura.

"I want to do the Trentham Run with you, for the Stroke Association. You're going to have to help me though. I'm crap at running."

'*Yes!!*' Mike said to himself excitedly, and checking no one was looking, did a little happy dance on the pavement.

Driving to work that morning, Mike thought about the training plan for the next few months.

His runner's mind took over, and he decided the first plan of action was to get Laura kitted-out properly. She would need trainers, running tights, proper socks, short sleeve and long sleeve running tops, a sports bra, a running jacket, plus the essential gadget: the fitness watch.

"I think a shopping trip is in order very soon," he said out loud, confidently.

Mike loved encouraging new runners. He had done so with two of the Trentham Trotters. Matt, the only other younger guy in the group, and Lucy, who was about the same age. Luckily they had both been very keen to be taken under Mike's wing, and had learned fast.

This time however, it was different. This was Laura. The love of his life, the woman he wanted to spend the rest of his life with. It was imperative that he didn't balls it up, just as things were going so well.

Ron, he thought would hopefully make a full recovery, with love and expertise. It would take some time, but they would all get there in the end, and Mike was more than happy to help out. Not only did he genuinely want to do it for Ron, he wanted to support Laura, and from now on, she and Gracie would be the centre of his Universe.

Once at work, Mike busied himself with finishing off paper work from the day before, doing obs, and taking one elderly guy to the toilet. He found a quick ten minutes to go and see Ron, who, when Mike entered the Stroke Unit, was propped up on an armchair of pillows, looking very comfortable indeed. He waved at Mike with his good hand when he saw him, and Mike's heart surged. He felt incredibly sorry for Ron, not only because he really liked him, but because he had been so very strong for the family when Jim had upped and left, with very little warning. Mike couldn't help but feel that the stress of it all had brought on the stroke, and he felt angry again.

"Hi Ron, how are you doing today? Feeling a bit better?" he asked cheerily, and sat on the chair next to the bed.

Ron just nodded very slowly. He offered his good hand over to Mike's and held it briefly.

Mike could see tears rolling slowly down Ron's cheeks, and he felt another surge of anger mixed with raw emotion.

"Listen. It's going to be ok, I promise you. I really do promise, if it's the last thing I do, I'm going to make sure you get better. You'll soon be pottering about in your shed again, and doing loads of great stuff with Gracie and Laura," he said quietly.

"Hey, shall I tell you a secret?" he added, and put his face closer to Ron's ear. "Laura's going to start running. I have it in black and white, cast iron proof Ron, she wants to do the Trentham Gardens run with the Trotters in October. Raise some cash for the Stroke Association." He looked for a reaction, and got one.

Ron simply raised his eyebrows as if to say, 'Bloody hell, *Really?*"

'Straight up. She really is." Mike beamed from ear to ear. Not only because he had gotten a good reaction from him, but also because there was no way Laura could back out of it. Her father would not let her.

CHAPTER SIX

Over the next few days, Ron continued to improve, albeit slowly. The use came back slightly in his arm and leg, and he was able to say a few words. It was slurred and slow, but they were there.

Laura, Carol and Gracie visited every day, twice, taking it in turns. It wasn't that far away that they couldn't manage to visit twice, and it also brought on Ron's recovery seeing his family so often.

At Mike's suggestion, Gracie brought a book to read to him. She decided on something nice and light, so from her bookshelf at home, picked out 'The Wind in the Willows'. Ron spent many a happy afternoon listening to the escapades of Ratty, Moley and Badger, and even laughed at the sheer naughtiness of Toad. When Ron laughed, everyone beamed with delight. They were clutching at every little sign that he was still in there, somewhere.

One day, Laura texted Mike and said, "Ok, I'm ready to start training. What do I do? Where the hell do I start!!!? LOL."

Mike smiled to himself. "Firstly, you need the proper kit. I have a little gift for you, to start you off, give you some incentive," he replied.

Rightly, or wrongly, he had bought her a fitness watch. He had deliberated long and hard over whether to, but in the end he threw caution to the wind, let his guard down a little, went on EBay, ordered one in black, and it had arrived four days later. Job done.

By the second week in May, the stage was set. Mike had taken both Laura and Gracie into Stoke on Trent and they had spent not only quite a lot of money, but also a lot of time in the sports shop, getting Laura kitted out. Gracie came away with a set of gear too, because Laura thought it important she felt included.

Before introducing her to the Trotters, Mike decided to take Laura for her very first training session to the Gardens. It was, after all her favourite place, and such a beautiful setting.

They picked a warm sunny afternoon, when they were both off work. Mike had secretly splashed out on an annual season ticket, so showing their passes to the lady at the entrance, stepped into the Gardens.

To Laura, the place was a sanctuary. Somewhere she could go, and did frequently to think about things. It was peaceful, beautiful, serene. She felt like she was stepping back in time, to a magical secret garden, *her* secret garden. She didn't know quite why she loved the place so much, but felt blessed that it was on her door step and she could visit as often as she wanted.

Mike watched her as they walked over the threshold. How many times had she been here? Twenty or thirty? Probably every other day? And still she breathed in the air, joy spreading over her face as if it was the first time she had ever encountered it.

"Right!" Mike said, breaking the moment. "Now, I've bought you something, as I said. Little present, to give you some incentive to keep going. Marvellous things…you won't regret it for a minute. Close your eyes!" he said, trying to keep his excitement under control.

My God, this was like a bloody proposal, he thought to himself. Resisting the urge to go down on one knee with a boxed fitness watch in his hand, he simply retrieved it from a bag, and put it in her eagerly awaiting hands.

"Oh my word!" she exclaimed excitedly. "Mike, oh my goodness me, I don't know what to say!" She put her hand to her mouth "That must have cost a fortune, I've been looking at them on EBay," she said.

"It's a gift from me to you," he said. "But you've got to promise me one thing."

She nodded.

"That you finish the race. Finish the 5K, whatever it takes. Ok?"

"I promise," she replied, and gave him another one of those hugs of hers.

* * *

Their first training session was a gentle one, because although Laura was reasonably active, she did struggle with her weight, and food was never far from her thoughts. Ever.

Mike had decided on the couch-to-5k training plan. He explained to Laura that he thought it was the best way forward. Despite Laura saying many times that she was crap at running, he noticed she had a very easy relaxed style and to see her run for the first time, in full kit, made him immensely proud. He had got her this far.

They began with a brisk walk around the lake for five minutes, then alternated 60 seconds of running, and 90 seconds of walking for a good 20 minutes, by which time they had reached the little café at the far end of the lake. Laura was quite out of breath, but Mike knew that would improve with time.

"Are going to stop for coffee and a cake?" she asked suddenly.

"Absolutely not," he replied. "Come on, let's try the same thing again, and we'll be back round to the other café by then. I might let you treat me to a coffee there. But no cake, Ok?"

Laura giggled. "Ok, boss!" And gave him a salute as she walked briskly off in front of him. "I can see you are going to be a hard task master, Mike Snow," she joked.

"Nothing ever worth having was gotten easily, you know," he replied. "I'll set your watch up on your phone for you when we get past the giant dandelions."

"Okey doke," she replied breathlessly, and they continued on their way.

It had started to get a little cloudy and cool towards the end of their first run, so Mike suggested they go and sit inside for coffee. You could get one to take away from the little kiosk next door, but the wind was getting up, and he was mindful of them both getting a chill. They had a good five-minute stretch afterwards, and then proceeded inside.

Whilst Mike set up the app on her phone, she got them coffee. She had a brief look at the cake, but thought better of it. They spent the next half an hour chatting, and Mike explained the app to her in detail.

She asked only a few questions, but seemed to get the hang of it fairly quickly.

"Thanks Mike, you're a gem," she said taking a sip. "That's all I seem to say to you, all the time. Thanks, Mike!"

He didn't reply, just gave her a reassuring smile. They sat in silence for a moment.

"How's your dad today? Sorry, never asked," he said.

"Oh, actually doing really well. He and Gracie have finished 'The Wind in the Willows' now and they're onto 'Toad of Toad Hall'," she laughed. "He should be able to come home tomorrow, but Mum's a bit nervous, so I said Grace and I would go and stop the first night, just to settle her mind, you know."

"That's great news, brilliant. If you need anything, you know where I am," he replied. "Any news from Jim, dare I ask?"

"Yeah, actually. He's asked to see Gracie at long last; took his bloody time. She's not sure if she wants to go 'round to Julia's house though, feels a bit funny about it, so Jim's going to take her to the pictures instead." She stared into cup for a moment, and Mike thought she looked a little sad.

"Seems Julia's pregnant, as well," she added after a moment.

Mike looked at her. "Whoa, really?" he added, surprised. "How do you feel about that?"

"Surprisingly ok," was all she would say in reply.

CHAPTER SEVEN

The following day, Ron was indeed ready to go home. It was Mike's last day off work, so he offered to take Laura and Carol to the hospital.

As Mike drew up at Laura's house, Carol came out, cigarette in a finely manicured hand, sweeping hair away from her face like a film star. Although eccentric, Mike thought she was marvellous.

"Morning, driver!" she said cheerily and sat in the front seat. He had hoped she might opt for the back, he being the chauffeur and all. She wound down the window, took one last drag, and blew a cloud of smoke out of her expertly glossed lips. She opened the door one final time, stubbed the cigarette out on the pavement, and placed the butt in a small plastic tub, which she had retrieved from her handbag.

"Do hate litter, don't you?" she said, smiling.

"Oh, yes. Absolutely," Mike replied. *'I also hate bloody smoking, but I'm not going to tell you that,'* he thought to himself.

A few moments later, the vision that was Laura

stepped out of the front door. Today, she had her hair down, and was wearing a little make-up. Mike cleared his throat nervously, and swallowed.

"Morning, Mike," she said as she climbed into the back seat. "You ok?"

"Morning!" he replied, his voice a little higher than usual. He cleared his throat again. "Yes, not bad. How are the legs feeling today?"

"Oh, a little bit achy, to be honest," she said, touching her left calf muscle. "But I slept really well. I love this fitness watch, Mike. I sat having a look at the app with Gracie last night, it does loads of stuff."

"They are wonderful things Laura, nothing like a fitness watch to motivate you," he said smiling.

They all chatted quite happily and easily on the way to the hospital, and Mike noticed Carol was watching him thoughtfully out of the corner of her eye. Every now and then she shot him a knowing smile.

'Shit,' he thought. 'She's twigged.'

They continued their journey chatting about how great it was that Ron was finally coming home, his progress, and about the 5k. Laura, it seemed was still as keen as ever, and between her and Mike, decided on the best training days. It was going to be at least a month before he would introduce her to the Trotters. She needed one-to-one for a little while longer.

Carol had been silent for a while, but eventually spoke. "So, when's shit-face seeing our Gracie next?"

The tone of easiness went down a notch in the car, and Mike felt a little uncomfortable.

"At the weekend, he's taking her to the cinema," Laura replied.

"Wow," Carol replied curtly. "Bastard," she said under her breath, and shot another look at Mike.

They continued the journey to the hospital in silence, but Mike was very pleased when they finally arrived and eventually found a parking space.

Immediately Carol leapt out of the car. "I'll pay for the parking, Mike," she said. "Thanks so much for offering to drive."

"Ah, no need Carol. Staff permit holder," he replied.

"Great!" she said cheerily and proceeded to walk off in the general direction of the main entrance.

"She's nervous, believe it or not," Laura said to Mike as they tried to keep up.

"Heard that," replied Carol, as she marched ahead, shoulder length blonde hair flowing like a cloud behind her.

* * *

They collected Ron from the ward, and Mike had managed to get hold of a wheelchair to transport him back to the car.

Once they had spoken to the nurse, and an appointment had been made in the Stroke Clinic for the following week, they set off back to Ron and Carol's house.

By now, Ron was able to walk very slowly; he still had some weakness in his left arm and leg, but his speech was coming back well. Mike only detected a slight paralysis in his facial muscles, but it was all encouraging.

The journey back was quite jovial, and Carol sat with him in the back, holding his hand. Laura was up front with Mike, and it occurred to him how 'right' it felt. How 'together'. For the first time in years, he felt a sense of belonging to a family, and he realised just how lonely he had been. Sidney Greenstreet was a wonderful companion, but to be part of a proper family would be something else.

Once back at the Beresford home, they settled Ron on the sofa, made cups of tea, and Carol seemed to relax a little. She went outside into the back garden for another cigarette, leaving Ron and Mike alone, whilst Laura disappeared upstairs to unpack hers and Gracie's overnight bag.

"There we are then, Ron. Back home. Bet it feels nice. You'll sleep a lot better in your own bed tonight," Mike said as they sat together on the sofa.

Ron nodded. "Too noisy."

"Ah yes, always something happening, even at night time on the wards. Busy places," Mike agreed.

"Thank you, Mike," the older man said slowly, and took the younger's hand, "for everything."

Mike felt that old familiar hard lump in his stomach again.

"It's a pleasure. Any time, really," he replied.

Ron inched his way across the sofa, so he was closer to Mike, not letting go of his hand, and whispered in his ear. *"I know."* Ron winked at him, and did a thumbs-up. "It's ok by me," he said.

Mike felt himself flush a deep red. He left shortly afterwards, feeling bare, and exposed, but somehow relieved. He'd kept his secret deep inside himself, only confiding in his best friend, Sidney, for nearly 6 years.

Obviously, he had let his guard down too much, but was it ok to do so now? He didn't want to scare Laura away, especially when things were still raw with Jim and Julia.

There was a new baby on the way too, which threw

an enormous spanner in the works. How would Grace react to another half-brother or sister? She had been the only child for 9 years, and the fact that her dad was having a baby with another woman, and her teacher, at that, would be something she might find difficult to handle.

Carol was very open about her feelings towards Jim. She always followed a sentence involving him with a cursory 'Bastard'. Mike thought this was actually rather funny, because Carol was such a strong character there was something almost comedic about it. And she only ever referred to him as 'Shit-face' these days when Grace wasn't around. In front of the child he was referred to as 'her dad' but it was always through gritted teeth, because Carol did love a good swear, and found it hard to mask her feelings.

When Mike arrived home, he sat down in his kitchen and thought very carefully.

At some point in the future, he and Jim, his best friend were going to come to blows. Mike was certainly no fighter, and neither was his opponent, but it would undoubtedly be a war of words.

That was the part he was least looking forward to, because Mike was always the one to walk away from confrontation. He actively hated it.

CHAPTER EIGHT

With the rest of the afternoon ahead of him, Mike decided to get changed and have a really long run. It always cleared his head and helped him get things into perspective.

He picked up Sidney Greenstreet, who immediately purred, churped and nuzzled into his master's neck.

"My God young man, I'm feeding you far too well!" Mike said out loud as he carried a rather overweight feline up the stairs.

He changed into his running gear as Sidney looked on. Mike ruffled his friend's head. "I'm going on a long one matey, might be a couple of hours, ok?" he said fondly.

Sidney responded with another churp, and settled himself down in a tight ball at the bottom of Mike's bed. He purred loudly as Mike ran down the stairs and out of the house.

Setting his watch, he decided to run from home all the way to the Gardens, around the lake, up past the giant dandelions, through the Italian Garden, and back home. It would probably take him an hour or so, but he was really in the mood for a long run.

Mike was one of those very lucky runners who could just keep going, and would only tire after about 8 or 9 miles. It was a little overcast and cool, which was perfect. Not too hot, and not too cold. He quickly warmed up, and enjoyed listening to the sounds of the outdoors. Birds tweeted, dogs barked, cars and vans drove by, people passed him; some smiled and said hello, some didn't.

He crossed the main island with care, ran through the car park, and getting out his pass, flashed it at the lady on the door, and entered the Gardens. He stopped briefly, his heart pounding in his chest, and a thin film of perspiration on his skin. Looking around, he smiled to himself. *'I can see why this place is so special to her, it is bloody lovely, even on a dull day.'*

He ran off to the right, through the Italian Gardens, deciding on the opposite direction from where he and Laura had run a few days previously. It struck him how immaculately the gardens were kept, not a weed in sight. The wild flower meadows were in bloom now, and he proceeded towards the giant dandelions, then passed the waterfall, the myriad of colours that represented the waist high flowers, and then through the woods, which housed the tree carvings.

When he arrived at the café at the top end of the lake, he remembered Laura asking if they could stop for cake, and he allowed the memory to linger in his mind a while. With the miniature railway to his left he passed some more of the wire fairy sculptures. Every time he came, he saw something different. The lake was peaceful and calm, and a canoe glided across it sending silent ripples towards the edge.

Mike was sorry to come to the end of this part of the run, and contemplated going 'round again. He didn't take much persuading and did one more blissful circuit before heading home. His legs were getting a little tired and hunger was gnawing at his stomach. Tea time beckoned, and Sidney's tummy would remind him too that food was needed.

Mike returned home, relaxed, happy and pleased with his time. It would be his last run before meeting up with the Trotters the following Monday.

Once showered and changed, he stood briefly in the kitchen, looking out at the garden. Whatever happened, he decided, nothing was worth falling out with Jim over. He would not hold a grudge against him, or Julia. Life was just too dammed short. He would remain totally neutral, and let Carol do all the fighting, if that was going to be the course of things.

* * *

The next few days were taken up with three, twelve hour shifts, and Mike was offered two nights, which were always welcome for a bit of extra cash. This of course meant that he had to try and fit in training runs with Laura, and the usual Monday night Trotter meeting. By the end of that week, he was shattered, but could concentrate on a lovely sunny weekend with Laura and Grace, and really ramp-up the training.

Grace, being only 9 years old, had all the energy in the world, and didn't even seem to get out of breath, but Laura, on the other hand, was struggling. They were nearly a month in, and although she had made some progress, Mike wasn't sure she would stand up to a 5k with the Trotters for a while yet. On the Sunday afternoon, after a particularly tough session, Laura stopped and sat on a bench trying to get her breath. Mike and Grace were up ahead, so turned back to make sure she was ok.

"You ok, Mum? What's up?" Gracie put her arm around her mother.

"I don't know, I just don't feel like it today. Sorry Mike, I'm just finding it really hard," she gasped.

Mike sat next to them on the bench. It was true, he had upped their game as far as training was concerned, but that wasn't the only problem, he sensed.

"Is everything all right otherwise, you know?" he asked.

Grace looked at him, and then back at her mum. "Dad and Julia are moving away," she said quietly.

"Oh?" Mike replied surprised.

"They want a completely fresh start, apparently," Laura said. Sorry Mike, it's just all so up in the air at the moment. Not only do we feel abandoned, but our whole lives have been turned upside down because of Jim's choices. It's just not fair." For the first time, Mike detected a tone of anger and resentment in her voice. "It seems everything has to be on Jim's terms," she added.

"Do you want to stop the running for a while?" he asked.

Laura thought for a moment.

"Actually, no, I bloody don't. I want to carry on. I'm dammed if he's going to stop us doing things we enjoy, and even when I do find the training a bit hard going, I never regret it afterwards. Weird, but it's a bit like therapy, gets all the anger and frustration out. I guess we're just on a downer today Mike, really sorry you had to see it," she said.

"Listen, the last one to the café past the big dandelions, buys the hot chocolate! Who's up for it? Then tea on me at the diner on the way home. Sound like a good plan?" he said trying to lighten things up.

Laura and Gracie looked at each other, and their faces lit up at the mention of tea at the diner.

"You're on." Laura took Mike's hand and shook it, pulling him up off the bench. "But the hot chocolate's on me!" she shouted back to him.

The atmosphere lightened then, and they continued through the woods, past the beetle carving, chatting about whether they would have the deluxe version of hot chocolate with cream and marshmallows or be really virtuous and not.

Gracie trotted along effortlessly, and Laura finally got into a good rhythm. Mike was pleased all was going well. They were close to the café, when Laura stopped dead. Her face changed instantly and her jaw hardened. Mike looked in the direction of her glare, and his heart sank. Grace stopped in her tracks too.

Directly in front of them, were Jim and Julia, arms around each other, strolling along, lost in each other's eyes. A picture of togetherness.

This, Mike thought, *'is probably going to get really, really messy.'*

He wasn't wrong.

CHAPTER NINE

Jim, Julia and the opposition stood by the edge of the lake, staring at each other. It was like 'High Noon', Mike thought, without the wild west bit.

No one else was around, and he could feel the tension building. Should he try and diffuse the situation? By the look on Laura's face, he thought that was probably not a good idea, and looked from one to the other.

Laura was the first to speak. "Mike, would you mind taking Grace for a hot chocolate please? I have some business I need to attend to," she said curtly.

"Sure. No problem. Will you be ok?" he added.

"YYYYYep!" she replied, not taking her eyes off the loved-up couple.

"You're not joining us Laura?" he asked her. She didn't reply. "Take that as a no, then," he said under his breath, and signalled to Gracie that it was time to go.

He encouraged her to run to the café, making light of the chaos.

"She'll be along in a minute, don't worry," he said not daring to look back.

"I think I heard a splash, Uncle Mike," Gracie added.

'That wouldn't surprise me,' he thought but said aloud, "Some big fish in that lake, Grace."

Mike couldn't help thinking that it was a large fish going by the name of James Eddison.

They were halfway through their drinks when Laura appeared at their table. She stood looking liberated and rather pleased with herself.

"We sort of need to go now, and I need wine and chocolate when we get home," she announced, hands on hips.

"Is everything ok?" Mike asked, quickly followed by Grace asking the same question.

"Yep, fine. We sort of need to go quite quickly though," she replied cheerfully, flashing a look over her shoulder. "Let's run back, shall we?"

Mike and Grace looked at each other, drained their cups, and joined her in the run back to the car.

"Is Dad all right, Mum?"

"Yes, yes, absolutely fine," Laura assured her daughter.

"Bit damp, is he?" Mike asked quietly, as he ran up alongside her.

"Just a tad," Laura replied, a huge smile lighting up her face.

Once back at the house, Laura asked Grace to go upstairs and change. The little girl asked if she could go on her computer for half an hour, and Laura nodded. "Just half an hour."

With Grace upstairs, Laura reached inside the fridge and produced a large bar of milk chocolate and a bottle of white wine. She poured herself a glass, but when offered, Mike refused. He wanted a clear head.

"So, what happened?" he asked.

"There's one thing you will learn about me, Mike, the more you stick around. I'll only take so much shit off people, then I blow. I'm fairly mild mannered, but if I think someone's taking the piss, that's it," she told him, taking a large gulp of her wine.

"You pushed him in the lake, didn't you?" Mike said flatly.

"Yes. Yes, I did," she replied. "He asked me what I was 'doing there' and particularly why was I there with you. So, I told him to mind his dammed business and concentrate on his pregnant girlfriend. Anyway, I sort of shoulder barged him, he fell back and into the lake. Absolutely bloody soaked to the skin he was. Julia and I both started laughing at him. He wasn't best pleased at that, so I left her trying to pick duck weed off his jacket." She started to laugh hysterically then and Mike could feel the corners of his mouth twitching.

"It felt absolutely awesome Mike, I have to say. He looked *so* pissed off."

Her laughter was cut short by a loud, sharp knock at the front door. Mike's heart skipped a beat. He just *knew* who it was, and mentally prepared himself.

Laura put down her glass and answered the door. Within seconds, Jim was in the room with them both. Bits of duck weed stuck out from behind one ear, and his hair was partially dry, but matted. He had bird pooh on the arm of his leather jacket.

Mike stood his ground, and Jim stopped about six feet away from him. Out of the corner of his eye, Mike saw Laura send a very quick text. The three of them looked at each other.

"You deserved that," Laura told Jim after a moment. "You had it coming."

Jim was visibly trying to keep his temper under control, and straightened his jacket.

Mike cleared his throat. "You've erm, you've got duck weed in your ear, Jim."

"Just what exactly are your intentions towards my wife, Mike Snow?" Jim asked flicking away the weed from his ear angrily. "Because it seems to me, you moved in bloody fast once I left this house. Pretty much wearing my slippers, it would appear! Not only did you completely take over when my father-in-law had his stroke, but now you're taking my wife and daughter running?" Jim stood with his hands on very wet hips.

"I've just been helping them out, Jim. Because if I remember rightly, it was you who walked out, left them both high and dry, and couldn't be reached for love nor money when Ron had his stroke."

'Stand your ground Michael, don't let him fluster you,' he thought to himself.

This seemed to knock Jim slightly off kilter for a moment, and it was Laura who spoke next.

"So now I'm 'your wife' all of a sudden, am I? And my dad's your 'father-in-law'? Bit bloody late for that, don't you think Jim? You're nothing to do with this family any more. You denied yourself that privilege the day you told me you were shagging Grace's teacher and you were moving in with her. You have failed us *all*, Jim. Every single one of us. Me, Grace, Mum, Dad and Mike. I'd like you to leave now please. Your girlfriend is waiting for you, I'm sure." Laura went to stand next to Mike.

"This guy has done more for us in the last month

or so than you ever did in years. He's been a rock for this family. Now take your soggy arse back to Julia's. Oh, and the next time I see her, I must give her a really big hug, and thank her."

Jim looked puzzled. "What for?" he spat.

"For taking you off me. I'd been looking to get rid of you for a long time, Jim. She's done me a massive favour."

'Bloody ouch!' Mike thought. *'That was a massive kick in the balls.'*

Jim's face dropped and he looked away, ashamed for a moment.

"Off you go, please," she added with a flick of her hand, as if swatting away a fly. "You're dripping on my carpet."

Laura now had the upper hand, was the mistress of the put-down, owned the room: *nailed it.*

"I thought you were on *my* side," Jim hissed at Mike as he turned to leave.

"No! He's on *mine!*" shouted Laura, suddenly losing her temper. "Now *piss off!*"

With her final verbal arrow sticking firmly in Jim's throat, he turned and made a squelchy exit, leaving duck weed and wet footprints in his wake.

She returned to the kitchen, poured herself another drink and leaned on the work top.

"Feel better now?" Mike asked.

"On top of the world, thank you Michael" she replied triumphantly.

'Excellent,' He thought to himself. *'Never will I get on the wrong side of this one,'* and his heart swelled a little more for his warrior Queen.

Once Laura had returned to normal human strength, and consumed the best part of the bottle, they ordered a takeaway, and chatted some more. Grace, it seemed had missed the whole thing as she had been wearing her headphones in her room, so was blissfully unaware. Carol had been on standby as Laura had sent her a text of possible imminent danger.

Mike decided it was high time he had a glass of wine to steady his nerves, and after two was slightly more mellow.

"I'm sorry, Mike, dragging you into all of this. It's not pretty. I'd quite understand if you walked away," Laura said when they had finished their meal.

"Look, these things are always messy. I've never heard of one that wasn't to be honest. Things will settle down, I promise. Diane and I speak to each other now, but at the time, we locked horns a bit. It's natural. Tempers run high, emotions are at their peak. I just mean, I understand. Ride it out, and all will be well eventually," he said sympathetically.

Laura looked thoughtful. "You and Diane speak often?" she asked.

"No, not really. I saw her at work funnily enough last year. Her partner, Rose was on our ward. Felt a bit weird at first, but it was fine. We buried the hatchet a long time ago. You have to, because if you don't you can get bitter and resentful. Life's too short for that, Laura," he said.

"Yeah, you're right. I think I'll probably look back on this whole period in time in years to come and have a good laugh about it. So will Jim, I should think. Dripping all over the bloody carpet." They both laughed.

"Did you mean what you said to him, about Julia doing you a favour?" Mike asked, taking another sip of his wine.

"Yes, I did," Laura replied. "I'll tell you all about it one day. He was doing my head in on a daily basis, and I just wanted rid. So yes, that bit was right." She got up and started clearing away the takeaway containers.

"You sure you still want to run…do the 5k in October? I'd understand if you didn't, what with everything that's going on," Mike asked, not looking at her.

She came back to sit by him on the sofa. "Running's really important to you, isn't it?" she fixed him with her pale blue eyes.

"Yes, it is. It's a massive part of my life," he said.

"Then let's do it," she replied, putting her hand on his shoulder. "Let's bloody do it, Mike."

CHAPTER TEN

Before Mike left that evening, they had drawn up a training schedule on a big piece of card, and stuck it on Laura's kitchen wall. Dates, times planned all the way to the actual race. Mike had told her to register her and Grace in August online then their running numbers would arrive about a month before the big day. Soon, it would be time to introduce her to the Trotters, and he was looking forward to that moment.

It seemed to him that the events with Jim at the Gardens and afterwards had been a turning point for Laura, almost as if she had needed to get it out of her system. Once she'd given him a dammed good soaking in the lake and a big piece of her mind for good measure, she was ready to draw a line under some of the betrayal and move on.

Certainly the next time they met, Laura appeared stronger, determined and calmer. She was waiting for him at the entrance to the Gardens one afternoon at the beginning of June, and he noticed she had bought herself new items of running kit. Beige Keith was going to love her, as she sported a pair of black lycra shorts, and matching muscle back top. Mike smiled to himself; she had evidently lost a little weight too, but he was too much of a gentleman to ask how much.

"Come on slow coach!" she called cheekily to him as they set off on their usual route.

'The old Laura's back,' he thought to himself. *'Excellent.'*

He noticed her strength as a runner was increasing, the muscles in her legs becoming more defined and her body generally was toning up well. Before his very eyes this remarkable woman was becoming a proper runner, and not just in body, but mind also. That's when it really got you, he knew from experience. Once running got into your head, it never left, and you were hooked for life.

In a matter of weeks, they were running nearly three quarters of the way around the lake without stopping. Laura still got out of breath and had to power walk a little bit of the way, but generally he thought she was now ready to meet the Trotters. So, the following week, Laura joined the group. It was a momentous occasion for Mike, and he beamed with pride, as he introduced his student.

"Good evening everyone, lovely night for it!" he said excitedly. "Now, we have a new member I would like to introduce to you all, this is Laura."

There were handshakes and introductions all round, and a particularly firm one from Beige Keith, who had difficulty in taking his eyes off Laura's legs. When he began to smack his lips, Mike quickly moved her on to Pam, who gave a handshake like a sumo wrestler.

"Welcome to the club," Pam smiled. "You won't regret it. Done me the world of good since I joined," she added.

Laura smiled back and started up a conversation with Pam.

"Right folks, is a 3k ok for everyone tonight?" Mike asked. "Being as we have a new recruit; Laura's doing the couch-to-5k plan."

A general, "Yeah, fine Mike," rumbled through the group, and off they went.

They were only a kilometre in, and Mike noticed a change in the dynamics of the group. It seemed happier, lighter in mood. Maybe it was because of the beautiful evening. It was a lovely sunny night, with a warm breeze. They would surely enjoy an equally lovely sunset. Mike decided as it was Laura's first time with the Trotters to run at the very back with Pam so he could make sure everyone was ok. Suddenly though, joining them was Keith. Tonight, he was sporting beige shorts, white top and his lime green trainers. Mike realised why Keith had dropped back. It was because Laura was a little way ahead. Keith had a perfect view, and never took his eyes off her for a second. He even took the time to look across at Mike and give him a knowing wink.

As they turned a sharp left corner and proceeded down a fairly steep hill, Keith seemed to be in a spot of bother. He dropped back quite some considerable distance, and appeared to be flailing his arms around in the general area of his nether regions. Continuing to run, Mike turned to see what the problem was, as did Laura and Pam. The others were too far ahead to hear Keith screaming like a girl with both hands down the front of his shorts.

"You ok, Keith? What's the matter?" Mike stopped and shouted.

Keith wasn't really paying attention to anything other than the problem in his shorts. Not looking where he was going, he lost his balance and fell sideways into someone's front garden, disappearing completely into a large privet hedge.

"Oh my God, Keith!" shouted Pam. The trio ran towards the spot where poor Keith had disappeared.

Pam hauled him out of the foliage and started picking bits of twig and leaves out of his hair. Keith however, still had hold of his privates, and seemed to be in some discomfort. He was red in the face and wincing.

"Have you pulled something, what's wrong?" Mike asked worriedly. "Pam and I are both nurses, so don't be shy," he added.

The poor man proceeded to point in the general direction of his nether regions and managed to whisper 'wasp'!

Pam smiled. They managed to ascertain that whilst he had been running along, a wasp had flown up the front of his shorts, and as he had decided to 'go commando' that particular evening because it was hot, the little pest had stung him several times on his manhood. Four, to be precise. The persistent offender was now lying dead on the pavement, squashed.

Pam and Laura just about managed to keep straight faces as they helped Keith up, but his pain was clear to see.

"Will he need to go to hospital?" asked Laura.

Pam shook her head. "Shouldn't have thought so," she said. "Unless he develops a reaction; we'll soon see."

"Right. Keith, can you manage to walk, do you think?" Mike asked.

The invalid shook his head.

"Tell you what," Laura suggested after a moment. "I'll run home, get my car. Mike why don't you run ahead and tell the others; maybe Pam wouldn't mind staying with Keith?"

They all decided it was an excellent idea. Mike and Laura ran off in different directions, leaving Pam and Keith sitting on the kerb together.

"Think you're going to need some antiseptic on that, you poor chap," she said quietly.

* * *

By the time Laura returned with the car, Keith was still in agony. Pam had identified a fair bit of swelling, and so they decided the best plan of action was to get him home to his wife. Laura phoned Mike to let him know.

"Right, ok. We're on our way back now," he said. "How's he doing?"

"Lying down in the back of my car. Won't take his hand away from it. Must sting like hell."

Poor Keith. Of all the things to happen on a beautiful summer's evening, when all he wanted to do was run and look at Laura's legs.

A little while later, the invalid was taken home, and Mike, Laura and Pam decided a visit to the pub was needed. It had been quite a night.

They sat in the beer garden and Mike went to order three lime and sodas.

"Wouldn't mind popping a brandy in mine, would you?" Pam asked.

"No problem. Might join you," he smiled.

They enjoyed their drinks and breathed a big sigh of relief.

"Fancy that. What are the chances of a wasp flying up your shorts and stinging you on the willy, four times?" Pam said after a period of retrospective silence.

"The poor guy, honestly that's such bad luck. Will he be ok?" Laura asked.

"Oh yes, he'll be fine in a couple of days," Mike assured her.

He couldn't help thinking that it might be a week or so before they saw Keith back with the Trotters again.

CHAPTER ELEVEN

As it turned out, Keith refrained from running for two weeks after the incident. He re-joined the Trotters in the middle of June, and Mike couldn't help but notice a sobering difference in him upon his return. He also never wore shorts again, opting for jogging bottoms instead. A strong whiff of insect repellent seemed to hover over him like a cloud, and if you were unlucky enough to get down wind, it could be quite overwhelming.

Laura now regularly met up with the group, sometimes calling for Mike on the way. Sticking well to her couch-to-5k plan, she would only do 3k and then head home. That intermixed with their training runs around the gardens meant that she was growing in strength and confidence.

She also started opening up to Mike, and would often ask him his opinion on which course of action she should take, particularly on the subject of her impending divorce. Jim and Julia were moving to

North Wales, which was good in one way, but not in another.

"How does Grace feel about everything?" Mike asked one afternoon, after they had successfully completed a circuit of the lake. "It's an awful lot for a 9 year old to take in," he added.

"Had a few issues with her this week," Laura replied. "I'm a bit worried about her, Mike. Her dad's buggered off with her teacher, *and* got her pregnant, so there's a new little half brother or sister on the way. To top it off, he's moving away. I mean, I'm not surprised she's confused, poor kid." She paused for a moment. "He's always been a totally selfish bastard, but this, this is something else."

Mike looked thoughtful. He knew that Jim had been a little selfish over the years; he hadn't realised just how dreadfully self-centred he could be until recently.

"I mean, I did *everything* for him. Absolutely *everything*. He never had to wash a pot, hoover, dust, clean the house. The washing machine was like something from another world to him. The most he had to do was mow the lawn once a week, that was all. He had his packed lunches made for work, tea on the table when he got home. I'll tell you how bloody selfish he was Mike, first thing in the morning, he would make *his* side of the bed and leave mine. For Christ sake." She put her hand to her forehead exhaling a long and slow sigh.

"Sorry," she said after a moment.

"It's ok. You can always talk to me," he said unlocking his car, and he meant it. He *wanted* her to talk to him, to confide in him. He really didn't mind at all, because all this was therapy for her, the running, the venting. All part of the healing process.

"You're welcome to come and have tea with us tonight if you like," she added as they put their seat belts on. "I'm doing something very runner-friendly."

"Oh really?" he asked. "Now that sounds like an offer I can't possibly refuse. What is it?"

"Well, in my running magazine, they had this brilliant recipe for salmon, which apparently is a great food for runners, and spinach," she said excitedly.

'Oh my God!' he thought. *'This woman is seriously hooked if she's buying running magazines.'*

"Wow, sounds lovely!" he replied trying to appear calm and matter of fact. "What time you want me?"

"Around 6?"

"Perfect," he said. We could register for the Stroke run tonight if you like."

They agreed that was an excellent plan, and as they drove home, a few spots of rain appeared on the windscreen. They had timed their run just right.

* * *

Every time Mike was in Laura's presence, he felt nervous. But he remembered that old familiar feeling, the butterflies in the stomach. He hadn't experienced it for a very long time, not since Diane and he had first started dating. But only this time, it seemed more intense. He looked at Sidney Greenstreet whilst he was getting ready to go to Laura's for tea. The sky had gone very dark, and rain gently pitter-patted on his bedroom window. Sidney had curled himself up by Mike's pillow and was washing his ears with those big white paws of his. He looked up and for a moment, Mike thought he almost smiled at him. He returned a cheerful grin.

"You just keep those paws crossed, my little friend,

that she feels the same way about me. Because I'm going to be lost if she doesn't."

Within the hour he was in the company of his two favourite people, Laura and Gracie. They enjoyed the runners' tea, and once Grace was bathed and in bed they set about registering themselves on the Stroke run.

"Oh my God, I'm just so bloody excited!" Laura said. "I'm really doing it, my first race." She poured herself and Mike another glass of wine each and joined him on the sofa, where he had his laptop open and ready to enter.

He explained to her that she would receive a t-shirt or running vest, race number and details about a month prior. They filled in forms for himself, Laura and Grace too. She had desperately wanted to be part of it, not only to support her mum, but to help others like her grandad. She would ask anyone and everyone at school to sponsor her: teachers and kids.

Laura clapped her hands in delight once they were registered and finished. She was visibly delighted and encouraged. Mike felt her hand on his arm, and she planted a lingering kiss on his cheek.

He swallowed hard. '*Okay. Deep breaths, deeeeep breaths. Don't ruin it. Calm. What do I do now?*'

He swallowed again and looked at her, smiling.

"You're looking forward to it then? Great," he said. "Shall we see if we can find the route online? Give you a bit of an insight."

She searched his face intently with her eyes, and her smile faded a little.

"Great," she said.

It was at that point that something in Mike's brain clicked.

He knew. He knew there was something there,

between them. If he acted upon it now, he could potentially ruin everything. It could all be a rebound situation, and that was the last thing he wanted. Was she just trying to make Jim jealous? Getting back at him? But she had said several times that Julia had done her a favour, Jim's selfishness had been the downfall of their marriage. She was well shot of him. His head spun with possible scenarios and he felt suddenly nauseas. Little beads of sweat formed on his brow and he wiped them away with his hand.

He cleared his throat nervously, and Laura turned her eyes from him to the computer.

"Let's have a look at this route, then," she said.

CHAPTER TWELVE

The following three months were a mixture of training, work and healing for Laura and Grace. During the school summer holidays, Jim and Julia did indeed make the move to North Wales, choosing a very nice house in Aberdovey to settle. The beach was amazing, and they even promised Gracie a weekend visit once they had set up a room for her. Laura seemed to find a balance mentally, and found a certain closure with the departure of her ex-husband and his partner.

It was like a new chapter had begun. Ron continued to make very good progress, and his speech improved, although he did have a very slight slur, especially when he was tired. He and Grace had moved on from 'Toad of Toad Hall' and now were full steam ahead into the Harry Potter books. By September they were into the third one and Ron was lost in the adventures of the young wizard. He particularly liked his namesake, Mr Weasley.

Training continued to go well. The Trotters lost two of the younger female runners, as they had decided to go back-packing 'round Australia for three months, but the rest of them still met every Monday night, and were all registered, and had raised a couple of hundred quid each for the Stroke run.

The weather was starting to turn; September was warm and balmy. But the mornings were crisp sometimes, and they could feel the seasons were changing.

Sure enough, a month before the big day the race packs arrived.

Mike was at work early one morning, and in his 5-minute break, just managed to check his phone for messages, which he did more so nowadays.

Two texts from Laura read:

THE PACKS HAVE LANDED! WHOOOO! x
and the second:

Sooooo excited! Have you got yours yet? xx

He laughed to himself.

Will check when I get home! Does the vest fit ok? x

A thumbs-up from Laura signified all was well, and he put his phone away and went back to the ward.

* * *

They were exactly two weeks away from the big day, and the nerves started to set in for Laura.

"So, how much have you managed to raise?" Mike asked her one lunch time. He had popped in to the florist where she worked. They were just finishing some bouquets for a wedding for the following day.

He loved the smell of this shop. It had the wonderful scent of freesias and greenery.

"Two hundred and five pounds, exactly. Will that be enough do you think?" Laura wiped her nose with the back of her hand. She was hot, bothered and working to a deadline.

"Bloody hell, that's fabulous!" Mike laughed. "More than me, I've got £177.52." Though he couldn't remember exactly where the 2p had come from.

Grace had raised the princely sum of £53.47 and even her dad had sponsored her.

She was back at school now, with a new teacher and a new classroom. It had helped enormously with drawing a line under a messy year. Jim had made some attempts at contacting her regularly and they had set a definite date for her to visit them in Aberdovey in the autumn half term for two days.

The house was on the market, and Laura decided it would be good for both of them. A new house where they could make new memories.

On one of their last training runs, Mike went through a few things with Laura and Grace that he thought would be helpful.

"Now then," he said. "It's best we do our very last training session roughly 3 to 4 days before the race. It just gives your body time to recover before it runs the big one. An early night the evening before, no alcohol and maybe some pasta for tea. Breakfast is up to you. But I always favour porridge with honey and a sliced banana," he added.

Grace pulled a face at the mention of the banana. "I don't like them, Uncle Mike. Could I have strawberries instead?" she asked.

"Absolutely!" he replied. "Do you like peanut butter?"

"Erm, sort of. Mum does."

"Well, that's another alternative," he said helpfully. "Lovely on toast, and great running fuel. But just make sure you have it about an hour or so before you start, otherwise you're going to get a stitch, and that's not very nice at all, is it?"

She laughed and shook her head.

"Come on then, let's go!" shouted Laura who had seemed to be losing weight by the week. He was dying to ask her how much she had lost, but he would leave that one for another time. Watching her run, he estimated about half a stone since 'Jimgate' had started. That's what they had labelled it, but apart from the house sale, they talked about the split less and less these days.

In the end, the only Trotters who were registered on the Stroke run were Pam, Keith, Lucy and Matt. But Mike was happy with that. Beige Keith had been wearing his Resolution Run t-shirt since it had come through the post. He had three of them at home. It was a little bit like wearing the equivalent of a Christmas sweater in the run up to the festive season.

RACE DAY

Mike awoke at 7 am. Sunlight poured in through his bedroom curtains, and Sidney was sitting on his chest, as he always did, eagerly awaiting breakfast.

He lay there for ten minutes thinking about the day ahead. The weather report had said a chilly start, but giving way to fine and sunny, with a light breeze. It had been exactly the same last year. A flurry of excitement coursed through his veins, and he got up, managing to move Sidney Greenstreet to one side.

"Either I need to stop feeding you so much or you need to get on the treadmill, my lad," he said stretching.

Sidney looked at him and churped.

"Right! Big day today, Sidders!" he added. "I'll just have my shower and we can have some breakfast."

Once downstairs, Mike fed his hungry companion and set about deciding on his pre-run breakfast. After careful consideration, he opted for his favourite porridge with banana. He thought of Grace, and smiled to himself.

"She hates bananas, Sidney. Shame. Great running fuel."

Sidney wasn't interested because his favourite cat food was fast disappearing into his stomach, and it would soon be time to go and sit on top of the wheelie bin in the back garden. He'd got his whole day planned out, which generally consisted of lazing around in the sunshine.

Mike ate his breakfast standing by the patio door in the lounge. He was too excited to sit down. Race day was a big event for him, he absolutely loved it. The atmosphere, the people, and the run itself. He was always sorry when it was over.

He had packed his bag the night before, with the usual stuff. He had put his headphones in just in case, but he anticipated Laura and Grace might need some encouragement along the way, so he ended up taking them out of his bag and putting them back in the drawer. When it came to music Mike was a bit of a surprise. You would have been forgiven for thinking he was a middle of the road sort of guy, but no. Mike loved nothing better than dance music. He'd done last year's race listening to Ibiza Anthems part the way 'round, then swapped over to Ministry of Sound.

He was a little disappointed that this year his running buddy wasn't going to be Fat Boy Slim, but spending this awesome day with Laura would more than make up for it.

He checked his watch. It was 8.15 am. Time to go soon. He was picking Laura and Grace up at 8.30 and then on to the Gardens. They had to check in at the desk, and also give in their sponsor money, so it was a good idea to get there in plenty of time. He checked the contents of his bag, running number, sponsor money, safety pins, spare kit, sports tape, plus other bits and bobs he thought might come in handy.

Sidney Greenstreet was already ensconced on the bin, washing his face with his giant paws, and planning his next meal. Such was life for this very spoilt cat. He would probably be in exactly the same spot when Mike came home in the afternoon.

There was indeed a slight chill in the air, and Mike could smell Autumn was on its way. He looked up at a bright blue sky and took a deep breath.

'*What a beautiful day,*' he thought to himself. '*Make the most of it Michael, we might not get many like this from now on. There will be snow on the road before we know it.*' He stopped and laughed to himself. '*Hang on a minute, I will be 'Snow' on the road!*'

He put his bag in the boot of the car, and set off for Laura's house.

They were already standing on the pavement waiting for him when he drew up, sporting their purple Stroke Resolution Run T-Shirts. Mike thought they looked like twins in their matching outfits. Laura had bought them matching track suits.

"Bit nippy this morning, Mike!" Laura said excitedly.

She sat in the front next to him, and he could see how nervous she was.

"You ok?" he asked.

"Yeah, yeah. Think so. Just excited. Aren't we Gracie?" she replied.

"Mum's worried she might not finish it, and you'll think she's not very good, Uncle Mike," came the voice from the back.

Laura shot her daughter a disparaging look.

"Well, that's what you said!" Gracie whined.

"Right, right ok. We're both just a bit nervous, Mike, sorry," Laura tried to smooth things over.

"Girls, this is your first ever race. *Of course* you're going to be nervous. Honestly, you'll just love it. Try and relax and just enjoy the run. It's all about taking part, doesn't matter how fast or slow you are." He leaned over so he was facing them both. "Both of you, I just want to say how immensely proud I am. Despite everything you've been through in the last few months, you're incredible. Let's go smash it, and raise a few quid for the Stroke Association too."

"Thanks Mike," Laura said and she put her hand on his arm. "Means a lot to us. Doesn't it Grace?"

The little girl nodded.

"Are your mum and dad coming down to watch?" Mike asked.

"Too right they are!" Laura replied. "Just try and keep them away!"

* * *

They parked up and all three of them eagerly jumped out of the car, joining other runners in purple t-shirts going in the same direction.

It was still cool and crisp, so they moved quickly across to the entrance of the Gardens, and showed their numbers to the ladies on the door. They had a short walk up to the start line and registration desk, and Grace was pointing to the fairies made out of wire.

"That one's my favourite, Uncle Mike," she pointed out. "That one blowing the dandelion, it's lovely, isn't it?"

Mike nodded. "As we run 'round we can count how many there are."

They proceeded up to the start line where a good number of people where gathered already. Music was coming from the stage, and the compere was telling everyone that warm up would start soon.

"Let's go and put this sponsor money in," Mike said. "It's weighing a ton in my bag."

The lady behind the desk checked them in, and was delighted to see how much they had raised.

"My grandad had a stroke a few months ago," Grace told her.

"Oh, I see," said the lady. "How is he doing?"

"Much better, thank you. I'm reading the Harry Potter books to him," Grace added.

"Come on, love," Laura called. "It's warm up any time now."

They all just had time to pin their numbers to the front of their vests and set up fitness apps, before the rest of the trotters arrived.

"Mike! Mike!" Beige Keith was waving frantically as he pushed politely through the rapidly growing crowd. He was closely followed by Pam and the rest of them.

They greeted each other excitedly with hugs. Pam had really pushed the boat out and had on a purple wig. Lucy had a purple tutu and Keith was not beige today, he had bought himself some purple running tights.

"Wow, guys you look amazing!" Mike said with a big smile on his face. He just knew that today of all days, he could not have been happier.

A few moments later, Carol arrived pushing Ron in a wheelchair.

Laura screamed and ran towards them. "Oh my God, Mum, Dad!" she shouted. "We're starting in 20 minutes! I'm so excited, I really need a wee."

"You're going to miss the warm up, Mum!" Grace

said concerned. "But I really need one too."

They decided to run quickly down to the café and relieve themselves one last time before the start, and Pam joined them.

Mike was getting concerned that they might only get back in time to start at 10 am.

'Come on girls, cutting it fine,' he thought to himself.

Sure enough, through the myriad of purple he saw them striding back towards him. He felt a hand on his shoulder. It was Carol and Ron.

"We just wanted to say, bloody good luck Mike, and thanks. Thanks for everything you've done for the girls in the last few months. We're so grateful," Carol said and gave him a very tight hug. Why was it that most of the women in his life gave such strong hugs?

Mike shook Ron's hand, and Ron gave him a knowing wink.

"Good chap," he said slowly, and winked again.

"Desperate for a fag," whispered Carol in Mike's ear. "Anywhere I can go? Feel like I really shouldn't, being around all these fit people," she added.

"Erm, I'm not sure actually Carol, what the rules are for smoking," he replied quietly.

"Don't worry, ought to think about giving them up really," she said with genuine sadness in her voice.

"I know some people who could help you with that. If you like. No pressure."

"Thanks, I'll give it some thought."

Pam, Laura and Grace joined them and looked at their watches. They had 10 minutes before the start of the race.

"Oh my God, I feel a bit sick," Laura suddenly announced.

Carol immediately stepped in and took her aside.

From what Mike could see, she was telling her to get a grip and pull herself together. Within seconds, she was pulling Grace over to the warm up session, and Mike and Pam did a few stretches of their own.

It was then time to line up. Five minutes to go. Laura took hold of Mike's hand.

"You will stay with us, won't you?" she asked.

"Every step," he replied.

The race co-ordinator asked for those doing the 5k to stand towards the back of the large crowd. Laura looked around her and guessed there were probably 200 plus runners. She smiled to herself and took a deep breath.

"Those doing the 15k are at the front," Mike whispered. "Then the 10s."

"Why is that?" Laura asked.

"They stagger it so as to avoid lots of runners bunching up at any one point."

"Oh, I see," she replied.

"Have a great run everybody!" shouted the co-ordinator, and that was it, they were off.

Mike was glad he hadn't packed his headphones. Laura and Grace would need lots of encouragement, and all his attention in the next hour. He had agreed with Pam and Keith beforehand that the girls had his priority. Pam said she would be just fine plodding along behind and Keith said he would keep an eye out for the other Trotters on the way 'round.

It was going well. They had run past the café and were entering the Italian Gardens, and the weather was still good. Grace loved the fact that there were photographers along the way, and she waved and smiled at each one of them.

They were just coming out of the Italian Gardens,

towards the lake, when Laura touched Mike's arm.

"Need to power walk a bit," she said breathlessly.

"Ok, that's fine," he replied. He could see that she needed to get her breath back a little, so they slowed right down. A couple of the other runners were doing the same, so Laura didn't feel quite so self-conscious.

A younger lady in a blue wig ran past her and smiled. "You're doing great!" she said. "First time?"

"Thank you!" Laura replied. "Yes, it is."

"You can do it!" the lady shouted back.

Laura seemed touched by the fact that a total stranger was shouting words of encouragement, but Mike explained that the running community was a tight knit one, and highly supportive.

"Ok, let's go again!" Laura said and they started running again, but Mike slowed the pace down slightly.

"Hi Nannie!" shouted Grace as she caught sight of Carol on the side of the path taking photographs of them all. They waved frantically at each other. Carol was visibly moved by the whole occasion and blew them kisses.

"We're so proud of you!" she shouted after them.

They were now nearing the other café at the other end of the lake, and ran over the wooden bridge, up past the boating club.

"How are we for time?" Laura asked.

Mike looked briefly at his fitness watch.

"We're ok," he said. "Don't worry about your time, but we're fine. Eighteen minutes so far."

"Wow, that's bloody good," she replied.

Grace seemed to be having a great time, and kept up with them well. Once past the café they entered the wooded part of the race. Here, Mike thought, they may start to struggle, and he slowed the pace down. The water station was on their left, but they declined it as politely as they could.

Sure enough, Laura was showing signs of struggle. Mike could see that her energy levels were draining, and he knew just the thing to help with that.

"Here," he said to them both. "Stick one of these in each cheek." He handed them two energy sweets each. "Careful you don't choke though. Tuck them into the sides of your cheek by your teeth. They'll dissolve slowly and give you enough energy to get around."

"Bloody hell," Laura whispered to Mike as they came up to one of the marshals. "I'm gonna be like a chimp on acid by the time I get to the finish line then."

Mike laughed.

The run through the woods seemed long to Laura, but the energy sweets seemed to help after a while. Mike looked behind him briefly to see if he could spot any of the others. About half a kilometre behind he thought he could see Pam, or it could have been anyone in a purple wig, there were so many in fancy dress.

They were now faced with a slight hill up to the left, and Grace wanted to stop.

"I'm really tired, Mummy," she said.

"Look, we've only got about 1 kilometre to go," Laura assured her. "Come on Gracie, we can do this. Think of Granddad. I'll hold one hand, Mike will hold the other, ok?"

"Ok," she said quietly.

Laura knew that this was proving far more tough for them than she had first imagined. When she said the words '5k' it seemed to just slip off the tongue easily. Actually doing it was dammed hard, she thought. But Mike gave them both words of encouragement again.

"Don't think of how far you still have to go," he panted. "Turn and look how far you have already come!"

Laura took Grace's hand and Mike took the other, and they ran up the hill. A marshal was standing to their left cheering them on and signalling for them to turn right.

"You're nearly there, guys!" she shouted enthusiastically "Come on, you can do it!"

Laura was so tired by this time she just managed a thumbs-up.

A board was looming in the distance which told them that they only had 1 kilometre to go. Laura felt she could have kissed it.

"I'm tired, Mummy," panted Grace again.

"I know, darling," she could barely speak now. "So am I. We have to keep going, I can see the finish line!"

It was true. Their hearts lifted as the finish line was in sight.

Suddenly out of nowhere, the lady from earlier in the blue wig came bounding across the field shouting at them.

"Come on!" she called to them. "You're nearly there! You can do it," and proceeded to run with them. She had evidently already finished, and Laura couldn't believe that this mad woman was running a bit more. 'Oh, to be as fit as that,' she thought.

As they ran down the long pathway and turned right onto the home straight, Laura's strength seemed to return a little and she put every effort she had into the final stretch. She could see her mum and dad standing by the finish line beaming with pride. Mike looked across at Laura as they came closer, and he could see tears in her eyes. She wiped one away quickly with the back of her free hand and sniffed.

One last surge of energy taken from somewhere deep down saw them over the finish line.

It was done.

Laura's first reaction was to burst into tears. Grace took a bottle of water that had been handed to her and pressed it to her forehead. Mike stood and watched them both. The lady in the blue wig patted Laura on the back and they exchanged a hug.

"Thank you so much," she said.

Laura's attention then focused on Mike as she regained a normal breathing pattern.

He motioned to them to collect their medals, and Laura took hold of Mike's and placed it 'round his neck.

Without saying a word, she gave him a long, lingering kiss.

"I've been waiting five long years for that," he said afterwards.

"So have I," she replied.

They walked hand in hand with Grace over to Ron and Carol. Mike knelt down next to the wheelchair and let Ron hold the medal.

"That's for you," he said.

Ron was noticeably moved.

"Good chap," Ron replied slowly, and they all walked down to the café to meet the others for a well-earned drink.

EPILOGUE

It was the following summer, and Laura was sitting at a dressing table in a hotel room.

She applied her make-up with care and put up her hair.

"You look beautiful, Mum. Mike's going to think so too," said Grace sitting on the edge of the bed, all dressed up and ready.

"Thank you Gracie, so do you," she replied. "I'll just put my dress on and we'll be ready to go?"

Gracie nodded.

Today was going to be a big day for everyone.

END OF PART 1

Snow's
Angels

A V Turner

Book 2 of "In It for the Long Run" – the Mike Snow trilogy

CHAPTER ONE

Mike Snow was a very happy man. He was in fact, probably the happiest he had been in his entire life. He was standing by the window overlooking Aberdovey Bay, which was bathed in sunshine. He turned to look at himself in the full-length mirror, and adjusted his suit. The flower in his button hole had been freshly picked that morning, and the smell from it was heavenly.

It would soon be time to head off to the wedding, and he felt a surge of excitement in his stomach. Things had come an awfully long way in the space of a year, and he smiled to himself, happy in the fact that it was all working out just fine.

It is a cliché, but true, that time is a great healer. At the end of March, Jim and Julia welcomed their son, Noah. A half-brother for Gracie. Jim was the ex of Mike's girlfriend, Laura, parents of Gracie. Despite relations being strained for a long time, Noah's birth brought a peace to the five of them. Mike, in particular, decided life was too bloody short to bear a grudge, and

Laura agreed that a child should not come into the world surrounded by bad feeling and malice. So it was then, that Jim, Julia, Mike, Laura and Gracie decided to bury the hatchet and just get on with life. It worked out so well, in fact that today August 13th was Jim and Julia's wedding day. Mike and his new family were in attendance.

"Funny how life turns out sometimes," Mike thought to himself. He was just happy that he and Laura were together. They had officially started dating at the finish line of the Trentham 5k and had been pretty much inseparable ever since. Only a month before Jim's wedding, they had moved in together, to Mike's house. Grace was happy because Sidney Greenstreet was allowed to sleep on her bed. The fact that he took up most of the bed, sprawling out on his back with legs in the air, didn't seem to bother her at all.

"Are you ready then, handsome?" Laura asked as she stood in the doorway.

Mike turned to look at her, and his heart swelled a little bit more. He guessed his heart would soon be the size of a rugby ball, the rate it was going.

"Oh, love, you look beautiful," he said looking at her. Gracie appeared from behind her mum and bounced into the room.

"Thanks Mike!" she joked and ran up to give him a big hug.

"You both look lovely," he laughed and winked at Laura. "Come on then, we don't want to be late," he added and they left the hotel room.

The sun streamed in through the windows of the small registry office onto the happy couple. There were no bridesmaids and no best man. Julia's mum held Noah, who at four-months-old thought it was very appropriate to squeal throughout the entire ceremony. Laura privately thought this was hilarious. She glanced sideways at Grace and they exchanged a smile. She felt a sense of relief when Jim and Julia were pronounced man and wife, and she was genuinely happy for them. 'Let's just see how long it is before he starts messing you about, love,' she couldn't help thinking to herself.

A select few attended a reception afterwards; there were no speeches, but they all enjoyed a three-course lunch.

"Can't wait to get these heels off, and get off home to be honest," Laura whispered in Mike's ear.

"Me too," he whispered back. "Bloody shoes are killing me." They smiled and held hands under the table. *"Could life get any better?"* Mike thought to himself.

Three hours later they were indeed on their way home. Laura had phoned Carol to check in, see how her dad was doing, and if Sidney had missed them. Grace snored softly in the back seat.

"Hi Mum! We're just on our way home, how's things?" Laura asked.

"Absolutely fine darling, all good here. Just hang on a tick, I'm lighting my first fag of the day." Laura knew this was probably Carol's sixth fag of the day, but she let it go. Her mother had still not managed to kick the cigarettes despite trying two or three times. The truth was, Carol was hell to be around when she went cold turkey, she had repeatedly burnt the ironing, and had once put the kettle in the washing machine. Such was her addiction. So, they thought it probably best she just kept on smoking for the time being. Sometimes, it took a few attempts.

"Right! I'm back with you!" Carol said and exhaled

loudly on the other end of the phone. "Am I on loud speak?"

"No, Mum you're ok. Anyway, Grace's spark out in the back seat," Laura confirmed as she glanced in the rear-view mirror.

"Excellent. So! How did it go then? He now officially belongs to someone else!" Carol took another drag on her cigarette.

"Yep, he is now signed off to Julia. Big relief, I can tell you. It all went fine though. Noah screamed all the way through the ceremony. Classic." Laura giggled.

Her mother gave a loud throaty, smoker's laugh and even Mike could hear it from a few feet away.

"Ha, ha! Bloody marvellous. I bet Jim stood there looking like a turd in a trance, didn't he?" Carol asked.

"Yeah, pretty much. Anyway, all done now Mum, we're on our way home. Dad and Sid ok?"

Carol confirmed they were both fine and on the sofa together watching football. Ron had suffered another small TIA in the June, but was being closely monitored by the hospital, and Carol made sure he got plenty of rest and lots of fresh air. She had purchased a wheelchair and took him on walks 'round the lake at Trentham.

They said their goodbyes and Laura put her phone back in her handbag. All was well.

She and Mike sat in a comfortable silence for a while. The sun was shining and they were making good time. "Be a lovely night for a run," Mike thought.

"Do you fancy a run this evening?" Laura asked him.

"Excellent idea," he replied. "Could just do a two, three-miler?"

"Yeah," Laura agreed. "Feels like we've been

cooped up a bit over the last two days. Need to stretch our legs. What races have we got left this year?"

Mike thought for a moment. They had already done four park runs in 6 months, and were doing the Trentham Stroke run again in the October.

"Well, apart from Trentham, we haven't got anything booked at all now. Unless you want to do some more Shrewsbury runs on a Saturday?"

Laura thought for a moment. She loved the park runs, and they always combined it with a look 'round the shops followed by tea out.

"Tell you what, I'll have a look online when we get home to see what's going on locally next year. We could do Market Drayton 10k. Might be some spaces left." Mike reached over and held her hand.

"Bloody hell. A 10k? I've only ever done 5, I don't know if I've got it in me to go further." Laura looked concerned.

"With the right training love, you can do anything," he reassured her. "Honestly."

"I dunno. Bloody long way." Laura sighed and looked out of the window. "Quite fancy it though. Be the furthest I've ever ran. Be really proud of myself if I could do it," she thought.

"Would the training be hard?" she asked.

"Not really," Mike reassured her. "Think of it as a 5k, and then another one. As long as you build up gradually, you'll be ok. You can do a 5 now without blinking. Just remember how shattered you were when you did the first one. Come a long way since then."

He was right, of course. She could do a 5k without any bother these days. Her stamina was increasing. The last park run she had managed to do in 35:20. A personal best.

"Okay then," she said. "Deal." They shook on it.

Mike smiled to himself. *'That's my girl,'* he thought. *'I'll get her doing a half marathon, yet.'*

"Just don't even think about asking me to do a half," she added. "Because the answer will be a definite no."

Laura thought she heard him let out a disappointed sigh, but chose to ignore it.

CHAPTER TWO

That evening, whilst Laura was changing into her running kit, she allowed herself a quick look in the mirror. She had now lost a total of 14 pounds in weight. A stone off her small frame had made a massive difference. She was pleased that her bottom had decreased somewhat, her stomach flattened, muffin tops shrunk back down into their paper cases, and her boobs were acceptably strapped into the corset-like running bra. She was very thankful for that bra. *Nothin' was goin' nowhere* when she had that thing on!

It was another family affair, their run that evening. She was pleased that Grace joined them regularly, and it was the perfect end to a lovely day. They headed out at 6.30 pm into the last of the sunshine for a gentle run around the streets, combined with popping in to see Carol and Ron on the way back. Sidney was eagerly waiting his trip home. There's no bed like a human bed, when you're a cat of that size. Carol had insisted that he sleep in the kitchen at their house, on a proper cat bed. Oh, the indignity of it.

There were a lot of people out that evening, mowing lawns, walking dogs, neighbours chatting, washing cars and watering flowerbeds. Mike liked to wave and say hello, but stopping to chat was a no, because it interrupted the flow of his run. A quick polite "evening!" was all he was prepared to give, as he passed by. Laura was only a few paces ahead and Grace a little way behind.

"Mum! Mike!" she shouted suddenly and the whole family came to a standstill. Laura stood with her hands on her hips.

"What's the matter, love?" she asked. "It better be good, because I was on a roll there!" Laura glanced at her sports watch and paused it.

"I've got cramp!" Grace winced in pain, and started hopping around on the pavement. Mike immediately went to her aid, and whipped out of his running belt a small pot of muscle rub. Instructing her to pull her toes upwards, she then rubbed some of the liniment onto the calf muscle. "Oh, that's better!" she sighed. "Smells amazing too." Mike expected an "awesome" to be included, as it was her favourite word of the moment, but she was obviously saving it for another time.

"Just let me know when you are ready to go again," he said. Laura was now holding her daughter up by the elbow to give her tightened leg muscle a chance to recover itself. They all agreed that cramp was not a pleasant thing, with a stitch being a close second.

They were just about to set off again, when a young man walked by with a little dog. He smiled at them and said hello. "You ok, guys?" he asked, and the dog stopped to sniff the balm on Grace's leg.

"Oh, we're fine thank you," Laura replied. "She's just got a bit of cramp. Be on our way again in a minute. Thanks anyway."

He nodded and smiled again. Mike and Laura looked down at the dog and gave it a fuss. "Sweet," said Laura. "What's its name?"

"Winston," said the young man. "Border terrier. Only a year old."

By this time of course, Winston was lying on the pavement having his tummy tickled by all three of them and loving it. The fact that they were all cooing over him, made him love the situation even more.

"What are they like with cats, generally?" asked Mike.

"Pretty good, actually," the young man replied. "He lives with one. They get on fine."

Mike nodded. "Like exercise?"

"Yeah. He can walk for miles, this one."

They finished fussing over Winston, much to the dog's dismay, and the young man said a polite farewell.

"Ready then?" Laura asked Grace. "All right to run on, love?"

Grace put her brave face on and nodded. They had all been so preoccupied with the little dog, fifteen minutes had gone by. It was time to get over to Carol and Ron's and pick up the feline enigma that was Sidney Greenstreet.

As they ran towards the road that her parents lived on, Laura couldn't help wondering what that great big, fat, stubborn cat would make of a dog entering his house. She envisaged Sidney's eyes widening at the horror of one having the audacity to cross the threshold. That was a step too far.

"Nice dog," Mike said to Laura, sowing a seed. His

words hung in the evening air.

"Yes, really sweet," she replied after a few moments.

"Are we getting one?!" Grace asked excitedly. "It could come running with us! Please!"

Laura raised her eyebrows and looked at Mike. His expression was the same as Grace's. Pleading and puppy-like.

"Oh, for goodness sake," she said. "We'll have to talk about it. You can't just get a dog. It takes a lot of planning."

Of course, within a month, they were indeed the proud owners of a rescue Border Terrier. He was just six-months-old, and had no name, so after much deliberation, was called Humphrey Bogart. Mike thought it very fitting and it sort of suited him. It also went very well with Sidney Greenstreet, as Mike informed his girls that the real film stars had been in a movie together called "The Maltese Falcon" in 1941, a classic and one of his personal favourites.

It was true that they were all just a little bit in love with their new arrival. Despite only being a pup still, he was remarkably good-natured, and not too much of a chewer. Only one cushion from the sofa had bitten the dust so far. Laura could not quite believe how much stuffing possibly came out of a relatively small home furnishing, but it had gone everywhere. A puppy crate was purchased quite rapidly after that, and everyone relaxed, happy in the knowledge that all soft furnishings were now safe. Even Sidney seemed content to watch his arch enemy behind bars for part of the day. Laura fancied she had almost seen the cat smile, but of course that was all in her imagination, wasn't it?

It was obvious from day one who was going to be boss. Humph, as he was affectionately known, thought the big, fat, fluffy cat was great fun to play with and bark at. A swift smack on the nose without claws soon put him in his place. Next time, Sidney thought, the claws would most certainly be out. He had it all planned. One afternoon, shortly after Humph arrived and the hissing, spitting and arching back routine had ceased, Sidney retreated to his favourite place in the garden to sulk and contemplate his next move. As he washed his face with a very fat paw, he decided that no dog was ever going to knock him off top spot. New female humans were one thing, but a DOG? What on earth was Dad thinking?

He had listened to them talking about the fact that a canine running companion was a good idea. Of course, running was not something Sidney was remotely interested in, unless it involved food or fuss. He could run to his bowl, or Grace's bed. That was the long and short of it.

So, it was then, that very afternoon, sat on his throne: the patio table, Sidney decided he would continue to be King of his castle, and the hound would simply have to tow the line. End of story, and that's exactly how it came to pass. The pecking order was cast in stone.

CHAPTER THREE

Life for the Snow's settled down nicely and they were all very happy. Laura's previous existence with Jim was but a distance memory. Mike was a very different character to her ex-husband. More easy going and generous. A little serious at times, she thought but a real gentleman and most importantly, completely selfless. She had been unsure whether her wounded soul could cope with another relationship, but she had secretly always carried a torch for Mike. Whenever he had got himself a girlfriend in the past, there had been a little sting of jealousy in her head, but Laura had taken in a big breath and privately hoped it would come to nothing; which of course it did. Thankfully, he was now all hers, and she intended to keep it that way. She loved him for his kindness and gentle nature, and they were happy.

When he came home from work that evening, Laura could tell he was on some sort of mission, because he became all determined and business like.

"I've been thinking," he announced at the dinner

table. Laura and Grace looked up expectantly. Even Humph's ears pricked up in anticipation.

"If we're going to be doing a 10k sometime early next year, we need a training plan for you."

"Can I do it, as well Mike?" asked Grace.

"Unfortunately, not honey," he tried to break the news to her gently. "It's a bit different to the Stroke run. Kids can enter that, but when it comes to anything more than a 5k, the entry age stipulates only 15-years-old and over."

She pulled a face and looked very disappointed. "Got a few years yet then before I can enter."

"Yes. BUT! you can still train with us," Laura tried to reassure her.

"Yeah, but then all that hard work will be for nothing, Mum," she replied.

Mike took a sip of his wine and thought a moment.

"It won't all be for nothing Grace. You'll still be with your mum and me. You and Humph can help us. You'll both be an important part of our training plan."

Grace seemed to take great interest in the fact that Humphrey Bogart was on board. She looked over at him, and his big brown eyes glanced from one to the other. In his head he was sure that he had been signed up for something big, but he wasn't too sure what it was. As long as it involved a walk or food, he was up for the challenge.

Their conversation was interrupted by Mike's mobile ringing. He had left it in his jacket pocket, so Grace went to fetch it for him.

His face darkened somewhat when he looked at the missed call.

"Melvin," he said flatly. "I'll ring him later," he said and smiled at Laura.

Melvin or Mel, was Mike's older brother by four years. They seldom saw each other, because as with a lot of siblings, they didn't really get on. Mel didn't earn the name: "Snows-it-all" for nothing. He was quite the most pompous, opinionated and arrogant human being Laura had ever had the displeasure to meet. It hadn't always been that way of course. During their younger years, at home with their now deceased parents, the brothers had enjoyed happiness and harmony. But Mel's degree and highly paid job had swollen his head to ridiculous proportions, to the point where he had difficulty getting through doors, metaphorically speaking. Laura had only met him once, and wondered within 5 minutes of their introduction just how long he would last with that ego in the presence of her mum. Carol, of course would reduce the guy to mush, she was sure. Melvin was evidently used to being the top earner, and the most successful of the two boys, and even the slightest threat of Mike stealing his crown reduced the elder to a jealous, sanctimonious arsehole, who would belittle Mike in a heartbeat. Subsequently, despite only living 8 miles apart, their paths seldom crossed.

"What will he be wanting, I wonder," Mike said in a monotone voice.

"Why don't you and Humph go for a walk, give him a ring back?" Laura suggested.

"Good idea. Won't be long," he smiled and kissed her. "I'll load the dishwasher when I get back."

Mike threw on his hoodie as the sun was disappearing behind some ominous looking clouds, and headed out the door with Humph in tow.

A little way down the road, he returned his brother's call.

"Hi! You're through to the voicemail of Melvin Snow, IT Consultant. I can't take your call right now, because I'm busy helping improve someone's company with my IT skills. Please leave a message and I'll get back to you when I'm free."

The message said it all.

Mike groaned in embarrassment and hung up.

No sooner had he finished cringing than his phone started up again.

"Hi," Mike said flatly.

"Mikey!" said the voice on the other end of the phone. Mike hated being called that, unless it was by Laura in one of their cosier moments.

"What can I do for you, Mel?"

"Bro, how are you doing? Haven't seen you guys in ages." Mel was unusually amiable and friendly.

"We're fine thanks. How are you?" Mike was retaining his monotone voice.

"Well, actually not so great, really. I was going to ask you a favour, Mikey." Mel had that annoying sales thing where he kept mentioning your name in every sentence. It made Mike cringe a little bit more.

The silence obviously made the older brother feel uncomfortable, and he coughed nervously.

"What sort of favour?"

"Erm, thing is. I just wondered if I could come and stay with you guys for a couple of days?" he asked gingerly.

"How many?" Mike's voice sounded concerned.

"Oh, only a couple. It's just, well, Moira and I need a bit of space, you know. Just wondered if you would like to hang out with your brother for a bit!"

Mike did not like the sound of this at all.

"Have you split up?" Mike asked.

"No, no, no. Nothing like that. I just need some space, Moira's menopause is causing some friction in the house, you know how it is. Women's stuff. They get a bit paranoid, don't they? This time of life."

Mike bristled. Nothing was ever Mel's fault. It was always someone else's.

"I'll ask Laura first. Let you know. When do you want to come and stay?" Mike asked.

"Tonight?" his brother asked.

"What? Jesus Melvin, why didn't you give us more notice?" Mike was annoyed now and it showed in his voice.

"Well, things got a bit heated around tea-time," was Mel's reply.

Mike explained that he was taking the dog for a walk, then would head home around 8-ish and ask Laura. He agreed to ring his brother back and let him know. As they finished the conversation he fancied he heard Moira shouting something obscene in the background followed by the smashing of crockery, but he couldn't be sure.

He looked down at Humphrey Bogart and sighed. "Looks like we will be having a house guest for a few days, eh Humph? Do you want to offer him your bed in the kitchen? You could come sleep with Mummy and me." Mike smiled as the little dog looked up at him with those lovely brown eyes, and he cocked his head to one side. It started to rain very softly so they headed home, making a brief stop at the off-licence on the way.

"How long for?" asked Laura when Mike broke the news. He had made sure she had a drink in her hand at the time.

"Couple of days. He says."

"Well, it's your house love, I mean I really don't

mind. Will he be ok in the box room?"

"He'll have to be," Mike smirked.

He hugged her and they both wondered how the next 48 hours was going to pan out. It was certainly going to be very interesting.

Within a very short space of time, Melvin was indeed their new house guest. He must have had his bag packed pretty smart-ish, because his brother was sitting in their lounge within 35 minutes of being given the go ahead.

Mike also knew that Mel would most probably behave himself for the first 24 hours, then relax after that, and revert to being a complete knob. This had happened many times in the past. Mike and Laura also knew, however, that once he started behaving like a knob, that was probably the best time to introduce him to Carol. She would single-handedly reduce his overblown ego to quivering jelly, and all whilst sipping a gin and tonic and smoking a fag.

With Grace in bed, Mike was true to his word and loaded the dishwasher. He fed a permanently hungry Sidney and then joined Laura on the sofa, whilst his brother sat awkwardly in the armchair.

"So, things aren't going too well I take it," Mike said after a long silence.

"Noooo," Mel replied whilst exhaling loudly. He took another gulp of his wine, and sat back in the chair. The tips of his ears were turning pink, and a rosy glow tinted his freckled cheeks. The wine was relaxing him and he started to feel mellow.

He sniffed loudly, which he did often, Laura noticed. Taller than Mike by about 3 inches, he carried a lot of weight, and didn't appear to have much of a neck. Now he was sitting in their home and she had time to study him, she noticed more about his general demeanour than last time they met. The hair colour was the same as Mike's but Mel had more of it, typically. He was fairly tanned, but obviously overweight as his stomach was trying to force its way out between the buttons of his expensive shirt. She looked away.

"I mean, and no disrespect here Laura, as you are a woman yourself," he said putting his hand up apologetically, "but the menopause is causing some terrific problems at home." He nodded knowingly, took a deep overweight sigh, and another large gulp of his wine.

"You can pop another one in there, Mikey, if you wouldn't mind. I've brought a couple of bottles with me. Only the good stuff, of course," he laughed in an *I can get away with anything* sort of way.

"Have you eaten?" Laura asked, thinking he probably didn't need to.

"Oh yes, thanks Laura. Had tea with the boys earlier. Of course, we only eat organic, you see. Far better for you," he winked.

'If you think you're getting that here you can bugger off,' she thought to herself.

"So how are Moira and the boys generally?" Mike asked as he poured another glass of wine for his brother, and one for Laura. "Apart from the menopause."

"Oh, well the boys are doing fantastically well at school, of course. Both gifted and talented and showing all the signs of doing very well when they leave. They'll be going to University and getting degrees without much effort," Mel bragged.

'But of course they bloody will,' thought Mike. His

nephews, Simon and Melvin Jnr were 14-year-old twins. Simon was a pleasantly quiet, thoughtful boy, much like his mother, but Melvin on the other hand, was exactly like his father. Obnoxious and arrogant. In their father's eyes they were however, perfect in every way, faultless and never put a foot wrong.

They spent the rest of the evening mainly listening to Mel brag about his amazing sons, and talk about how much his wife had failed him.

By 10.30 pm Mike had had enough, and Laura felt like she had been squashed into a confined space by his enormous ego. Time to bring him down to earth a little.

"You'll be ok in the spare room, won't you Mel?" She smiled as she got up and stretched.

"Oh yes, it's only for a few nights," he replied slurring his words slightly. "I'm sure I can cope with a pokey box room for that long."

Laura felt like drop kicking him into the 'pokey box room' slamming the door and sticking two fingers up, but she reminded herself that this was Mike's brother, and politely showed him his new accommodation.

"Bathroom is across the hall, next to our bedroom. I've put some towels out on the bed," she whispered, so as not to wake Grace.

"Oh, it's ok. Brought my own. Egyptian cotton. Only the best," he replied wrinkling his face patronisingly.

"Of course. Wouldn't want you to get a rash now, would we?" Laura said through semi-gritted teeth. "Night then, Mel."

She climbed into bed and snuggled up to Mike, who was already asleep and snoring softly.

CHAPTER FOUR

When Mike got up the following morning, his brother was already at the breakfast table. He had been to the local supermarket, purchased organic bread, butter and jam, and was slowly munching noisily on it whilst reading The Times newspaper.

"Not working today, Michael?"

"No, not today. Just off out for a quick run." Mike's reply was terse.

Mel paused briefly and looked up from his paper. He sniggered to himself.

"Not still on with that lark, are you? Really bad for your knees you know. I knew a bloke dropped dead after one of those long marathon-y things. I'd be careful if I were you."

Mike thought for a moment, and took a deep breath. He could go about this two ways. Option 1 was to completely lose his temper and give his brother the bollocking from hell, or Option 2 was to ignore the inane crap that was currently spilling out of his mouth, and rise above it.

He chose the latter.

"See you later, Melvin. Come on Humph, let's go for a nice RUN," he replied and disappeared out the door.

It was early, only 7 am. Laura and Grace were still in bed, but Mike felt the need for an early one. Not only would it set him up for the day, but it would also relieve the stress that was creeping up on him by the hour.

He attached Humphrey's lead to his harness, and they set off for a gentle 5-miler.

Barely a mile in, Humph was having none of it. There were too many walls, clumps of grass and pavements to sniff, and all of them had to be urinated on. The amount of times Mike's arm had been yanked in the wrong direction was starting to make his shoulder ache.

"Seriously? For goodness sake dog, give me a bloody break, will you? You need the exercise as much as I do. Come on, stop the sniffing and let's just run." Mike was suddenly aware that he was standing in the middle of a pavement having a conversation with a border terrier, and the postman was looking decidedly uneasy as he walked by.

He sighed as Humphrey lay down and rolled over for his tummy to be rubbed. He wagged his tail for good measure.

"Come on matey," Mike said quietly giving the little dog a fuss. "Let's get on with it. Nice treat at home after, yes?"

The word treat saw Humphrey's ears prick up and he jumped into action. As long as Mike could keep him away from the interesting smells, they could do their run without it taking forever.

Mike loved this time of day. It was going to be fine and balmy, and he could already feel the warmth of the sun on his back. The trees were rustling gently in the breeze, and the flowers in the front gardens were waking up and pointing their heads to bask in the warmth of a new day. He and his canine companion had finally found their rhythm and the five miles became six. Mike felt so much more relaxed and ready for any challenge that lay ahead of him, so they headed home for a well-earned breakfast.

As it was a particularly lovely Saturday weather-wise, they had decided to stay at home, potter around in the garden, have a barbeque and invite Carol and Ron over for drinks at around 5 pm. Mike and Laura both thought this was a fantastic idea, in view of the fact that her parents had not yet met Melvin, or his ego. Secretly, they couldn't wait until early evening, so they could have front row seats to see Carol make absolute mincemeat of him. They would have quite happily paid good money for tickets, in fact.

Mel decided that another trip to the supermarket was in order. He couldn't possibly eat non-organic sausages. He shuddered at the very mention of Laura's home-made burgers, and recoiled at the idea of everything else they were planning to cook. So off he went, in pursuit of perfection for his plate. By the time 5 pm came around, Laura was on her first cocktail and taking her frustrations out on a poor unsuspecting salad. If she mixed it much more, Mike thought, it would end up being a smoothie.

When her parents walked through the front door, Laura greeted them with extra fervour, and Mike gave Carol an exuberant hug. He even hugged Ron, such was his relief.

"Having problems, darling?" she whispered in Mike's ear.

"Am I glad to see you, Carol. Have I told you lately that I love you?" he whispered back, desperation in his voice.

She gave a deep throaty laugh in his ear, and winked at Laura. "Do introduce us to your brother, Mike."

By now, Grace had joined them all in the garden, eager to see her grandmother in action. 'This was going to be awesome,' she thought to herself.

Laura placed a vodka martini in Carol's well-manicured hand, and breathed a sigh of relief. Her mother was here. Everything was right with the world.

"Carol and Ron, this is Melvin, my brother. Melvin, this is my mother-in-law, Carol and my father-in-law, Ron."

Mel stretched out his hand and shook Ron's then fixed his attention on Carol. Instead of a customary shake though, he turned on the charm and kissed the back of her free hand, not taking his eyes from hers. She said nothing, until he released her.

"I can see where Laura gets her good looks from," he said, oozing oil from every pore.

Still Carol stared at him, making no comment. The atmosphere was so tense, it was impossible to know if anyone was breathing or not.

They all sat down around the patio table. It had been a baking hot day, and the heat was still evident. Hopefully it would give way to a balmy night, and they could enjoy being out in the garden until late.

Finally, Carol spoke.

"So, Melvin." She took a cigarette out of a shiny silver case from her handbag, and lit it with the loud clink of her lighter. Taking her time, she inhaled deeply, and blew it out through her nose. Mike was transfixed. It was like watching Joan Crawford in one of those films from the 40's. God, she was wonderful. Was she going straight for the jugular, or would she play with him for a while, like a cat with a mouse. He hoped for the latter.

"Tell me about yourself," she said, flashing her eyes at him.

"The next hour is going to be bloody amazing," Mike thought. Laura and Grace were thinking something similar. Ron simply sat admiring his wife, a smile on his face, eagerly anticipating what might come next. Even the dog was holding his breath. Sidney however, was eyeing up the smoked salmon on the patio table. Nothing much deterred him from his love of food, and his rapidly expanding waistline mirrored this.

Mel noticeably preened himself in preparation much like a peacock would, and smoothed his sandy hair back with his hand. He did that really irritating thing that Laura had grown to hate quickly, sniff before every sentence that came out of his mouth. His overweight sighs were starting to grate on her too. She hoped that he would soon be gone from their 'pokey little box room' and take his arrogant egotistical arse somewhere else.

"Where do I start, Carol. May I call you Carol?" he said, one eyebrow raised in a particularly slimey fashion.

"Well it is my name, so you might as well, hadn't you?" she replied quickly.

As Mike and the others watched, it soon became a bit like observing a tennis match. Mel serving very weakly, and Carol slamming the ball back over his side with vigour.

"Well, Carol. I'm a businessman, first and foremost. Very successful. Have my own IT firm. I also have two very bright sons. Twin boys, age 14. They'll do amazingly well when they leave school. Make a lot of money. Because that's what it's all about these days, Carol, isn't it? Money. Myself, I'm very comfortably off. Had to work for it of course, but I'm reaping the rewards now. I like the nice things in life, and I can afford them. Do you see where I'm coming from Carol?"

She sat back in her chair, the cigarette in her hand was slowly burning away, and a soft grey smoke drifted across her face as she studied him.

"You don't have to keep mentioning my name, I'm not senile," she replied flatly.

Mike took a sharp intake of breath. "Drinks anyone?" he asked cheerily. It broke the intensity of the atmosphere slightly and he disappeared into the house to replenish everyone's glasses. He poured himself a neat brandy, knocked it back and quickly went back outside so as not to miss any of the match.

By now, Mel was in full egotistical mode. He was mentally preening himself so much that he failed to notice Carol's icy stare. It was evident that she was at some point in the very near future, going to verbally slap him.

Mike and Laura decided to busy themselves with the barbeque, keeping an eye and ear on proceedings. Mel didn't offer to help, but instead shouted orders from his chair about how his organic food should be kept separate from the rest. He had even taken the precaution to stick address labels on all his food in the fridge with his name on it. *'Could he get any more pedantic?'* Mike thought.

Whilst he was cooking, he overheard his brother's voice getting louder. The more wine he consumed, the worse he became.

He sniffed loudly and followed it up with one of his sighs. "Of course, I absolutely insist on eating organic these days. So much better for you. I only ever used the top class supermarket over the other side of town. I mean, I wouldn't dream of setting foot inside that ghastly cheap supermarket you've got near here, what is it, Supersave? Urgh full of plastic cheap rubbish," he shuddered.

"Our friends own Supersave," Carol said in a loud voice.

It was true. They did. The atmosphere changed in the garden, and Mike could almost feel a winter descend on an otherwise hot afternoon.

Carol took out another cigarette from her silver case, and lit it. Whilst the grey mist swirled around her face, Mel's mouth finally came to a standstill.

"Worked very hard, they have, Mel," she added. "Worked all hours, in fact. Reaping the rewards now of course and they can finally afford the nice things in life, much like yourself, Mel. But," she said taking another drag of her cigarette, "I never hear them bragging about how much they've got. Very modest people. Both keen runners too, just like Mike and Laura, so they have that inner strength and determination. Which I find very admirable in a person. Don't you Mel?" She stared intently at him, awaiting a response, but he was unable to give one.

Game set, and match to Mrs. Beresford. It was all Mike could do to not give her a round of applause.

"Food's ready!" Laura said cheerily. Carol got up from her seat and went inside to collect the over-mixed salad, and a bowl containing some nice looking dip that Sidney Greenstreet had been coveting for the past half an hour. He had moved himself into position to start licking the top of it, but his plot had now been foiled. Damm it. He repositioned himself under the patio table with Humph in case anything dropped onto the floor.

They all sat in comparative silence around the table now, after Mel's terrific faux pas. But it wasn't long before he was bleating on about his organic sausages, wholegrain and chia seed bread roll, and organic chicken.

In truth, Mike had mixed the meat up on the barbecue, and after a brandy, and two vodka martinis had completely lost track of which was organic and which was the ordinary stuff that common people ate. A little pissed, he also really couldn't give a toss.

"So, which is which, Mike? You did keep mine separate, didn't you?" said his brother, desperately trying to belittle him.

"Jesus!" shouted Laura suddenly slamming her knife and fork down on the table, and she got up and went over to the barbecue. Almost immediately she returned, with a face like thunder and a blackened piece of chicken. She slammed the burnt offering on his plate, and sat back down again.

"Now just bloody well eat it, for Christ's sake!" Everyone stopped and looked at her with open mouths.

"Is it my organic chicken?" Mel asked after a convenient pause.

"YES!" everyone shouted.

It bounced around his plate somewhat, but he felt he had to eat it. Reaching over the table he grabbed three of his special sausages, and began to eat. Almost immediately his face started to turn purple and little beads of sweat appeared on his forehead. Mike realised quickly that this brother was choking on his organic, good-for-you food. He leapt up out of his seat, and ran 'round to him. By now Mel's face was the colour of beetroot and he was gasping for breath, frantically pointing at his excuse of a neck. Carol, Ron and Grace all stood up to try and help, but in doing so tipped the table up on its side, sending both posh and common people's food flying in all directions. Mike stood behind his brother and applied the Heimlich manoeuvre, giving three big pushes on his diaphragm to try and dislodge the offending piece of sausage.

Finally, it shot out of his mouth with such force, it hit Sidney Greenstreet on the bottom, as he was happily helping himself to the rest of the food on the floor. He gave a yowl and ran off into the house, leaving Humph to help himself to a veritable banquet.

CHAPTER FIVE

The following Monday night when the Trentham Trotters met up for their weekly run, the main topic of conversation was Mike's brother choking on a piece of organic sausage. Pam had laughed so hard, she had almost wet herself, and Keith was positively purple in the face with hysterics.

"Of course, we shouldn't laugh, really," said Pam once she had calmed herself. "It could have been quite serious."

"It could have been Pam, but I was on it quickly. He was absolutely fine afterwards. Sweating with a face full of snot, but alive and well," Mike replied.

They were about a kilometre into their 3k run of the evening. It was a short one because Keith had to get back for a meeting with his History club, so they wasted no time.

A couple more of the younger ones had dropped out of the Trotters, much to Mike's disappointment, and they had been two of the girls, which saddened

Keith. Matt was however, still with them, and showed no signs of leaving.

"You're stuck with me Mike, hope that's ok," he said cheerfully as they ran together.

"Goodness, absolutely Matt. It's sad when we lose a few though. But we've gained my lovely Laura," he smiled, proudly.

It was true that the Trotters now only consisted of Mike, Keith, Pam, Laura and Matt, and occasionally Grace. Secretly, Mike would have liked some new recruits, but it was very much a casual affair, and he was grateful for small mercies.

"Sorry, Boss," huffed Pam from the back. "Need a wee."

"No worries," shouted Matt. "I'll tell the others," and he ran off ahead a little whilst Mike acted as lookout. It was becoming the norm now, these toilet stops for Pam, but he didn't mind so much. He did however, wish she would make sure her underwear was in order before they started off again. As fond of her as he was, he found it a little disconcerting knowing exactly what kind of knickers she wore.

Laura came running back towards him. "Come to keep you company, love," she smiled, jogging on the spot.

"Oh thanks, I think she's almost done," he said. "You ready, Pam?"

The bush she had disappeared behind was rustling violently, and there was a lot of huffing and puffing going on. Laura guessed that knickers and running tights had had a bit of a disagreement, and she was desperately trying to regain harmony between the two.

"Yep, nearly! Just be a tick!" came the reply.

Suddenly, Pam burst through the foliage with a

relieved look on her red face. "All ready to go, sorry both! I think it was all that laughing did it. Couldn't wait any longer."

Laura giggled. "Don't worry, come on," and the three of them set off to catch up with the others.

On the way, they discussed the Stroke run. It was fast coming 'round, and they had decided to do it again. This time though, it would be rather different for them all. Matt and Mike were running the 10k, and Keith, Pam, Laura and Grace were running the 5 … pushing Ron in the wheelchair.

It had been a mad idea dreamed up mainly by Keith one night, when they had all met in the pub. He had seen it done before, he recalled and didn't look too hard going. In fact, so easy did it appear, that he had struggled to keep up with the young lady pushing her mum around the lake. So, if Ron was in agreement, why not? Laura was up for it, and then Pam and Grace were soon game too. Ron was so laid back, he agreed instantly. They had a couple of trial runs around the streets, and discovered it was in fact do-able.

After breathless goodbyes, the group split in all directions to respective homes. Pam was on an early, so bed beckoned her before 9. Mike and Laura headed home, where Grace was watching TV with Uncle Mel.

It was true that since the ill-fated barbecue, Mike's brother had been somewhat subdued. He had even said a heartfelt thank you for saving him from death by sausage. He was visibly embarrassed by the fact that he could possibly have met his maker with snot and slobber all over his face, and half a pork and herb chipolata still stuck in his windpipe. It had certainly been a sobering experience.

Humph had benefited particularly well out of

proceedings, closely followed by Sidney Greenstreet. The little dog had eaten the majority of the food that had been left scattered over the lawn. After six sausages and a turkey burger he had started to feel a little bit sick, so Sidney stepped in to help with the clean-up operation. He had quickly recovered from being hit on the backside by a projecting pork product covered in saliva, and headed back outside to see what was left. Thankfully, the smoked salmon was hanging off a rosebush. He smiled to himself, licked his lips, and dived in. After that he moved on to the dip, and finished off his banquet with half a chicken, being careful to avoid the bones. Both pets then retired to the lounge. Grace found them an hour later at either ends of the sofa, on their backs, legs in the air, fast asleep and snoring, looking for all the world like lions after a successful kill. Quite how neither of them had been sick, was anyone's guess.

Mel stayed for another week, and then found himself a rather nice apartment. It was within reasonable distance to his ex-wife and sons, but not close enough for the long-suffering Moira to be able to launch missiles. Mike and Laura were relieved and happy to have their home back to normal, after what had been a very stressful time. As the Stroke Run was fast approaching, they increased their training accordingly.

One evening, towards the end of September, they were sitting at the dinner table counting up how much sponsor money they had raised. It was late, as Mike had not long been home from work. With a bottle of wine between them they calculated a grand total of £352.67. It always baffled Mike as to where the pence came from.

"I think we've done better than last year," he said excitedly.

"I can't remember," Laura replied wearily. "We off to bed shortly?"

"Definitely," Mike replied yawning. "We're both shattered. Still getting over the shock of Mel staying, I think," he grinned.

"What's that noise?" Laura said suddenly.

Mike listened carefully. "Can't hear anything."

"Hmm, strange. Could have sworn I heard something then." She looked over at Humph who was sleeping soundly in his basket. He would have been the first to stir at a sound.

They switched off the lights and went quietly up to bed, leaving the house in darkness and their canine companion dreaming of squirrels.

The following morning was much like any other. Mike was helping Grace get ready for school, Laura making packed lunches, and Humph was wading through a bowl of dog food. Sidney Greenstreet however was absent, and Mike was becoming worried about him. A creature of habit, and ruled devotedly by his stomach he was always there for breakfast. Mike looked out into the back garden, and breathed a sigh of relief when he saw his feline friend waddling across the patio.

"There he is," he sighed. "Come on Sid, come get your breakfast."

They heard the cat flap click, and expected him to stroll into the kitchen in his usual nonchalant way. But nothing happened. After a few moments, Grace stopped packing her school bag and called him again.

"Sidney! Your breakfast's ready."

Nothing. The only sound coming from the utility

room was muffled scraping. Within seconds, there was a loud clunk and high pitched yowl. Mike, Laura and Grace stopped dead in their tracks. Standing in the kitchen doorway was Sidney.

He was wearing the cat flap like a misshaped plastic tutu around his middle.

"Jesus Christ!" Laura shouted.

"Good God," Mike said under his breath.

"Awesome!" whispered Grace.

It appeared that Sidney had simply grown too fat for the cat flap, tried desperately to squeeze his way through it in search of breakfast, and somehow it had lodged firmly around his ample girth. Laura, despite feeling desperately sorry for the poor animal, dissolved into fits of hysterics, closely followed by Mike and Grace. The look on the cat's face said it all. The very pinnacle of humiliation in front of humans. He would never live this one down. Attempting to slope off into the lounge and hide in shame behind the sofa was proving difficult too. His new attire was heavy and cumbersome and it rattled when he tried to walk.

Mike sprang into action then and went over to try and help. Sid was having none of it. His eyes settled on Humph, who had stopped eating his breakfast and was staring open-mouthed at the scene before him. Sid thought that if there was ever a time when a dog would genuinely laugh at a cat, it would be now.

Half an hour later, Carol arrived to take Grace to school. The situation had not progressed any further, and Sidney had managed to get himself stuck under the dining table, with his back to everyone. Laura had gone to work, leaving the others wondering what the hell to do.

"Holy crap, Mike," Carol said after what seemed

like forever. "Can't you get it off him?"

"No. I can't get near him. We all started laughing and he seems to have really taken offence over it. I think I'm going to have to try and get him to the vet." Mike scratched his head.

"He's going to have to go on a diet," said Grace, staring at the sulking cat.

"Going to need a bloody gastric band, I'd say," Carol replied. "Right, time we weren't here. Gracie, come on darling. Mike, give me a shout if you need anything...chainsaw, clamps, pliers," she called after him as they disappeared out the front door.

Sitting in a crowded waiting room at his local vet's was not the morning Mike had planned. It was certainly not his intention to be holding a very fat, pissed off tabby wearing a cat flap.

An elderly lady with a sick budgie was sitting next to them. She smiled sympathetically at Mike every now and again.

"Not going to be doing any hunting today then, is he I suppose," she whispered from underneath her plastic rain cap.

"No," Mike replied politely. He was in no mood to get into a conversation about how or why this had happened.

"Is it a he or a she?"

"He."

"Mmm," she murmured.

There followed a period of silence. Everyone in the room was desperately trying not to make eye contact with him, but he felt their eyes flicker his way at any given opportunity. One young gentleman with a black Labrador had tried so hard not to laugh, he had to wait outside. Mike noticed he was now on the phone.

Probably telling someone about the bloke in the waiting room with a fat bastard of a cat wearing a cat flap. God, this was so humiliating.

After what seemed like an awfully long time, they were called in. By now Mike's arms had gone to sleep with the sheer weight of holding Sidney on his knee. He was glad to be in a private room out of the public glare.

"Goodness," said the vet, a tall dark-haired man of about 30. He stood with his hands on his hips, then rubbed his chin.

"Soooo, likes his food, does he?" he said in an annoyingly jokey sort of way.

"He's always been a large cat," Mike said defensively. "Yes, he does like his food a little bit too much, I suppose."

"If you can just hold his head steady for me Mr Snow, and I'll try and pull it off him." The vet grasped hold of the cat flap whilst Mike attempted to keep the cat calm.

After three big tugs, a few scratches and yowls later, Sidney was finally free from his plastic prison. The vet thought it prudent to put on his gauntlets halfway through the releasing process as Sid had not taken kindly to being messed about with, and had scratched him in a particularly aggressive manner.

"Feisty chap, isn't he?" said the vet, applying a plaster to his lacerated arm.

"Sorry. He's normally not like that," Mike apologised.

"Well, it's not every day you find yourself wearing a cat flap, is it?" he sniggered. "Anyway, we need to talk about his food intake, Mr Snow. I trust that's ok with you?"

Mike agreed. Sidney didn't and growled at both of them. This was quite possibly the worst day of his life.

Half an hour later, they were walking out of the surgery, and drove home via the local hardware store, to buy a new cat flap and some low calorie dry cat food.

CHAPTER SIX

It is well known by all cat owners, that when they are not able to get their own way, our feline friends will sulk for a very long time. Particularly if it involves food rationing, or losing a fight with another cat.

When the latter happened to Sidney, his bad mood lasted for several days. He wouldn't eat, converse with anyone or anything and growled if Mike touched him. True enough, he had lost out to three rounds with a neighbour's ginger tom in a bid to win a war over which one owned the tiny piece of tarmac at the end of Mike's drive. In the end, of course, Mr Binks, the aforementioned ginger ninja won the fight, and had since claimed the land, washing his privates there every morning at 9.30 ever since. So, the food rationing was absolutely the final straw for Sidney, and he sulked for a week.

Eventually however, he saw sense. It was sheer starvation that did it in the end. Ignore food, or just be grateful for what you have? He went for the latter. By the time the Trentham Stroke Run came 'round again, he had lost three pounds. Watching his family get into the car on that fine October morning, the spring in his step was lighter, and he went to spend the day on the patio table, sleeping and watching bees buzz around the last of the summer flowers.

Race day at Trentham was every bit as exciting and unnerving as Laura had remembered it. She recalled that at this point in time, exactly a year ago, she and Mike were not yet an item, but barely three quarters of an hour later, their fate was sealed. She was now standing with him at the start line, feeling the chill of the fresh October air. Inhaling deeply, there was just the hint of autumn in the breeze.

She had kissed Mike and wished him luck, told him she was proud, and loved him. He had returned the sentiment, but Laura could see he was side-tracked, mentally preparing himself for the 10k with Matt. Twice around the circuit. This race was a little different for her too. She had Grace at her side again, but in front of her, in his wheelchair, was Ron. Dressed from head to toe in purple, the Stroke Association colours, he was preparing himself to be pushed around the 5k course. They had agreed to take it in turns; Laura would start, then Pam, Keith and Grace would each do a stint. It was too late now to be thinking that this was a really bad idea, but as she looked around the hundred or so runners, she noticed someone else was doing exactly the same thing. They met her gaze, and she smiled and waved.

"Good luck!" they shouted over to her.

"You too!" she shouted back.

She felt a surge of excitement within her, that same feeling she always got at the start line. Whether it was a park run or this run, it was always the same. A mixture of excitement, fear, and intense emotion. She wiped away a tear with the back of her hand.

"What's the matter Mum, why are you sad?" Grace whispered.

"I'm not sad, love. I'm really, really happy," she replied.

"That's weird," Grace sighed. "You always cry at the start line."

"And at the finish, don't forget," chipped in Ron from his chair.

They had borrowed a special lightweight chair from a friend, which was easier to push. Ron was a man of slight build anyway, which today, Laura was thankful for.

They were off. The claxon sounded the start of the race, and Grace squealed with delight. A quick high five from Mike and Matt and the two men disappeared off into the distance in the direction of the woods, around the corner to left, and down past the lake in the direction of the Italian Gardens. Laura's backup team stayed close. It was proving very hard to push Ron, she quickly discovered. They had been on a few practice runs on concrete but this was something else. As they graduated to gravel it became a whole lot harder, and slower. Her arms were beginning to ache.

"Keith, take over for a little while," she shouted breathlessly behind her. "It's such hard going. We need to swap regularly."

Beige Keith, today braving it in shorts for the first time since his wasp incident, sprang into action. He was a strong man for his age, and Laura was impressed at how fast he could push her father along the tiny stones. They eventually came out of the Italian Gardens and were running with the lake on their right.

It was such a beautiful day. The sky was blue and clear, with just a wisp of light cotton cloud here and there. Sun shone on the still waters of the lake, as men in canoes glided effortlessly across it. Ducks and swans preened themselves and watched the multitude of runners pass by them, towards the perimeter of the monkey forest. The heat of the sun was becoming more intense by now, and Laura could feel it on her skin. She glanced over at a swan, looking cool and elegant on the water's edge. It dipped its head into the lake, shaking droplets of diamond-like liquid as it came up for air.

Keith was starting to slow down, growing tired. Grace took over for half a kilometre through the woods, where the ground was smoother, and then Pam decided to drive. She was a lovely woman, and Laura was incredibly fond of her, but speed was not her forte. They slowed down significantly, and the others started shouting words of encouragement. She was determined however, to keep hold of the reigns and not let go. They were by now deep into the wooded area, and it was thankfully cooler on this side of the lake. Normally, they would be taking in all the usual sights of the Gardens that they loved so much. Grace could not wait until they reached the giant dandelions, which were her personal favourites, so she had to be content for now with spotting the odd wire sculpture fairy or two. They were there, hiding in trees, their wings glimmering in the dappled sunlight. It appeared they enjoyed quivering lightly in the breeze, whispering words of encouragement to the crazy humans on the ground.

Laura decided to take over once again, but as they passed the 3k marker and a marshal spurred them on, she felt the strength in her arms draining. It was hard enough running 5 kilometres, but pushing an 11 stone man in a wheelchair was something else.

"You ok, sausage?" Ron turned his head slightly, but not daring to take his eyes off the path ahead.

"I'm buggered, Dad," she panted.

"You can do it, love," he said. "We're not far from the finish line. I can see it through those trees."

It was true, in the distance, there it was. But coming up before them, was a bit of a hill to the left. Laura's heart sank.

"Oh Christ," she said, stopping. "Forgot about this bit, didn't we?" She stood gasping for breath, hands on hips.

"Come on, everyone!" shouted Keith, "All hands on deck!" All four of them put a hand on the chair and pushed with all their might up the hill, which seemed to go on forever. Their arms ached and they were sweaty, tired and sore. It had been far harder than they had imagined.

Once at the top of the steep incline, they stopped briefly for a breather, and decided quickly who was now in the driving seat. Grace volunteered, but the ground became rough again. Darker rough stones lined this part of the course, and it was a little uneven in places. The shade of the trees was welcome and protected them from the growing heat of the day. In the distance, they could hear the cheer of spectators for those crossing the finish line.

"Come on people…1k to go! Let's do it!" shouted Laura. Pam looked utterly knackered, but they couldn't give up now, it just wasn't an option. Even Ron looked tired.

"Keep your arms in, Dad," she said suddenly.

We're going for the burn."

"Ah shit," replied Ron and held on tight.

The five of them burst out into the sunlight again, as they said a silent farewell to the trees and their welcome protection. It was hot. Laura did not dare look at her watch, there was no time. Sweat was now dripping from her nose, and she could taste the salt on her skin. Downhill now, and on the home strait. She looked around her briefly to check everyone was together, and indeed they were. She felt a surge of immense pride.

They turned right around the corner at the bottom of the incline and were happy to see the finish line up head, barely 500 yards in the distance. From somewhere deep within her she pulled some extra strength. With a wipe of her face from an already sweaty hand, she charged like a bull in the general direction of the waiting crowd, looking for all the world like Boadicea going into battle. Mike would be so proud.

They burst over the finish line in just over 1 hour. 1:1:16 to be precise. Yes, 5k, in the bag, and pushing a 70-year-old stroke survivor in a wheelchair! Not a bad achievement they decided, and all before lunchtime too.

Mike and Matt had done 10k however, in 45 minutes. They had cheered their colleagues and loved ones over the line looking fairly cool and calm, not at all like they had just ran 6.2 miles.

Medals, patted backs, hugs and smiles were in abundance. Carol was on hand to provide drinks and towels. She was so very proud of her family that day. A tear ran down her cheek as she wiped a line of sweat from Laura's brow. Her little girl had done good.

Everyone was happy. It was the most beautiful day and they had achieved wonderful things in a wonderful place.

After a picnic in the grounds, Mike and Laura followed the same routine as they had the previous year. A walk around the shops, a few treats purchased, and then home. The only difference this time was that they were throwing a barbecue for the Trotters back at their place in the evening. Thankfully, it was a much more relaxed affair than the previous one, and less food ended up on the floor for the animals to eat.

As the light faded and everyone sat around chatting and laughing, Mike went to switch on the fairy lights which adorned the outside of the house. He looked back at the crowd of people he held most dear, and stopped to take it in.

His beautiful girlfriend Laura, whom he never thought would ever love him the way she did now; the funny quirky Grace, who occasionally called him 'Dad'; the feisty and magnificent Carol; Ron, the gentlest and kindest of men, Pam, his friend and work colleague of many years; Matt his friend and running buddy, and dear old Beige Keith, loyal wasp hater.

Mike's heart swelled, and he felt a rush of emotion. It hadn't been all that long ago that it had just been him and Sidney Greenstreet against the world. But now their lives had changed so much for the better, and for that he was eternally grateful. He looked up to see the stars starting to twinkle against the deep rich violet of the night sky. Taking a deep breath in and out, he headed inside to get everyone a nightcap.

Carol and Laura lit the fire pit and everyone huddled 'round, talking about the day. They were starting to feel weary now, as it was almost 10 pm. Grace had been in bed for almost an hour, so the adults were left to make a decent hole in Mike's bottle of good brandy and half of his good whisky.

"I'd like to propose a toast, if that's all right by everybody else," said Matt.

A general murmur of agreement went around the circle.

"To Mike," he said raising his glass. "Not only a thoroughly deshent and nishe chap, but the very backbone and essence of the Trentham Trotters!" His words were a little slurred, but they all got the idea.

A cheer went up and they drank the rest of the bottle. There were certainly going to be some delicate souls around the following morning.

CHAPTER SEVEN

Inevitably, after the Stroke run, Christmas was soon on the horizon. This was Laura's favourite time of year in the florist's. She loved making the wreaths for customers. The shop was filled with the smells, sounds and sights of Christmas. Burnt orange and cinnamon filled the air, and the sparkle of fairy lights, glitter and tinsel made it all the more welcoming. Thankfully, her boss Trudy had not insisted on a loop of Christmas carols blasting from the cd player in the office, but had gone for a more subtle approach of Celtic woodland sprite music instead. She had found the ethereal CD in the ethnic shop next door, and thought it was less commercial.

Trudy was not only Laura's boss, but was also one of her closest friends. At 6 ft tall, she towered over her friend and colleague. She also wore heels all day, every day, which baffled Laura. Quite how anyone could stand up in those things, and run around the shop in them until closing time seemed to her, superhuman. It also added another few inches to her height, making the overall presence rather intimidating. Trudy had a very unique style and dress sense, but the entire package seemed to work, somehow. Her strong facial features were enhanced by immaculate but heavy make-up. Her hair, although short, was a different colour every week, and always adorned by a headband of some description. Since the mermaid hair colours had come out, her repertoire had increased, and this week it was the most beautiful shade of lilac. Laura loved it.

"You should so keep your hair that colour, Trude, it's really pretty," she said whilst they grabbed a quick coffee break between wreaths.

Trudy touched her lilac tresses. "Oh, thanks babe," she replied through heavily coloured lips. "Helene loves it as well, thinks I should keep it a while longer. I was gonna go for the pale blue in time for Christmas, I dunno. Last time I managed to get some on the bathroom carpet and the dog, so I wasn't too popular. A white poodle with a purple back looks a bit odd, you know," she laughed.

Laura smiled. Helene was Trudy's partner of 20 years. They had met at an art and pottery class in their twenties, and had been together ever since. When it had become legal for them to marry, they had done, in a quiet ceremony with just close family and friends, and of course their poodle, Lancelot.

To say that Trudy and her partner were very different, was a bit of an understatement. They were complete opposites. Helene was 5ft 1, a little wide around the middle, dark, plain and wore very thick glasses. Think Thelma from Scooby Doo after a few extra doughnuts, and you'd be on the right track.

"Soooo, how's you and Mike these days?" she

asked, her eyes widening. "Been a bit busy to ask you, lately." She drained her coffee cup and set it down next to her on the work bench.

"Great actually," beamed Laura, and she wasn't lying. "He is 100 times easier to live with than Jim ever was. It's weird because the more I lived with Jim, the more I disliked him. The selfishness, everything having to be on his terms, going places he wanted to go, listening to music he wanted to hear, watching films he wanted to see. I got tired of it, you know? Just so dammed tired. Wore me down. Wore Gracie down too. Didn't see it until he left and we were given the freedom to do, see, go wherever, whatever. I was blinded by the fact that he'd been shagging someone else, and then I thought, 'Hang on a sec. This girl has done you a massive favour. You're free'. Then Mike came on the scene. I mean, I'd liked him for years. Liked his gentleness; he had something about him I couldn't put my finger on, but I knew he was more suited to me than Jim. Bit scary at first, but it just seems he wants to do whatever makes Grace and I happy. Can't ask for more than that, can I?"

"Nope, you bloody can't, babe. But that's how it should be. He's one in a million, your Mike. Really happy for you both, you know we are. You going to tie the knot, do you think?" she asked twiddling with a bit of wire.

"I'd like to. Dunno if it's Mike's thing though. He seems perfectly happy as we are. But it would be nice to be Mrs. Snow." She smiled again as his face came into her mind.

Trudy's attention was suddenly diverted outside the shop. She turned her head to the window. "Oh, my

God Laura, look!" she said excitedly. "It's bloody snowing!"

They both ran towards the front of the shop and opened the door. It was indeed snowing heavily, and they squealed with the excitement of little children. Only a week until Christmas, and it was already settling on the pavement. A quick check on Google confirmed snow on and off for the next seven days. Perfect.

"You guys fancy coming over to do sledging tomorrow? We could have bacon sandwiches and hot chocolate afterwards," Trudy asked.

"Mate, wild horses would not keep us away from that one," Laura confirmed.

The following day by happy coincidence, was a Sunday. As Google had promised, they woke up to a beautiful white wonderland. The sky was still heavy with snow, and it looked bitterly cold, but they didn't mind.

They spent a blissful day over at Trudy and Helene's house, sledging, cooking endless batches of bacon, and making umpteen mugs of hot chocolate. Mike and Grace were having a fantastic time whizzing down the bank in the back garden, and Laura had managed to get a photograph of the two of them, and Humphrey on the sledge in mid-flight.

"Let me take a picture of you all together," called Trudy from the kitchen. Mike grabbed Laura and sat her on his knee, whilst Grace and Humph sat on the other.

He groaned slightly. "My God, you three weigh a ton," he joked, and Trudy took the photo.

"Let's have a look!" Grace asked impatiently. "Ah, Mum, this is amazing. You can see right up Humphrey's nose though." True enough, it was a lovely photograph, but the little dog's snout was indeed the dominant feature.

Mike studied it for a few moments.

"That's great, Trudy," he whispered thoughtfully. "All of us together." He hugged the two most important women in his life close to him. "My little angels," he said proudly and gave them both a kiss.

"Snow's Angels," Trudy added.

They all laughed and decided it was getting very cold, so they headed back inside the house seeking the warmth and comfort of the open fire.

The run up to Christmas was as busy for Mike and Laura as it was for everyone celebrating the festive season; present drops to friends and colleagues, the odd glass of mulled wine with them, as it would have been rude not to, and of course the big food shop, not forgetting the ever essential parsnips. It was exhausting and stressful, but when Christmas Eve came around at lightning speed, Mike decided it was high time to relax, unwind and enjoy the holiday. He was back to work the day after Boxing Day, so time was of the essence.

Grace was incredibly excited, and therefore seemingly incapable of going to bed at a decent hour, so they played games and chatted the evening away.

"I always think," Laura said after three glasses of Irish cream liqueur, "that it's a real shame Trentham isn't open on Christmas Day for a walk."

"They need a holiday, just like the rest of us, love," Mike replied.

"Sure do," she agreed. "I'd love a walk up there tomorrow though. Be amazing wouldn't it?"

They were united in saying that Trentham Gardens on Christmas Day, in the snow would be like having all your Christmases at once, with a cherry on top. And sprinkles. Flake. Extra cream.

"Sauce," said Grace. "Don't forget the toffee sauce."

"Oh my GOD!" said Laura jumping up suddenly. "I forgot to get the bloody bread sauce!!"

Humphrey looked up from his bed to see what all the fuss was about, yawned and deciding it wasn't worth getting up for, went back to sleep.

* * *

They woke up bright and early on that Christmas morning, and after tea and toast in bed, they decided what better way to set things up for the day than to go for an early run. It had to be said that Grace took some persuading, and Humph had to be virtually dragged out of his basket. He thought, as he was pulled, sliding on his backside past Sidney's bed, he saw the cat smile, but he couldn't be sure.

As a fresh layer of snow had fallen overnight, Mike thought it prudent to run trail rather than road; it would be much safer underfoot.

"Right girls," he said when they had reached the nature reserve, and he had locked the car. "How far do you want to go?"

"I feel really up for a long one, to be honest, how about you two?" said Laura, looking remarkably refreshed despite her sinking the best part of a half bottle of Irish cream the night before.

"Fine by me," said Mike. "Grace?"

The little girl shrugged. "Yeah, ok."

They let Humph off the lead, as there was no traffic to worry about, and they set off slowly along the grassed path that led around an old racecourse. It felt comfortable underfoot, and Laura soon got into a rhythm. The air was cold and crisp, and it hurt their lungs for the first mile or so. Grace's face began to glow pink, and her eyes shone in the sunlight. She had chosen to wear a Santa hat, in keeping with the festive spirit. Both Mike and Laura had their heads cosily encased in beanies and thick running gloves kept their hands and fingers warm and protected from the elements.

It was still very early. Mike looked at his watch briefly, it was only 9.30 am. Humphrey wore his new dog coat, and ran alongside them happily, sniffing the occasional clump of frozen grass, but the snow had masked most of the interesting smells, so he was content just to run.

After 3 miles, they were warming up nicely, and as all three of them were comfortable with it, decided to go back to the car the long way around, not cutting through the woods. The sun was out, and made the snow sparkle on the ground and in the trees like icing on a Christmas cake. Laura's mind was pre-occupied with turkey, stuffing and the lack of bread sauce, so Mike suggested making their own. He was full of good ideas like that. She didn't know how on earth to make it, but she was sure her mother would have a recipe somewhere.

Grace was starting to get tired, so the trio walked a little.

"How far have we done?" Laura asked breathlessly.

"Not sure," Mike replied. "I'll have a proper look in a bit. It's half ten, so we must have covered a fair distance."

By the time they had got back in the car, and the windows had steamed up within seconds, Mike checked to see. He and Laura always compared distance and steps on each other's fitness watches.

"Mine says 5.5 miles," she exclaimed, surprised.

"Yep, so does mine," confirmed Mike. "You do know that's just short of a 10k, don't you?"

"Ten-k," piped up Grace from the back of the car, "is 6.2 miles. And I'd really like to go home now."

"Wow," said Laura quietly. "Didn't think I could do that far all at once."

Mike smiled to himself.

"Let's go home and concentrate on opening all those presents, what do you say to that?"

They all agreed that was one brilliant idea.

CHAPTER EIGHT

By midday, the turkey was in the oven, a bottle of Cava Brut had been opened, and was partly consumed.

They had sat around the tree opening presents, still glowing from the morning's exercise. New running kit mostly dominated the present theme of the day, but they were all happy with their gifts. Even Humph managed to tear open a new dog bed, and a packet of treats for himself. Sidney Greenstreet however, seemed disinterested in the squeaky mouse and brightly coloured cat toy, because it didn't involve food. He was slightly comforted however, by the lovely smell coming from the oven. He had seen what went in, and he was looking forward even more to what would come out. He sat up and stretched, his nose and whiskers twitching as he caught the scent of roasting turkey, and he seemed to smile.

"In your dreams, Sidders," said Mike, reading his mind.

"Oh Mike, it's Christmas Day, can't he have just a little bit? He's lost loads of weight, and doesn't get stuck in the cat flap anymore," pleaded Grace.

"Well, maybe just a little bit, then. But not too much," Mike relented. "Don't fancy the shame of sitting in that waiting room for a second time, with a cat wearing a plastic tutu."

Grace unwrapped a PS4 game from its cellophane case. "Will you play this with me?" she asked.

Mike looked at Laura. "Yes, carry on you two, everything is as it should be with dinner," she confirmed and went into the kitchen.

Harmony was broken by the doorbell. They were not expecting her parents until later, so Mike went to investigate.

There on the doorstep, stood his brother, with a bottle of champagne in his hand. "Happy Christmas, Mike!" he beamed.

Mike's heart sank.

He managed a very weak smile and a bland reply. "Melvin. To what do we owe this pleasure?"

Before he could say anymore, his brother was inside the house and already halfway to the kitchen. "Happy Christmas, Laura!" he bellowed, planting a kiss on her cheek. "Hi, Gracie, how are you?"

Now, either Melvin Ralph Snow had had some sort of personality transplant, or taken a happy pill. But he had just asked how someone was. That was very unusual indeed.

"Did you ask him over?" hissed Laura.

"No, I bloody didn't, he just turned up!" Mike hissed back.

The four of them stood in the lounge, and there followed a rather awkward silence.

"Brought you a bottle of bubbly!" Mel said finally and thrust it towards his brother to open.

"Thanks. Erm, I thought you were spending the day with Moira and the boys?" Mike asked curtly.

Mel gave one of his overweight sighs, and then sniffed.

"Well, yes I was. But then things got a bit, you know," he said waving his hand around, "bit heated. I've never had a Yorkshire pudding thrown at me before! Ha ha. But there you go!"

"Why did Moira throw a Yorkshire pudding at you, Melvin?" asked Laura, flatly. She just knew this bastard was here to stay for the day, uninvited, and most probably would ruin it.

Another sigh followed, accompanied by a deeper sniff than usual.

Mel scratched his head. "Well, I can't really remember what set her off, to be honest." He shuffled his feet nervously now, and took off his coat. He handed it to Mike, who quickly handed it back.

"Look. I'm really stuck for somewhere to go today, and I just don't want to be on my own. Could I just stay for a couple of hours?" he pleaded.

This time, it was Laura and Mike's turn to sigh deeply. Even Humph grumbled and took to his new bed.

"Right," said Mike suddenly taking complete control of the situation. "I'm going to be very straight with you, Melvin. You turn up here, unannounced and uninvited. We were planning Christmas dinner with just us, Carol and Ron. The deal is, if you stay here A) it is just for a couple of hours, B) you don't annoy anyone and C) you eat whatever is put in front of you. Is that crystal bloody clear?"

Laura looked at him. Blimey, he certainly wasn't taking any prisoners. There was a new-found firmness to his voice and for the first time in a long time, he had a real air of authority about him. She was proud. Maybe it was the two glasses of Cava giving her partner courage, but she didn't really care. Mel was promising to toe the line, and that was all that mattered.

"Is that ok with you girls, if he stays?" he asked.

They both nodded. It was true that when Mel was behaving like a perfectly normal human being, which he was capable of doing, he was a reasonably pleasant person. The problem was that he had to be reminded to stop acting like a complete knob all too frequently.

"Go and hang your coat up in the hall," directed Laura, "then you can grab that apron and come and help me make some sense out of the veg." She went back into the kitchen and started laying an extra place at the dinner table.

"Thanks," he said quietly whilst he tied the apron around his ample waist. "Didn't want to go back to an empty apartment."

Laura felt she was now seeing the real Mel for a moment. Behind all the bravado and arrogance, was just a sad lonely guy who didn't want to be on his own on Christmas Day. She decided that the only way to deal with him was to be blatantly frank, and in her mother's words: not take any more shit.

She stood with her hands on her hips, and then poured him a glass of Cava. "Here," she said handing it to him. "Can you peel parsnips?"

"Yeah, sure. Do your spuds as well if you like," he replied after taking a glug of wine.

"Deal," she replied. "So, come on then. How did you come to have a Yorkshire pudding thrown at you this morning? And for Christ's sake don't blame it on the bloody menopause, or I'll personally wrap my turkey 'round your head for good measure." She had the upper hand here and wasn't about to lose it.

Mel started to peel the parsnips thoughtfully and with some precision. He wiped his nose with the back of his big fat hand, and sniffed.

"Things started ok when I got there, opened presents and that, you know. Then I guess we just rubbed each other up the wrong way, and it all went a bit tits up after that," he said quietly, not looking at her.

"Did you say something to upset Moira?" Laura asked.

Before he could answer, the doorbell sounded again; this time it was her mum and dad. Mike opened the front door with a relieved smile.

"Am I glad to see you," he whispered.

Ron pointed to Mel's Jag sitting on the driveway and Carol frowned.

"Just turn up?" mouthed Ron.

Mike nodded and rolled his eyes, "Come on in, both."

He helped Carol get the presents from the car, and the six bottles of champagne she had bought from Supasave. Now that was going to be interesting, he thought. But Mike had a plan. He was now top side of the situation with his brother, and knew finally, after all these years, just how to play him. Decades of pussyfooting around this guy, and taking all the crap that was hurled, he had finally had enough. Time for him to be in control.

Once inside, the atmosphere lifted somewhat, and Carol shook Mel's hand with her vice-like grip, and fixed him with her icy stare. It said, "behave yourself" and he knew it.

For the rest of the day they enjoyed their Christmas

like any other family, unwrapping more presents, eating a lovely dinner, crackers and party hats. Afterwards, Laura settled herself on the sofa with a large box of chocolates between her, her mother and daughter, whilst Mel, Mike and Ron set about clearing up. The light of the day was gone, replaced by the thick inky darkness of a winter sky. The lights on the tree twinkled and cast shadows on the wall where they caught the tinsel.

An hour later, Ron, Mike and Laura were asleep in front of the TV, leaving Grace to read one of her new books. Carol got up and went to get a cigarette out of her bag. "Want to join me?" she asked a surprised Mel.

He nodded.

"Get your coat on then. Cold out there," she ordered.

Carol had worn her special coat today, being as it was a special occasion. She had picked it up from a charity shop in the summer. It was a thick, oversized fake fur coat, as white as the snow on the ground. It was completely over the top, but she had loved the warmth and comfort of its softness, and at £15 was not about to let someone else nab such a bargain. She wrapped it around her, put on some leather gloves, and headed outside to the patio armed with a packet of 20 cigarettes, her trademark lighter, a bottle of Supasave whisky and two glasses.

He stood next to her as she sat at the table, not quite knowing what to do.

"For Christ's sake man, sit down," she barked. "Drink it neat, can't you?" she asked him when he had gingerly placed his backside on a cold patio chair, and she had unscrewed the top of the whisky bottle.

Mike then opened the patio door, and said he would

143

light the fire-pit for them, which he did quickly and quietly, and then disappeared back in the house to join a sleeping Laura on the sofa.

Carol poured them both a large whisky. The amber liquid looked even darker in the moonlight, and Mel took a sip of it, wincing slightly as it burnt his lip.

"Good stuff that, Melvin," she said watching him carefully.

From inside the house, Mike kept a close eye on what was going on. He longed to be out there with them, mainly to see Carol in action, doing what she did best. He wanted to watch this modern-day Joan Crawford work her magic on his brother. But he had to be content for now, with a vague view of the back of their heads and clouds of cigarette smoke.

Carol pulled up the collar on her fur coat, and lit up. She offered Mel one, and to her surprise, he took it.

Mike had realised that they didn't have an ash tray, but the fire-pit, he soon thought, would act as such.

He watched them for what seemed like a very long time, taking sips of their drinks, pouring more, gesticulating, laughing occasionally, blowing clouds of smoke into the frosty air.

After their third refill, Carol turned to Mel and looked at him thoughtfully.

"You see, this is the Mel we all want to be around," she said pointing to him with her gloved finger. She put her feet up on the opposite chair and crossed her legs.

"You can be a nice guy when you want to be, and that's the Mel that people want. Do you understand what I'm saying?"

He nodded. "Yeah. I guess so," but it was a reluctant gesture.

"I'm going to be very frank with you, Mel. If you don't like it, then tough, I don't really give a shit. No skin off my nose. But your arms must have got real heavy over the years," she said taking a drag of her cigarette.

"Sorry, what you do mean?" he replied taking another sip of his drink.

She looked at him with that determined stare of hers. "From throwing all that crap at your brother, and don't say you didn't because I know you did. I've seen it. I'm not being funny Mel, but you can't treat your siblings like that, you just can't. Now you could walk away from this conversation now, go back inside, take the huff for the rest of the time we're together, or you can sit there and listen to what I've got to say to you, and hopefully come out the other side a bit better off. Choice is yours."

He thought for a moment, and decided to stay. He was interested in what she had to say, and was even a little bit in awe of her, but most of all secretly admired her directness.

"Go on," he whispered.

"Got a little story to tell you," she said quietly, and poured him another shot of whisky. She blew clouds of smoke through her nose, and then looked away down the garden.

"Once upon a time, there were two sisters. They grew up in a very nice house, with very nice parents. They had everything they wanted, were well loved and cared for. As children, they were happy together, played games, shared dolls, looked out for each other. When they were aged 10 and 12, they sat in the garden one summer's day and promised they would always be there for each other. Always and forever. No matter what. They hugged and thought everything was going to be just fine. A few years later and one went to college, the other who was not so academically bright went out to work, ended up in an office job. The sister who went to college came home with a degree. She had changed somewhat, grown distant and superior. The dynamics of their relationship had altered.

"Over the next ten years, they grew apart, only seeing each other at family gatherings. The sister who had gone out to work tried in vain to get the other to go places with her, do sisterly stuff, but the sister with the degree felt she was too good for her sibling. Somehow a rot set in to their relationship, a jealousy. Instead of being kind to each other, they fought and bickered. It became a way of life to the point they lost sight of what really mattered.

"They both married, had children of their own. Lived barely 5 miles apart, but still hardly saw each other. Deep down, they still loved each other dearly, but by now it was too late. They had gotten into the habit of being horrible to one another. Then one day, things took a turn. The eldest sister, the one with the degree, she was crossing the street. Didn't look, as she stepped off the pavement, to see if anything was coming. In the blink of an eye, a lorry hit her. Died instantly." Carol wiped away a tear from her cheek swiftly. "Died not knowing that her sister really, really loved her. They had wasted all those years Mel, pissing about, being horrible to each other, because it had become a habit." She took a deep long drag of her cigarette and knocked back a whole mouthful of whisky.

"Don't let that happen to you, and your brother. He's a good man, Mel. A really good man. Ok, he's got his faults like everyone else, but Ron and I think the world of him. Laura adores him, so does Grace. You know the most important trait in a human being? Kindness. A kind heart. It's lacking in so many people, but your brother has it in abundance. For Christ's sake Mel, take a step back, look at things carefully, and start appreciating him for the good guy he is. Truth be told, you could take a leaf out of his book." She poured another glass of whisky for the two of them. They were both fairly mellow now, and the warmth of the amber liquor kept them from feeling the cold night air.

"I'm sure your wife, Moira is it … would have you back in a heartbeat if you cut all that crap out, you know the arrogant 'I'm a salesman' shit. You're the father of her children. Just stop acting, Mel. Be yourself. People will like you a lot more for it. Admire you, even." She lit another cigarette for them both.

"I think it's gone too far for that now Carol," he said, his guard down completely. "She thinks there's more chance of her picking up a turd the clean end, than me dropping the corporate arrogant veneer and just being me."

"Try it," she replied blowing out grey swirls of smoke into the night air. "You may just get a surprise. You only get one chance in this life, Melvin. Remember that." She studied him hard. "You know what? I like the real you. You're ok," she nodded.

"Won't people think I'm boring, if I just be me?" he said quietly.

"No," she replied firmly.

Getting up suddenly, and collecting her lighter and almost empty cigarette packet she turned to him.

"Bring that whisky in, will you? And the glasses. I want my future son-in-law to have a taste of that. My ass is cold and I need the loo."

With that, she breezed inside, her white fake fur coat enveloping her, looking for all the world like the Snow Queen retreating into her castle.

CHAPTER NINE

By the time New Year's Eve came around, Mel had indeed taken on board what Carol had said, and finally, after several decades of dealing out mental abuse, had started to treat his only sibling with respect and kindness. There were no more put-downs, sneers, or bad mouthing behind his back. Instead he was quietly supportive and thoughtful. He also found that just being himself was far less tiring than being a dickhead, and the people around him slowly, but surely started to warm to him for the first time in his life. Of course he knew how to behave, how to treat people properly. But he had gotten out of the habit of not doing so. Melvin Ralph Snow was soon no longer known as "Snows-it-all". Friends and family wanted to spend time with him, and he liked it. Now, when Mike announced his race plans for the coming year, his brother listened, took an interest, and most importantly gave him some positive and supportive feedback.

Mike couldn't thank Carol enough. Whatever she

had said to him that night, had worked a treat. He just hoped and prayed that it was permanent.

Mike, Laura and Grace spent New Year with her parents. It had started off as a fairly quiet evening, but very quickly escalated into a boozy night complete with karaoke and Mike giving his best rendition of a few Tom Jones' numbers at 1am. Grace had decided she really couldn't take much more of his singing and had gone to sleep in the spare bedroom with the dog.

With the festive season over, the dullness of January set in. The nights were long, the weather was damp and miserable. Snow had given way to the dreariness of persistent rain, and going out for runs was proving a challenge.

One Saturday afternoon, the Trotters had decided to meet up for a 5k. It was cold, wet and the sky was grey. None of them were in particularly good spirits, and Matt looked like he had every layer he could get on his slight frame. He stood waiting for the rest of them in a beanie hat, his hands tucked neatly under his armpits for warmth, hopping from foot to foot.

"All right guys?" he said trying to keep cheerful, his breath catching the cold air.

Mike, Laura and Pam nodded bleakly. "No Keith?" asked Matt.

"Said he was coming," replied Mike. "Ah, here he is…bloody hell."

In the misty drizzling distance they could just make out the figure of Keith. Obviously he was really feeling the cold today, and was sporting an SAS style balaclava. He had on a long-sleeved running top, a short sleeved one, plus some thick yellow running tights. He looked like a bee.

"Well, we certainly won't lose you in that gear,"

smiled Laura. "Where did you get those running tights from?"

"eBay. Get anything from there, it's amazing!" he replied excitedly. Evidently, he had just discovered its delights. Over the next few months, the rest of the group would be treated to a vast array of brightly coloured running kit. Somehow, the name Beige Keith seemed no longer relevant.

It had to be said, that the weather that day would have challenged even the most devoted of runners. The cold was the type that got into your very bones, and the wind was getting stronger, with a freezing drizzle just for good measure. But still they persevered, this close-knit group of friends, determined to have a good run under the circumstances. Pam was wearing her glasses and had to keep wiping the rain off them with a tissue. By the time they had completed their run, the tissue was drenched, and she invariably needed the toilet.

"Well done people, that was a tough one. Anyone fancy a coffee 'round at ours?" Mike asked.

Matt made his apologies, but Pam and Keith were keen, so followed Mike and Laura back to their home.

"No Gracie?" asked Pam as she made a bee-line for the downstairs loo.

"At her dad's" called Laura, "back tomorrow. Tea or coffee Pam?"

"Coffee please!" came the muffled reply. "Four sugars."

"Bloody hell," muttered Laura under her breath. "Coming right up."

Mike lit the fire, and busied himself with making cups of tea and coffee. Humph made himself popular with the visitors, by giving and receiving lots of fuss and licking their freezing hands. He liked it because they tasted slightly salty after their run.

"So, Mike, what races have we got lined up this year?" asked Keith sipping the strong hot coffee he had requested.

"Well, I guess we are all happy to do the Trentham run again in October?" he asked.

They all agreed.

"I had heard on the grapevine," said Keith after a few more sips of his drink, "that there's going to be a new 10k starting up, fairly locally. I'll have a look into it, if you like."

To Mike's surprise, Laura took an interest. "Where's that then, Keith?" she asked.

"Well, I'm in this running chatroom community online, and they reckon there's going to be an inaugural 10k in Whitchurch, around April time," he said warming his hands on the cup.

"That's not too far away, say half an hour? Nice town too," Mike replied. "Can you keep us posted then, Keith?"

He nodded. "Sure thing, Boss. Like you say, not too far away from here, the other side of Market Drayton."

A little buzz of excitement filled the room, on an otherwise dull and dreary January day.

"I'd love to do a 10k," Pam piped up.

Laura put her arm around her shoulders. "Yeah, me too," she added.

Mike's heart did a little flutter.

* * *

A bleak January gave way to an even bleaker

February. Storms hit the UK, and high winds brought down trees and caused havoc on the roads.

After a quick chat with Matt at their next Trotter meeting, he was soon on board for the 10k, and a little more research from Keith meant that they were now in a position to enter the very first Whitchurch 10k race. Days later, they were successfully registered; now it was just a matter of training.

They say that the road to a race can be a hard one, particularly during the winter months. The Trotters were no exception.

Pam developed plantar fasciitis in her left foot, so purchased some KT tape, and a special boot to wear at night. It was uncomfortable and hot, but Mike assured her it would most certainly work. She sat every evening with her foot on a bag of frozen peas, and rolled it over her mother's old rolling pin. After about two weeks Mike was watching her walking around at work, and could see a significant improvement.

Laura developed a nasty cold which turned into a chest infection. She had needed two lots of antibiotics and a week off work. It pained her not to be able to run until it was completely cleared up, but her determination was steadfast, and once the cough had eased and the tightness in her chest was just a distant memory, she was back out there, pounding the streets with the rest of them.

Beige Keith had picked up a rather unpleasant tummy bug from his grandson, and had been caught short at one of his history society meetings. It had transpired his talk on King Richard III had been cut cruelly short, and the poor man spent the next 3 hours in the toilets of the local church hall. His wife had eventually gone to fetch him armed with a bucket, spare trousers and several bath towels. He didn't talk about it much, only to say it was probably the worst stomach bug he had ever had, and it came on unannounced.

So you see, the path of training for the 10k did not run smoothly. Illness and injury set them back a pace.

By the beginning of March, none of them felt ready. They met on an unusually sunny Sunday afternoon at Trentham Gardens, feeling despondent and underprepared.

Grace had joined them this time, determined to keep up with the adults on their quest to at least complete a training run of 5.75 miles. Just short of the required 6.2.

Laura looked up at the sky. At least it wasn't raining, and only a little bit cold. There was a pleasant breeze, and she thought she detected a promise of spring in the air. She smiled and closed her eyes for a moment.

"Jeez," muttered Pam under her breath, which snapped Laura out of her daydream. "Will you look at that?"

They all turned to see Keith jogging slowly towards them. Evidently, online had been his shop of choice once more, and he was not one to disappoint this time.

There was no balaclava in evidence, but instead a very bright red running vest with the words. 'Run the UK' emblazoned on the front of it. His running tights however, were something else. He was surely feeling very patriotic, because they had the Union Jack all over them. Mike's mouth fell open. He felt sure that even satellites in our orbit would have picked those up.

'*I'm not running with him today,*' he thought to himself. "Matt, fancy running with me today?" he asked.

"Was just thinking the same thing, actually," replied Matt quickly, after he had successfully placed his eyeballs back into their sockets.

"Come on, Keith," shouted Laura. "You run at the same pace as me, let's go," she turned and winked at Mike who shook his head.

Pam and Grace were bringing up the rear, and they soon settled into a steady run. Pam was more relaxed she said, because there were plenty of toilets nearby. She took the opportunity of going twice. Once at the kiosk by the monkey forest, and again at the café past the wire dandelions.

It was lovely now that the nights were starting to draw out, and spring was indeed on its way. There was a smell of the change in season in the air now, and evidence of buds appearing on the bushes and trees. The lake was still and serene, and swans glided effortlessly up and down, dipping their heads from time to time in the cool water.

They ran past the wire fairy sculptures again, Laura's favourite, the one blowing the dandelion seeds was swaying gently in the breeze. It never failed to fascinate her, and today the sun shone on it making it appear all the more ethereal.

Mike checked his watch, they had only done 3 miles; another 2.75 to go, so it was up around the Italian gardens again, and back down around the lake for another lap. He was giving Keith a very wide berth, but noticed several visitors doing a sharp double-take as the patriotic runner jogged past them.

He smiled to himself, and felt that he had privately been a little harsh on poor old Keith. He was at heart, a lovely man … loyal, kind and a good friend who would never let you down. Did it really matter that his taste in online running gear was a little lurid? He was certainly making people smile.

Mike's thoughts then turned to other things. He had a worry on his mind, something was troubling him. He spent the next mile or so mulling it over, trying to come to some sort of conclusion.

He checked his watch again, and put up his hand. "That's it guys, 5.75 miles. Well done, just short of the 6.2 required for April 9th." They stopped under the shade of the trees and stretched a little. They had found it hard, but were pleased to have done it. Laura's legs ached and Grace was shattered. Pam had done amazingly well, despite two loo stops, and sporting a face the colour of uncooked beetroot.

"Once or twice more folks, then we can taper off slightly the couple of weeks before," Mike announced.

"This is harder than I thought it was going to be," whispered Pam to Laura, who nodded in agreement.

CHAPTER TEN

The taper runs couldn't come soon enough for some of them. Pam certainly was enjoying the three and a half miles in the build-up to the big day, as was Laura.

Mike had started behaving oddly she had noticed, and it worried her. She had caught him on the phone in the garage one evening, talking in a very low voice. He had cut the call short when she appeared in the doorway, and looked embarrassed.

"Who are you talking to?" she asked, a lump rising in her throat.

"Work," was all he would say.

She knew he was lying, and her heart felt heavy. She had confided in Trudy one morning at the shop, shedding a few tears, because she was concerned. Was history repeating itself? Would another relationship be going down the pan? She felt sure her fragile emotional state could not possibly cope with yet another failure. Laura convinced herself that this was going to be her very last romantic liaison ever. If this went wrong, there would be no more. A single life would be much less hassle. She loved Mike with all her heart and soul; a split would be utter agony.

Trudy allowed her to vent her concerns and worries, listening intently. Her hair was by now silver, another good choice, Laura thought briefly through her angst.

"Your hair looks great, by the way. Love that colour."

"Thanks, honey," replied Trudy quietly. "Listen, I'm sure it's something and nothing. Is he stressed at work at all?"

"Not particularly," she replied tearily.

"Everything okay in the you-know-what department?" her friend winked, intimating their cosier moments.

"Yes, absolutely. He's very loving, my Mike. It's just something I can't put a finger on, you know. Pardon the pun," she laughed weakly, wiping her nose. "Caught him on the phone to someone the other night, whispering in the garage."

Trudy blushed, but it went unnoticed.

"Try talking to him about it. Wait until Grace is in bed, have a chat, tell him you're worried." Trudy was trying her best to give encouraging advice.

Laura nodded and thanked her. She walked out of the office, straightened her hair, and proceeded to start making up a bouquet for a wedding.

Once out of sight, Trudy carefully typed a text message:

She knows there's something going on.

She pressed 'send' and went to help Laura with the flowers.

* * *

The week before the race, the weather started to improve significantly. Some unseasonably warm sunny days were enjoyed by many. Mike looked up the long-range forecast, and felt mixed emotions. It promised a warm, sunny 24 degrees for Sunday 9th April in Whitchurch.

Great for spectators and marshals, not so great for those running.

He looked again at the route sent to them by email. It described it as fairly flat, which was good. He was worried about Pam, more than anyone. Would there be enough bushes to have a wee behind? He suspected not.

Other concerns drifted into his mind too. Sunday was going to be a momentous day in more ways than one. Big race, big finish, and big changes planned for the rest of his life. He swallowed hard and sighed, then picked up his phone and rang Carol.

"You ok, Mr?" she said immediately after two rings.

"Yes, I'm all right, thanks. All set for Sunday? So glad you are both coming, she's going to be very emotional. Important you are there for her," he replied seriously.

"Don't worry, Mike. Everything will turn out just fine," Carol replied coolly.

"Thanks for understanding," Mike said and hung up.

He took another deep breath and went upstairs to get ready for work.

RACE DAY

The previous night had been busy with getting their kit ready. Both Mike and Laura always followed a set routine and laid out their running outfits of choice on the ottoman at the bottom of their bed, ready to put on the following morning.

They had gone to bed early, after checking travel arrangements with the others, times and pick up points. Matt had the bright idea of hiring a mini bus, which would accommodate everyone. Parking was on the Rugby Club field opposite the school where the race was to start, and they were to register no later than 9.30, picking up their chip and bibs from the sports hall.

They ate their breakfast in silence. Grace busied herself getting the dog ready, and Laura and Mike hardly said a word to each other. She noticed he kept checking his rucksack regularly, for what she couldn't tell. He was extremely secretive about what was in it. He wouldn't allow her to share it either, insisting that she take her own.

On a beautiful sunny day in April she should have been happy and cheerful, but instead felt empty and sad. Tears were never far from the surface, and her stomach felt unsettled. She looked over at Mike and smiled, flatly.

He returned the smile, but looked on edge somehow, like something was troubling him still. She went over to him on an impulse and wrapped her arms around his neck.

"You do still love me, don't you?" she whispered in his ear.

"Of course," was all he would say. It was, Laura felt, non-committal, and she wished she hadn't asked.

The doorbell rang then, and Matt was standing in the doorway, ready to drive them to pick up Carol and Ron.

They grabbed their things, and left.

Matt had certainly not been lying when he said they were going to be travelling in style. It was quite the nicest of mini-buses Laura had ever seen. Already inside, seated and ready to go, were Pam, Keith, Trudy and Helene. For some reason unknown, her friends had decided to come along, not something they would normally do, but they wanted to this time, which was fine.

"Morning folks," said Trudy with a glint in her eye. She looked at Mike a little longer than she should have done, Laura thought.

"Right, just got to pick up your mum and dad then, Laura and we can be off. Takes about 45 minutes roughly to get to Whitchurch, should be there by 9 am," said Matt cheerfully.

"Excellent," replied Mike.

Mike looked at Matt in a knowing sort of way, and

sat down, strapping himself in. Grace sat next to her mother with Humph on her knee.

They drove over to Ron and Carol's house, and were then finally on their way to Whitchurch.

Mike continued to hug his rucksack. Sadness was now being replaced by irritation in Laura's emotions. What the hell was in that thing?

"What's in there today, that you love to hug?" she asked after they had been on the road for some time.

Laura didn't notice, but everyone looked at the rucksack, and then looked away, guiltily.

"Wallet, spare pair of trainers, change of clothes," he replied vaguely.

Laura sighed deeply and turned away, deciding to gaze out of the window for the rest of the journey. Everyone else was strangely quiet.

The weather promised to be stunning. They had woken up to a beautiful blue sky, and the warmth of the sun was already heating up the frosty atmosphere in the interior of the minibus.

Soon, they were there, and ready to park up on the field.

"Right, everyone. Let's go and find registration," said Mike breathing a sigh of relief as he stepped off the bus. The atmosphere had been tense.

They had taken Ron's wheelchair with them, so Carol and Laura made sure he was comfortable and the group moved en masse towards the school.

Mike walked on ahead quickly, leaving the others behind.

"He's doing my bloody head in at the moment," Laura said to her mother under her breath.

"Why, what's the matter?" Carol replied.

"I don't know, Mum. That's just it. He's been

acting strangely for weeks. Look at him! Walking off without me, he is, and it's my first 10k. Gonna give him a right bollocking tonight when we get home; this has got to stop." She was angry now, and Carol just cast a sideways look at her daughter, but remained tight-lipped.

Ron, Carol and Grace settled themselves at a table, and within minutes they had in front of them hot bacon rolls and steaming cups of fresh coffee. The smell was amazing, and Laura's stomach tightened in a little pang of hunger. She looked away, and got out a banana from her backpack.

Mike seemed to be faffing about in the registration hall talking to somebody over in a far corner, so she ate her fruit on the field, making sure she was up wind of the food smells emanating from the food stall.

Pam was just making her way back from the toilets and went over to Laura.

"Ok?" she asked cheerily.

"Yeah, not bad Pam. Ok if I run with you today? Mike will be up front with Matt and Keith, I expect."

"Yes, absolutely fine by me, love. Where's your friend Trudy gone?"

"In the queue for bacon bloody rolls, lucky buggers," she replied and rolled her eyes. The fact that she couldn't have one until after the race had finished was making her more irritable.

"I'll get you one for when you finish," shouted Trudy from the queue. She could read Laura's mind, evidently.

"It's the smell," she whispered to Pam. "Gets me every time."

Pam agreed. There was nothing like the smell of cooking bacon, or chips to make you instantly hungry.

Mike was striding back from the sports hall, and looking happier than he had in weeks. He went straight over to his girlfriend and kissed her cheek.

"Ok love? All ready to go?" he asked cheerily.

She looked at him and frowned.

"You're happy all of a sudden," she replied, haughtily.

He said nothing, and looked a little crestfallen.

He put his lips to her ear and whispered, "I love you, bunny," kissing her cheek again. She softened noticeably then and managed a smile.

"It's time to go," shouted Matt.

A sudden rush of excitement filled the field, as it was now ten minutes to 10 am and almost time. They had realised it was going to be a hot one. The temperature was already rising. Laura and Pam decided between them that just getting over the finish line was their priority. Doing a PB was not on the menu. Two bacon rolls and at least one coffee was, however.

Mike gave Laura one last hug. Matt, Keith and Pam all shook hands, and wished each other luck. Trudy had bounded over with Helene, breakfast baps in hand, and given them all a greasy kiss. Carol, Ron and Grace gave pats on backs, and encouraging words.

It was time.

Laura felt that familiar surge of excitement. It was intertwined with a feeling she might cry. It was happiness, not sadness that made her feel this way. She was always this emotional at the start line, and then again at the finish.

She grabbed Pam's hand and squeezed it. "Good luck, my friend," she said.

"Good luck to you too, love. I'll stick with you all the way 'round."

Laura squeezed her hand a bit tighter.

A little way in front, Mike turned to look at her, and time seemed to freeze, momentarily. He gave her that look he used to give her when they first started dating, and for a moment there, they were alone in that crowd of runners.

Then they were off.

Within five minutes, and still on the field, it struck Laura that this was going to be tough. Although a lovely day, it was baking hot, with no breeze. She could feel her energy was not going to last without some intervention. The fuel that the banana had given her was fast running out.

She looked over at Pam, who was already sporting a red face. Her training took over now. She thought back to all those runs they had done, around Trentham Gardens, through the streets in the winter time. Mike had given her many tips on how to pace herself on this one. She panicked slightly, but quickly calmed herself. His voice was in her head, telling her it was going to be fine.

'Run the mile you're in. Just think, this is me for the next however-long it takes. Relax, and above all, enjoy it.'

With those words buzzing around in her head, she looked over at Pam, and reiterated what Mike had told her.

The route itself was certainly proving to be very pleasant. They were already onto a housing estate, and probably 2k in. As they ran, Laura and Pam started to take in their surroundings, and they agreed it was a nice little town.

The marshals were lovely, and the two ladies thanked them regularly.

"Pam, please tell me you don't need a wee," said

Laura as they jogged down the hill past a large supermarket.

The crowd had dispersed somewhat now, and it was just them and four other women together, and another male runner behind.

"Surprisingly," replied her friend, "I don't. It's so bloody hot, I think I've sweated it all out." It was true, Pam was sweating profusely, and Laura was a little concerned.

"Here, have one of these," she passed over a glucose sweet. "Put it in the side of your cheek and let it dissolve. Mike swears by them. They're really good for giving you a bit more energy. The water station is half way around."

Pam thanked her. "I'm ok," she added. "Probably look worse than I actually am."

Laura laughed breathlessly. "You tell me if the heat gets too much, promise?"

Pam nodded, her head down. Laura could see this lady was probably finding it very hard, but was determined to finish.

The route was now taking them uphill back into the centre of the town, and down the high street where all the shops were. Laura kept a close eye on her colleague, who opted to walk a while, which worked well for the both of them. Laura passed her another sweet, and a couple of jelly beans. The sugar seemed to kick in after 20 minutes and they ran again, albeit at a slower pace.

A marshal cried out words of encouragement at the top of a hill, which led them into the park.

"Water station coming up ladies, well done you're doing fabulous," she said, reaching out her arm to guide them in the right direction.

They were in the park now, running past the bandstand and off to the right, up a particularly steep pathway. At the top of it, Pam could indeed see the water station, as promised.

"Yesssss!" she shouted, and Laura smiled.

Two boys passed them a bottle each, and the route then took them down out of the park, and past a row of houses.

Pam unscrewed the lid of the plastic bottle and tipped half the contents of it over her head. Laura did the same.

"That feels amazing!" the older of the two exclaimed.

Droplets of water ran down the back of their necks, and onto their vests. They wiped it away from their eyes, and could taste the salt from their skin. With their hair now soaking wet, it had done the job of cooling them down sufficiently.

"Are you going to drink any of it?" Laura asked.

"No," replied Pam. "Makes me feel sick if I drink while running. Just going to chuck it over my head."

Laura thought this was an excellent plan.

She wondered how Mike and Matt were getting on. Looking down at her body briefly, she could see the sweat gleaming on her thighs. Her bib, number 478, was fluttering gently in a welcome breeze, that had just started up.

They continued through the streets of the town, and on to another housing estate, asking a marshal how far they had to go.

"Another 2k ladies and you're there! Well done, you're doing great!" he shouted to them.

By this time, they didn't feel that great. Everything was starting to hurt. They walked a lot, ran a little.

More jelly beans, another glucose tablet, the rest of the water tipped over their heads, leaving it to cascade down their faces.

Laura wiped it away from her eyes. Her legs were hurting. She was exhausted, and the sun was beating down on them. Where they could, they ran on the shady side of the street, but this was not always possible.

The residents of the town lined the roads, and hung out of windows shouting encouragingly at the runners. Pam and Laura passed another lady, and the man who had been running close to them earlier.

Instead of talking to each other, they decided on silence to conserve their energy. This was tough beyond belief, and to just get that foot over the finish line was going to be amazing. Laura's mind again drifted in the direction of bacon rolls. She dearly hoped they would have some left, and looked at her watch. If they sold out, she was going to have a massive meltdown.

Coming out of the housing estate, they took a sharp turn to the right. Pam's heart leapt as the school came into view, they were nearly there.

Another marshal confirmed this, and from somewhere, they had a new burst of energy. The man's voice over the tannoy could be heard, it was so close.

Laura reached out for Pam's hand again as they ran back onto the field. Her skin was slippery with sweat, but they managed to hold on to each other.

The mixture of water, salt and sweat was in Laura's eyes, which made her vision a little blurry, but she could just make out the finish line in the distance.

Someone was shouting and running across the line with what looked like pink tape. She thought she could see Mike standing there too.

As they got closer, Pam dropped her hand and smiled, "Go on, darling. I'll catch you up in a sec."

"No way! We're crossing together!" Laura stopped, turning to her friend.

"Look!" replied Pam. "Look there!"

They were literally feet away from the line, and Laura turned to see what was waiting for her. She stopped dead in her tracks, and put her hand over her mouth.

Across the finish line, was a pale pink banner. In blue letters were the words, "Laura, will you marry me?"

Standing with the race organiser were Carol, Ron, Grace, Trudy and Helene, Matt and Keith. To their left, slightly was Mike, not on one knee, but in the middle of the finish line holding out his hand.

In his hand, was a small white box.

Time seemed to stand still. Everyone held their breath.

Laura managed to recover herself enough to run through the banner, and cross the line in 1 hour and 22 minutes. Pam was shortly behind her.

She stood looking at Mike, holding out the box, his hand was shaking a little.

"Will you marry me, Laura?" he said quietly.

"Of course I bloody will," she replied. "I thought you'd never ask!"

She hugged him tightly in a sweaty grasp, and the crowd that had gathered cheered and clapped. The man on the tannoy system congratulated the couple through his microphone for all to hear.

The next half an hour was a blur of hugs and kisses from family and friends. Mike placed the ring on her finger, and it glistened in the sunlight.

There was no doubt it was a beautiful ring, and would surely have cost him an arm and a leg. He had done his homework to get the sizing correct and had chosen a tear-shaped diamond, with a much smaller stone at the larger end. Laura could not take her eyes off it.

With race chips removed from their shoes, they walked over to the registration hall to collect t-shirts.

"Is this why you've been acting funny for the past few weeks?" Laura said when she had managed to tear her eyes away from her engagement ring.

Mike sighed. "I'm so sorry," he said. "I know I've been acting a bit strange for a while but I was just so nervous, and wanted everything to go smoothly. Also, I was worried you might say no."

"You daft bugger," Laura said stroking his face. "I was always going to say yes if you asked me." She gave him a salty kiss. "But there is just one more thing you can do for me."

"Anything."

"Can you go and get me two of the biggest bacon rolls they have on that stall there, I'm bloody starving."

They both laughed. It was the perfect end to a perfect day, and Laura couldn't have wished for better.

END OF PART 2

Snow at the Summit

A V Turner

Book 3 of "In It for the Long Run" - the Mike Snow trilogy

CHAPTER ONE

It is true to say that weddings have a special atmosphere. Certainly, for the couple getting married it is a momentous day, and for those family and friends who celebrate it with them.

The June morning of Mike and Laura's wedding promised to be a warm and sunny one. A perfect 25 degrees at 11am in Trentham Parish Church.

Laura had risen early, and Gracie not long after. They had eaten a simple breakfast on the patio with Ron and Carol, and by 8.30am the hairdresser had arrived and the flowers were on their way.

Laura's best friend and Boss Trudy had done the flower arrangements, carefully choosing blooms which were highly scented. It would always remind them of their special day when they caught the smell of freesias or roses in months and years to come. The warmth of the day made them seem even more aromatic, and Laura lifted her bouquet and took in a deep breath of the heady scent.

With hair and make-up done, Laura and her

daughter stepped into their dresses. Gracie looking beautiful in lilac, a sash about her waist, and fresh freesias in her curled hair. Laura had decided on a full length ivory lace dress with capped sleeves and a round neckline. A crystal necklace nestled softly around her throat that Mike had bought her especially. Her blonde hair was curled and pinned in soft waves, also adorning fresh freesias.

Ron and Carol stood in the doorway to the bedroom.

"We're ready," Laura announced and smiled at her parents.

Ron had tears in his eyes.

"Don't cry, Dad," Laura said. "You'll set me off, and the make-up lady has gone. I don't want to get to the church looking like a panda."

"Well, don't you both look a picture," Carol said after linking arms with her husband. "So proud. Come on, let's go downstairs, have some photos in the garden before the car gets here."

* * *

A few streets away, Mike was also getting ready. He had been awake since 5am, and up and about since ten past. Humphrey and Sid were taken by surprise at how quickly their breakfast was served, so much so, that they virtually had to be dragged from their beds.

To calm his nerves, Mike had decided to go for a run. It would set him up for the day, and clear his head.

It promised to be a beautiful day. He had checked the weather a total of 12 times with different apps, just to make absolutely sure.

He tried to brush his pre-nuptial nerves aside, and

headed off in the direction of the local park with a reluctant Humphrey in tow. The little dog had been woken up at the crack of dawn, dragged out of bed, and virtually force-fed his breakfast, and now faced a run he did not particularly want. His bed beckoned again once they returned home, of that he was certain.

There is something so very peaceful about running at 6am, especially on a fine sunny morning, when you just know that the weather for the next 24 hours is going to be glorious. Mike promised himself he would do 5k, then go home for a shower, shave and change into his suit. He had been alone for the first time in ages, and it felt strange. The house was so quiet and empty without the girls there. Even quieter than before they had come to live with him. His single days had been fine, but life as a couple had been even better, and he thought how very fortunate he was now, with such a wonderful family around him. He smiled to himself, and looked down at Humph. The little dog's eyes glistened in the sunlight, and his black shiny nose twitched at the early morning smells.

"Now don't forget Humph," said Mike, quietly. "Your aunty Angela is coming in a couple of times today, to let you out and give you a fuss, Ok?"

The little dog looked up at his owner, as if he understood what was being said. In reality, all he heard was 'fuss', and that was all that mattered.

'Aunty Angela' was the lady who lived next door. She was a 60-year-old spinster who lived alone in a two bedroomed bungalow. Mike had started talking to her one day many years ago when they were both putting their bins out.

It was one of those meetings where he discovered within 30 seconds that she was completely barking mad. Think Joyce Grenfell after a bag of Haribos and ten cups of very strong coffee and you'd be there.

Angela was very much old school. Conservatively dressed, and always in a twinset and pearls. Never had Mike seen her wear trousers, and summer, winter, spring or autumn, she had a cardigan draped across her shoulders. Now this fascinated him, because whatever she was doing, it never, ever slipped. It was almost like she had stitched it on that morning, ready for the day ahead. She could be gardening, cooking or walking to her car in a high wind, and the cardie never moved. Her hair was blonde and naturally wavy. She wore it in a short bob style, and probably it had been that way since birth. A plain brown hair grip held the fringe in place, and she tottered around noisily in modest heels. Her manner, when she spoke, was quick and nervy. She spoke so fast that Mike had a job to catch what she was saying, and she closed her eyes when she was talking to you, which he found rather irritating at first. She interjected each sentence with a nervous laugh, and never stopped smiling. She was however, a very nice lady, and was the first person to offer to keep an eye on the animals whilst the family were at the wedding.

"Are you sure you don't mind Angela?" Mike said one morning as he was off to work, and his neighbour was weeding her front garden, cardigan perfectly in place.

"No,-no-no-no-not-at-all-Michael-perfectly-happy-to-look-in-on-them-at-least-a-couple-of-times-during-the-day-for-you," she replied at breakneck speed, her eyes fluttered shut, and she smiled broadly. "Just-tell-me-from-what-time-and-to-when-and-I'll-alter-my-schedule-accordingly!" she laughed.

"Well, if you're sure, only we don't want to put you

to any trouble," he said, slowly.

"No-no-no-that's-no-problem-at-all. As-long-a-I-don't-need-to-do-any, you-know, toileting-things-for-them, I-don't-really-have-the-stomach-for-that-sort-of-thing," she laughed again, looking at him through closed eyes.

"No, that won't be necessary Angela, if you can just let Humphrey out say three times, and give them their tea around 5 o'clock, we'd be really grateful." He wondered for a moment just how Angela managed to get through life, really. She obviously led a very cocooned existence. She was a retired secretary, probably had never had a relationship, and hated anything remotely to do with toilets. *'Maybe she didn't have to use one,'* he thought to himself. She probably slept in a single bed with sheets and blankets and wore a button-up to the neck, brush cotton nightie and a hairnet. His mind was racing now, and he shook his head slightly to bring him back to the present.

"Are you going straight back to work afterwards? No honeymoon?" she asked a little slower.

"No, we've decided to have a holiday later on in the year," Mike replied. "Grace is going to her dad's for a week in Autumn half term so we can grab a last minute deal then."

"Oh, righty ho," she laughed. "I thought you'd both be having it off."

"Pardon?" Mike was taken suddenly unawares by her choice of words, but she seemed unphased.

"The time off," she clarified. "Work. Straight after your nuptials." Her eyes were closed again, her head tilted slightly and her hands clasped together. She looked like she had nodded off whilst praying.

"Oh, erm no," it was now Mike's turn to laugh nervously.

So naïve was Angela that she hadn't realised her double entendre one bit. Mike looked at her for a moment or two longer and decided he'd had enough. It was getting too much like a scene from a Carry On film. Making his excuses, he left for work, leaving Angela to her weeding.

It was then that the pets were well and truly taken care of on the big day. There was one thing about Angela, she was an excellent time keeper, and always true to her word. She had fed Sidney Greenstreet before when Mike had gone on holiday, so he knew she was reliable. He would buy her a bunch of flowers and a bottle of Elderflower cordial, to say thank you. It was her favourite, she said. An odd tipple for anyone else, but if you knew Angela, it would most certainly be the norm.

After a good run round the park with Humphrey, Mike headed home to shower and change into his wedding suit, and at precisely 10.30 his brother Mel was coming to pick him up to take him to the church.

As his best man, Mike had deliberated long and hard. Although things had been fine and dandy with Mel for a while, he felt he owed his good friend and running partner Beige Keith the honour of the job, just so long as he didn't wear his Union Jack running tights.

By 9.30 he was almost ready, and had another full hour to wait. Should he text Mel and get him to come early? He had already spoken to Laura and Grace at 7am.

He decided, as it was his wedding day after all, to have a glass of wine, just to steady the nerves. Only the one, you understand. Special occasion and all that.

But one turned into two. He was starting to feel a bit mellow, and even nearly tripped up over the cat. Better have a coffee, he thought, sober up a bit.

By 10.15 he was sober enough to hold a decent conversation, but his fluid consumption was sloshing around in his stomach somewhat uncomfortably, and the desire to pee had taken over. Mel did indeed arrive early, a full ten minutes in fact. After slapping his brother hard on the back several times and bellowing excitedly in his ear about the 'big day', Mike wasn't feeling too well at all, and had to be excused to go to the bathroom for a third time.

The mixture of nerves, wine, coffee and breakfast had all been too much for his tummy, and fifteen minutes later he emerged from the smallest room in the house, feeling a whole lot better.

Mike locked the house, took a key 'round to Angela's and went to sit in Mel's car. His brother had done him proud. On the back parcel shelf was an arrangement of flowers, and the interior of his Jag smelt of a fresh valet. He had even put an ivory ribbon on the front of the car.

"Looks amazing. Thanks Mel."

"You're more than welcome," his brother replied. "Ready to go?"

Mike nodded.

Finally, the day had arrived, and within the hour, Laura, the object of his affections for so long, would become his wife.

His stomach fluttered again as he stood at the altar with Beige Keith, briefly glancing at the small congregation in the church. Pam, Matt and his girlfriend, Trudy and Helene, people from work, even Mel's ex-wife Moira and the boys. Jim and Julia were sitting at the back with a lively Noah, who had just recovered from chicken pox, and still looked decidedly spotty.

Carol came and sat down quickly, giving Mike the thumbs up. He took a deep breath and standing at the back of the church were Ron was Laura.

'Do not cry, Michael. It will look silly, and you will show yourself up in front of everybody. Do not cry. Your lip is quivering, bite it quick before it goes any further. Oh, and wipe that tear away from your left eye whilst you're about it.'

With his mind racing, and emotions on an all-time surge, he took another deep breath and bit his lip hard. Keith did his best man duties, passing him a handkerchief.

"Best not use your sleeve Mike, not today," he whispered jokingly.

By now they were standing side by side, and Ron was sitting happily and proudly next to his wife. Grace stood behind her mother, looking very elegant and grown up.

"You both look beautiful. I'm so proud," Mike whispered.

"So do you," Laura squeezed his hand.

They said their vows then, in front of the people they held most dear. Family and friends. Once it was over, and the congregation stood outside the church throwing confetti and congratulating the happy couple, Mike and Laura Snow could enjoy the rest of their day.

"Right, ladies and gentlemen! If you would all meet at the entrance to Trentham Gardens, my wife and I would like you to join us in having our photographs taken in the grounds," Mike cried cheerily. The pressure was noticeably lifted from him, and he smiled as broadly as any man would, who had just married the love of his life.

Everyone cheered, and hurriedly dispersed.

As the happy couple and well-wishers stood at the entrance to the Gardens, a hush came over them. Some had not yet experienced its beauty. Today was warm and sunny, and the gardens showed its full potential to all that graced its presence. Laura felt a flutter of excitement, a sense of belonging. The scent of the flowers filled the air, and they stepped out into the sunlight.

There were relatively few of them for the photographs. Mike and Laura wanted it to be a quiet affair, and Jim and Julia had made their excuses, leaving shortly after the ceremony. Jim thoughtfully had guessed they didn't really want him on their wedding photos so had declined, heading home to North Wales. He did have the capacity to be thoughtful now and again, Laura thought.

They were spoilt for choice as far as location around the gardens was concerned, but decided to use the Trellis walk for their first few shots. The wisteria was in full bloom and fluttered gently in the warm breeze. They then moved on for a couple of lakeside pictures, plus some by the wire fairies, and finally under the giant wire dandelions. The photographer thought they were done, but Laura managed to persuade him to take another three under the snowdrop sculptures, just for good measure.

It was time to well and truly let their hair down after that. Carol and Ron had opened up their large home to guests. An open house was offered for the rest of the day.

Laura kicked off her shoes, and guessing that it

didn't matter now, opted for her slippers. The full-length wedding gown hid them perfectly, and she could eat, drink and be merry in comfort, instead of tottering around painfully in 4-inch heels.

Her parents had asked the caterers for a full buffet, but the wedding cake had been a surprise present from Carol and Ron.

"Gather around everybody, it's cake time!" shouted Carol, winking at her guests.

As the crowd entered the lounge, a large round wedding cake dominated the centre of the table. On the top of the single tier were two pairs of running shoes, one in white, the other in blue, hand-made skilfully out of icing. Mike and Laura's names had been carefully interwoven in the laces, and colour coordinating flowers adorned the rim. It was a work of art, and everyone gasped.

"That's awesome," was all Grace would say, wide-eyed.

"Incredible. Thank you so much, both," Mike said as he stared at it. "Shame to cut it."

But cut it they did, after taking many photos from all angles. Laura was delighted to see her mother had opted for sponge, not fruit.

"Like eating rabbit poo. Horrible stuff." Carol's description was graphic, but somehow accurate.

Day gave way to a balmy night, and those left went to sit outside. Fairy lights hung around the garden like fallen stars. The daytime breeze had gone, leaving a comfortably still evening air.

Mike, Laura, Beige Keith and Pam sat together talking and laughing. Matt came over to join them with his girlfriend, and soon Mel completed the circle.

"So, then. What have we all got planned for the rest

of the year?" Matt asked enthusiastically.

"Where my next Crème Egg is coming from," chipped in Laura. "Bastards have stopped selling them. Can't get one anywhere."

Everyone laughed, but Laura only smiled. She was serious. After Easter, those little handfuls of deliciousness had been scarce.

"Walnut whips are my favourite," said Pam quietly. "But they have changed somewhat over the years. Got smaller."

Mike and Beige Keith nodded.

"Disappointing," added Keith. "I'm fond of a Curly Wurly myself. Stayed the same size pretty much."

Matt looked wide-eyed at the rest of them. "I was actually wondering what you'd got planned running-wise. You know, races," he blushed.

The tone lightened then, and Laura laughed. "Oh, sorry, Matt!" she said slapping him gently on the back. "I was just thinking about chocolate. Which I often do, as you know. Anyway, what have we got planned Mike? What does everyone fancy doing?"

Matt's girlfriend, who obviously wasn't remotely interested in running, glazed over and went to the far end of the garden for a cigarette with Carol.

Mike thought for a moment, putting an arm around his new bride.

"How about," he said quietly, giving Laura an extra squeeze, "we all train for a half?"

"Bloody hell!" exclaimed Beige Keith, who was still in Curly Wurly land. "That's two 10k's merged into one."

"Yes, it is. Good way of putting it, actually. Two, back-to-back," Mike replied calmly.

Laura looked at her new husband with a playful

frown on her face. "If I hadn't had four glasses of champagne, and a vodka and Coke, Mike Snow, I'd probably tell you that you were completely nuts. I couldn't even contemplate doing a half marathon as I think I have mentioned before. A 10k is enough for me. Pam? Are you in agreement?"

They all looked in Pam's direction to see her half asleep in the chair, snoring softly. A fly buzzed around her slightly open mouth and she attempted to swat it away. "Hmmm, fine by me," she muttered.

Everyone laughed, and decided it was probably the end to a well and truly perfect day.

CHAPTER TWO

The months after Mr and Mrs Snow tied the knot, saw the best weather in years. Day after day of warm sunshine, and clear blue skies. Beige Keith likened it to the Summer of '76, when the hot weather seemed endless.

The Trotters met regularly during this time, and talked a little more about upcoming races.

"Of course, we will be doing the Stroke Run again at the Gardens, won't we?" asked Pam one balmy evening, as they tried a new local route.

"Oh, absolutely," Mike called to her over his shoulder. "What does everyone else fancy, apart from that?"

Mike let the question hang in the air momentarily. He had a secret longing to do a half marathon. But was finding it hard persuading his new wife to do it with him.

They ran along in silence for some time. Laura was at the back with Pam, and Beige Keith settled between them and Mike. Matt was always slightly ahead, being the youngest of the bunch.

"Anyone fancy a pint after?" he asked.

"Yes!" was the answer from the rest of the group. They had certainly worked up a thirst on this training run. Mike checked his watch and confirmed that they had indeed completed 7k that evening.

"Well done, everyone!" he smiled. "Brilliant job. Last one to the pub door buys the first round."

There was a general murmur of good humour buzzing through them then, and thought it an excellent idea to sit in the beer garden with their drinks.

The last runner to the pub door had been Pam this time, so the first round was on her.

"I'm going to be really good tonight and have a lime and soda," she announced proudly. "Laura, what are you having love, white wine?"

"Erm, no I think I might have the same as you, Pam if that's ok?" She wiped the sweat away from her brow. "Need a hand?" She helped Pam carry the drinks outside to the garden.

The last of the day's sunshine warmed the group of happy runners, and they chatted together like good friends do. Mike sat back and watched them all, smiling to himself. He never took these people for granted. They were the closest he had had to family for many a year.

Eventually of course, the conversation came around again to races, and that inevitable half marathon.

Laura looked over at Mike, who smiled sheepishly back at her.

"Look. If everyone wants to do a half, then let's bloody do one," she said quickly. "Mike, go and get me a large white wine please, before I change my sodding mind."

Pam, Beige Keith and Matt sat with their mouths open, drinks in mid-air. Mike, who had been completely caught unawares, jumped up, but in doing so knocked his drink over, which spilled all over Keith's Union Jack running tights.

A chaos of apologies followed, and poor Keith would be forced to walk home looking like he had wet himself, but being the good-natured guy he was, laughed about it. He was secretly happy too, that Laura had agreed they would all train for a half. It was their ultimate goal as a running group.

After Mike had covered his wife in a thousand kisses, and bought her a very large glass of the best wine the pub had, they sat down to talk some more about the training.

"Mike, you're the only one of us who has ever done one. What's it like?" Matt asked.

"Well, it's actually a nice distance, to be honest," he said thoughtfully, playing with his beer mat.

Laura let out a stifled squeal, and took another sip of her wine. "It's two 10k's darling. Do you think we would all manage it? What about you, Pam? Keith?"

"With the right training, yes we can. We need to pick a local one, preferably later on in the year, and work towards it," Mike replied.

"I would absolutely love to do one," said Pam quietly. "It would be my life's biggest achievement."

"Me too," said Keith. "Just imagine that feeling of accomplishment, Laura. Remember how we all felt after the Whitchurch 10k? I've never experienced anything like it. I felt I could conquer the world," he smiled to himself, and Laura put her hand on his arm.

"I'm in, then," she said, a tone of determination in her voice. Mike knew that once she had her mind set on something, that was pretty much it.

"I've got an idea of which one." Matt had been quiet for a while, but looked up excitedly.

They turned to look at him.

"Lake Vyrnwy half. It's in September sometime. I will check on dates if you like. Gorgeous spot in North Wales, about an hour away by car roughly. I cycled it some years ago. I think it's about 12 miles 'round the lake? Anyway, if it's a hot day, you're sheltered by trees, and it's fairly flat. What do you reckon?"

"Sounds good Matt; actually I have heard of it, but never ran it. Shrewsbury is a nice half, but a bit hilly. What does everyone think? The registration fee will be more, obviously." Mike was convinced that not only was it the right time of year, but also a great location.

"We won't make it this year though, Boss," said Keith. "August now, we aren't ready."

"No, but it will be something to work towards. If we up our game in the Stroke Run at Trentham in October…do 10k instead of 5?"

They all nodded. It was agreed then that the plan was set. A familiar buzz of excitement surrounded them. They were seasoned runners now, this group. Great friends united in their passion for the sport.

Laura groaned good humouredly "Bloody hell. Training through the winter time again. It's not my favourite." She pulled a face at Mike.

"Don't worry, love," Pam put an arm around her as they left the pub. "At least Keith will keep us smiling with his wonderful array of outfits."

They all laughed, and watched as Beige Keith walked the half mile home, waving to his friends, sporting a large wet patch in his running tights.

***

Some weeks later, Mike and Keith had a plan. They were going to drive over to Lake Vyrnwy, take a packed lunch, and walk the full distance that Matt had cycled. Pam and Laura managed to get the time off work, and one fine, but cooler, September morning, they stood waiting for Keith to come and pick them up.

The weather was noticeably changing again. Morning air felt crisper, sharper than it had previously. Pam took a deep breath in and exhaled loudly.

"Love it when the Autumn comes," she smiled.

In the distance they could hear a faint rumble, a deep throaty rumble that could only mean one thing. A high powered sports car was fast approaching.

Mike looked towards the end of the road, and glinting in the sunlight was a bright shiny red Aston Martin, with the hood down.

Now it has to be said, that no one had ever seen Keith in his car before, or accepted a lift from him.

"That's not him," said Laura and looked away, waiting for something more sober.

The sports car sped up alongside them, and came to a smooth halt.

"Morning all," said Keith, smiling from the driver's seat. "Hop in."

"Fucking hell," said Pam and put her hand over her mouth quickly. "Oh my, so sorry," she blushed. Mike looked at her in astonishment. In all the years he had worked with Pam, never had he heard her swear, ever.

The three of them stood on the pavement staring at the shiny car in complete disbelief. Keith removed his Ray ban sunglasses and flashed another smile at them.

"You getting in?" he asked furtively.

"Erm, yes, yes, thanks Keith," Mike said when he had eventually found his voice again.

Laura and Pam sat in the back, the two men up front.

"Fasten your seatbelts folks, ETA one hour, ten!" Keith announced, and off they went. It flashed through Mike's mind that his friend resembled Toad of Toad Hall, with his passion for fast cars.

To say that he drove fast, could have been the understatement of the year. He was confident with it though, which unnerved his passengers even more. After five miles, Laura had the guts to open her eyes, but she and Pam held each other's hand tightly in the back seat. She looked over at her companion; Pam's expression did not change, nor did she look at Laura. Her eyes were wide, her expression fixed on the road ahead, her jaw set like stone.

The wind in the back was ferocious, and their hair, which had been perfectly calm and tame before, was now whipped around their heads like candyfloss in a hurricane.

Laura managed to reach out and put her hand on Mike's shoulder, thinking that possibly this could be the last time she would ever have physical contact with her beloved husband before they perished in some catastrophic accident. He took hold of her fingers tightly, and kissed them, not saying a word.

Forty-five minutes into the journey, Keith started to relax even more, but proceeded to drive his beautiful car like Lewis Hamilton with a herd of zombies behind him. The gears were changed up and down with lightning speed, and he began to tell his passengers about his precious vehicle.

"Gift to myself on my retirement," he shouted.

"Saved up for years for this baby. Susan loves it of course. Wouldn't have got it without her say so," he grinned.

Mike's entire life flashed before him as they approached a busy bypass. He was thinking of offering to look left for his friend, as he looked right, but there was no time. A quick cursory glance either way, and his foot was hard on the accelerator pedal, the engine roared and they were momentarily stationary in the middle of the bypass.

"Oh shit, oh shit," Laura said under her breath and closed her eyes again.

Within seconds they were speeding down a leafy country lane, and Keith was chatting away, his left arm, gesticulating and changing gear nonchalantly.

"How. Much. Further??" asked Pam from the back. Her voice was weak and quivering.

"Not much further now. Another fifteen minutes, I'd say," Keith replied cheerily.

"Thank Christ for that," she said under her breath, closing her eyes tightly.

True to his word, Keith spun the car 'round into the car park at exactly 11.10am. He applied the handbrake, switched off the ignition, and turned to his terrified friends.

"Great ride, don't you agree?" he said proudly.

Laura started to cry softly. Her mascara was half way down her cheeks, and her hair looked like she had been backcombing it for a week. Pam's was similar. Mike opened the passenger door, but his legs were so weak, he fell out of the car, and stumbled slightly, only just managing to recover himself to let his wife out of the back. She clung onto him like a life raft.

Both women spent half an hour in the toilets, by

which time Mike had bought everyone a very strong coffee.

It took until midday for the trio to calm their nerves, but after two coffees, and a good lunch they headed off for a walk around the lake.

It was certainly a lovely spot; Matt was right. The water looked like glass, it was so still. Trees stood majestically on either side of the road, and the leaves fluttered gently in the breeze, whispering softly. Here and there were picnic spots, and at one point you could get right down to the waters' edge with ease. Laura thought it was a little bit like being at the seaside in some places.

The sun came out after a while, and they kept a steady pace.

"I wonder if you get much crowd participation on this one," she threw the question into the air, seeing who would catch it.

"Don't know. Maybe not," said Mike almost immediately. "Lovely place, though." He looked up into the trees as they walked.

After about six miles, Pam suggested a short rest, so they sat on a bench and got out the flasks.

Stopping only for fifteen minutes, they then pressed on, after Pam had disappeared for a toilet break behind some bushes. The usual grunting, huffing and puffing ensued, so the rest of the party stood a little way away.

Once the walk resumed, they made good time. The trees did certainly give you respite from the heat of the day, intermingled pleasantly with periods where the sky was clearly visible. The sunlight was dappled in places, and as the afternoon wore on, the warmth was replaced by a distinct chill. It was just before 4pm when they got back to the car. It had taken them a little under four hours, with only one stop. They were tired, and their feet and legs hurt. Pam was visibly shattered and sat on a low wall rubbing her legs.

"Blimey, bloody long way. Don't know about you guys, I'm certainly going to sleep tonight," she sighed.

"My God, you're not wrong," Laura agreed. "We are going to have to do some dammed serious training Mike if we are ever going to manage to run it."

"We'll manage it. I promise," he said stretching.

It was true that the first half of the walk had been very pleasant indeed. The scenery was so very beautiful; Pam had likened it to 'being like the Lord of the Rings' in places, because the trees were tall, and majestic. There was certainly something very magical about its atmosphere. Once they had reached the water tower, they were extremely tired, and Keith was complaining of a blister. Laura was desperate for an ice cream, and they had run out of drinks. When the dam finally came into view, they all cheered wearily. The end was in sight.

They almost forgot about the hair-raising return journey home that was possibly ahead of them.

'Bugger it,' Mike thought. *'I'm just going to have to say something, otherwise our nerves are going to be shot to bits.'*

"Erm, Keith. Do you think we could go nice and slowly on the way home? Only I want to take in the lovely scenery once more, you know. Savour it a bit. So beautiful around here, don't you think?"

Keith looked a little crestfallen momentarily, but quickly recovered and smiled. "Absolutely Boss. To be honest, I'm a bit knackered myself, so we'll take it steady on the way back. Shall I put the hood up?"

"Oh yes please, Keith," replied Pam and Laura together. "That would be really great. And nice and slow, Keith, please," Pam added.

"Sure thing, ladies," he cried cheerily and started the ignition.

They headed home, an awful lot slower this time. Even Keith was too tired to drive fast, and the women fell asleep in the back, happy in the knowledge that they could complete a 12 mile walk without the need to summon the emergency services.

CHAPTER THREE

Barely three weeks later, the Trotters were at the start line of the Stroke Resolution Run in Trentham Gardens.

The weather was again beautiful, and clear blue sky smiled above them. This time, of course, there was to be no 5k. That, as Keith said, was now behind them. It was 10ks all the way, if they were to have any chance of attaining their goal of a half marathon the following year.

Laura looked around her. Some faces she recalled from the previous run, and she could see her mother and father on the grass at the side of them smiling. Grace had decided she was just doing the 5k, so Laura would make sure she was safely in the hands of her grandparents before heading off for another lap of the lake to complete the 10.

She had chosen Pam as her pacer once more. During the Whitchurch 10k, they had worked well together, she thought, and had been great mutual support when things got a bit tough. Thank goodness today was not as hot. It drained her body of energy before she had even got off the start line, and the thought of running 6.2 miles had filled her with dread. But today, although fine, there was a strong breeze, which promised to keep them cool. Mike and Matt were standing alongside her, with Beige Keith, Pam and Grace the other side.

'Together,' she thought, *'we can conquer the bloody world, us Trotters. Ten-k, in the bag, then I'm going to drink the cafe's coffee supply dry and put 10 sugars in each cup. Yes, I am. AND I'm going to eat four iced buns, or something equally as sweet, one after the other.'* She felt a little pang of hunger, but shook it off. First, she had a race to run.

The claxon sounded, and she felt that familiar surge of overwhelming excitement. She wiped a tear away from her cheek quickly and concentrated on the path ahead, which was now such a familiar one. No one spoke. There was just the sound of their breath, and the crunch of the stones beneath their feet. Many, many feet, all running towards the Italian Gardens. A blast of cool air whipped around their bodies, and Laura smiled as it cooled her sufficiently to increase her pace very slightly. Surprisingly, Pam and Grace kept up with her. Mike, Matt and Keith were up ahead. She could see the back of her husband's head, and the beads of sweat forming on his neck. She remembered his advice once more. 'Run the mile you're in. If it helps, just switch your brain off for an hour, don't think of anything really. Just put one foot in front of the other. Relax. Think: this is me for the foreseeable, and enjoy it.' She applied this mantra, and decided to take in the scenery, which was as ever, breath-taking. The wire fairies seemed to smile down at her from their lofty seats, and the sun sparkled as it caught the fragility of their wings. Her heart filled with a sense of peace as she remembered having their wedding photographs at various points around the lake, and up ahead she could see Mike was doing the same. How lucky they were to have such beauty on their doorstep.

Lost in her thoughts, she suddenly came back to reality as they reached the entrance to the monkey forest. How quickly that seemed to have come around! Grace was tired, so they walked briskly for a short while, then Laura encouraged her daughter to run some more. They could feel the sweat on their foreheads now running down the side of their face, stinging their eyes, and soaking their hair. To a spectator it would seem that this was a chore, but how very wrong they could be. Appearances can be deceptive, can't they? We all know that. If you see a runner, breathing hard, with an expression of deep concentration on their face, sweat oozing from every pore, you can guarantee they are having the time of their lives. This was so, for the Trotters, and all the runners that day. It was soon time to say farewell to Grace and deliver her quickly over the finish line and into the hands of Carol and Ron. Laura looked back to see her daughter collect the well-deserved medal, and hug her grandmother.

Turning her attention to Pam then, she motioned to her companion that for the rest of the race, earphones were the way forward. Slowing down briefly to press the start button on her phone she put one ear piece in so she could still hear Pam if a toilet break was needed. They had an unwritten rule, these two, that neither would leave the other behind, for any reason. A strong bond had formed between these women over time, despite the age difference. But that was the thing about running, it brought people together, united them in a passion no matter what their age.

Laura looked over at the lake, her legs were starting to ache, and she was hungry. A swan was following them upstream, and seemed to bow as they ran by. *'Maybe it recognises me,'* she thought. *'I've been here enough times.'* She smiled to herself, and gave the majestic bird a salute.

Her throat was dry, and she took a sip of the weak solution of orange cordial from her sports bottle, then offered it to Pam.

"I'm ok, thanks love," she declined breathlessly. "I'll be needing a wee otherwise. I'm doing so well, don't want to spoil it."

"Not much further now, Pam. Nearly there. I can see the finish line for the second time today!" Her laugh was tinged with exhaustion and relief. They were almost there. The men would have finished by now, received their medals, be waiting anxiously for the girls. She hoped Mike had plenty of change on him, if he was going to buy her that lorry-load of coffee and buns.

A hunger pang hit her head-on again, and she reached inside her bum-bag for another jelly bean.

"No! Shit. None left. We've eaten them all!" she cried to Pam.

Pam's face fell to her knees. "Give me a quick swig of juice then. I'll make it until the finish line before I need the loo. Not far now, look!"

It was true, their hearts leapt as they looked across through the trees; there was the end of their race, shining in the sunlight like a beacon.

"Come on, mate," Laura could barely speak now. "Let's just go for it. We can collapse later."

The two women laughed in only a way a knackered

runner can, and ploughed on regardless of their exhaustion.

"For the next kilometre, let's talk about what we're going to eat, when we finish," Laura said. "If you've got enough breath,"

"Fry-up," gasped Pam, her face red.

"Beans?" asked Laura.

"Hell yeah," she replied, "and shit loads of toast."

Blimey, thought Laura. Pam was certainly getting very bold with her expletives these days. Maybe it was something to do with getting older, and not really giving a crap.

There was a slight incline in the last few yards towards the finish, and Laura could feel every inch of it. Sweat poured down her face and neck, soaking her race t-shirt. Reaching out to her companion, she took hold of her hand, as they burst over the line, completing their 10k in 1:12:14.

After they had collected their medals, gun and chip time, downed a Mars bar each and given sweaty, salty hugs all round, they headed off in the direction of the café, with the sole intention of drinking their coffee supply completely dry.

* * *

Laura had figured that once she had made her mind up to do the half marathon, some cross-training was needed. So, mindful of keeping her daughter in the loop, Grace went swimming twice a week with her mother, and accompanied her on long walks with the dog.

They were out one afternoon, after school for a walk around the lake at Trentham Gardens. There was a promise of tea and a cake at the café afterwards, so Gracie walked a little faster than usual.

It was October now. The leaves on the trees were once more starting to turn, and a nip in the air was faint, but noticeable. Half term was looming. Soon, Grace would be leaving her mother and step-father for a week's holiday with her dad, Julia, and the noisy Noah, and secretly, she didn't want to go.

They walked arm in arm for a while, a comfortable silence between them.

"Mum, can I talk to you about something?" Grace asked.

"Anything, sweetheart, you know you can, always," she replied, stroking her daughter's hand. "Something bothering you?"

"You sure you won't be annoyed?"

"No. Promise." Laura stopped walking and looked concerned. "What's up?"

Grace avoided her mother's gaze.

"I don't really want to go to Dad's next week. You won't make me go, if I don't want to, will you?"

Laura stopped for a second and looked at her daughter intently.

"Of course we won't make you go, love, but your dad will be really disappointed if you don't. For what reason? Something putting you off?"

"I'm really scared, about leaving you and Mike. I feel safe at home. I don't really like it there. It smells, and Noah cries all the time, and I feel lonely. They don't talk to me much, or do anything with me."

The little girl was clearly worried, and Laura thought carefully. It wasn't fair to force Grace into going, despite the fact that she and Mike had planned to go somewhere together with the dog; a last minute honeymoon.

"Is it really that bad, that you don't want to go? Shall I ring Dad tonight, have a chat with him?"

Grace shrugged. "I just keep getting this really bad feeling in my tummy every time I think about it. I'm dreading it, Mummy. I just don't like it there. Julia ignores me, and I'm hungry all the time."

Alarm bells rang in Laura's head.

"What? Why haven't you told me this before?" she frowned and looked at her daughter, face on.

"I thought you'd be really annoyed with me. I don't know why. I'm not fibbing, honestly, Mummy."

"I'm not saying for one moment you're fibbing to me love, but I have to get my facts right before I talk to your dad, ok? But one thing is for sure, if you aren't entirely happy about going there next week, you're coming away for a week with us. That's a definite."

"I don't want to go, Mum. I feel sick every time I think about it. The house is really dark, as well. I miss you and Mike. I wish he was my real dad." The little girl's face crumpled.

"It's ok love. Don't worry, Mike and I won't force you to go. I'll ring Dad tonight, have a chat."

Laura's first reaction was to call Mike, but he was at work and not contactable. She felt a surge of emotions following their conversation. It was a mixture of guilt and wanting to protect her only child. Anger welled up inside her, and the urge to call Jim immediately was strong.

She left it until later that night, when Grace had given definite instances of blatant neglect, that Laura picked up the phone and spoke to her ex-husband. Julia answered first, and it took all the restraint she could muster not to lose her temper. Luckily, she passed the call straight to Jim, and their conversation reiterated just what a complete idiot he was.

"Look Jim, I'm not being funny, and I don't want to start a row, but Grace isn't entirely happy about coming to you next week. Without losing your temper from the off, so we can have an entirely adult conversation, can you think of any reasons why she is reluctant to come?"

There was silence on the end of the phone while he was mulling over the question.

"No," he replied, "I can't think why she wouldn't want to come. We always have a nice time."

"Well, she says that you don't always have time for her, and she often has to go hungry."

There was a long sigh on the end of the line.

"Look, Laura. Julia isn't coping too well at the moment. Finding motherhood a bit hard. There may have been a couple of times that we skipped tea, ok? But it was only two or three times."

"Are you not capable of cooking, then Jim?" Laura asked again.

"Well, I was busy, wasn't I, I don't get time to cook." His stupid replies were getting more ridiculous by the minute, and the normally calm Laura's lid boiled over and flipped. It was a good job Grace was in bed, and couldn't hear her shouting.

"That's just bloody typical of you, though isn't it Jim? Isn't it? You selfish bastard. It's all about me, me, me, and sod everyone else. Well, I'm telling you now, there is no bloody way our daughter is coming to stay with you next week. A) because she doesn't want to and B) she would rather be with me and Mike, where, and I quote 'she feels safe, and wanted', unbloody quote. So when you decide you want to be unselfish and be a proper father to your daughter, you just let me know, will you?"

Her heart was pumping loudly in her chest, and her throat was tight. Again, she realised what a waste of time he had been all those years, and what a lucky escape she had had.

There was silence on the end of the phone, but she could hear him breathing.

"Look Laura. Who has to have the most attention? Noah or Grace? Noah of course, because he's only a baby."

"What?" she asked in disbelief. "They both need attention, you dickhead! Both of them. She's still only a child!"

She heard him tut and sigh on the end of the phone.

"I don't know, I can never do anything right....always my fault," he replied in a self-pitying kind of way.

Of course Laura knew this was the plan he usually followed. He would do something blatantly wrong, but when challenged, suddenly play the victim, and pretend how hard done by he was. It infuriated her beyond words.

"I've got to go, Laura, Julia needs me."

"Fine!" Laura shouted. "Go to your bloody Julia. You can tell her from me, she got 50 shades of dickhead when she started seeing you."

That last line had sprung into Laura's mind from nowhere, and she was immensely proud of it. Right at that moment, she hated Jim, really hated him, not only for being totally self-absorbed, but also for neglecting their daughter. She decided to wait up for Mike, as he wouldn't be home until gone 11.

His reaction of course, was what Laura had expected. Anger, and distress that Grace not only had kept her secret for so long, but that Jim felt it was ok to behave in such a way as to neglect his child.

"Well, she's not going there next week. She's coming on holiday with us, no question," Mike said after he heard the whole story.

By the following morning, Jim had sent them a text, back-tracking and apologising, saying he was tired and distracted during his conversation with Laura, and would Gracie still like to come and stay. This was typical of him, she knew. He lit the gas, then stepped back. He was a psychiatrist's dream.

Mike could see that for the second time in recent years, he and Jim were going to come to blows, and again, because of his selfishness. He picked up the phone, an option he preferred on this occasion, rather than texting, where a message could easily be misconstrued. He wanted to be firm, but not aggressive. He had a new-found confidence which had worked successfully on his brother. Surely, it could work on Jim too.

When Jim answered the call, he was calm, but taken aback slightly, that he was talking to Mike rather than Laura.

"Look, Jim. I don't want an argument, but we've had a chat with Grace and she has said she'd rather leave it, this time. Maybe come and see you for a couple of days over the Christmas holidays. Ok?" Mike was quietly firm and his voice did not waver.

There was a brief silence, and a sigh. "Yes, ok, if that's what she wants," was all he would say in a couldn't-care-less manner, and the line went dead. Mike thought it was a shame these days with modern technology, there was no option of slamming the phone down anymore.

"Nothing you do, Mike will ever be good enough for Jim. Ever. So don't even try. Damned if you do, damned if you don't." Laura was standing over by the kitchen window, her arms folded, and she had a sad, far-away look in her eyes.

"To be honest, love, I couldn't give a monkeys what he thinks. My priority is you and Gracie, and that's it."

"Look, we've got a week off, let's have a look online and pick somewhere to go. We can run, walk, play games, watch films, do whatever," Laura said.

"I want to give you and Gracie a really good holiday. Spoil you both a bit," Mike replied.

It was late, but they decided to open a bottle of wine, and search for a holiday. By 1am, they had booked 5 nights in Llandudno. A dog-friendly holiday cottage on the west shore.

Mike hugged his new wife. He was tired and stressed, but at least they had something to look forward to.

They went up to bed, looking in on Grace. She was snoring softly, her arms wrapped around her favourite teddy bear. She had taken him off the shelf where he had been for a year, and cuddled up with him in bed. For the next few days, he never left her side, which was a clear indication to Mike and Laura that she was feeling insecure.

She stirred sleepily from her slumber, just enough to open her eyes and smile at them both. "Don't worry about a thing," her mother whispered. "We're off to the seaside Monday, the three of us." She planted a kiss on Grace's soft cheek, and smoothed her hair.

"Night Mum, love you," the little girl smiled and hugged her teddy that little bit tighter.

CHAPTER FOUR

Monday could not come soon enough for the Snows. They woke early, packed up the car, and headed off in the direction of the North Wales coast. Sidney Greenstreet was to be well cared for by the ever-obliging Angela, and Humphrey was firmly ensconced in the back of the car with Grace. She beamed from ear to ear.

"Did you pack the running kits, Mum?"

"Certainly did," came the reply.

When they arrived in Llandudno, the tide was out. The mist had cleared, leaving a glassy sheen to the vast expanse of beach in front of them.

Getting out of the car and stretching their legs, the four of them took in a deep satisfying breath of sea air. Mike closed his eyes, and smiled. It was a peaceful quiet day, apart from the odd seagull here and there. They cried overhead, in the vain hope the few humans on the ground might be harbouring food.

"Why don't we get unpacked, and all go for a run along the beach?" Mike suggested after his third deep intake of ozone.

Laura agreed that was a perfect idea, and Grace didn't need much persuading. Humphrey was eager to go straight away, but was forced to wait until his companions were ready.

There is something very special about a run along the beach, as anyone who loves the sport will verify. The sense of freedom, the wind swirling around you, playing with your hair and whispering playfully in your ears. It tempts you further and further along the stretch of sand, until you turn around and see where you started is but a tiny spec in the distance. But you smile to yourself and think, no matter. I will go back when I'm done, but for now I am as free as a bird.

This was Mike Snow and his family, the faithful Humphrey running at their side, no need for the lead today. His eyes shone bright, tongue lolling in his mouth, a few grains of sand on his shiny black nose. The strains and stresses of everyday life simply melted away, and happiness filled their souls.

Those five blissful days on the Welsh coast were an uplifting tonic. Days filled with never-to-be-forgotten memories, carried far into the future. The weather stayed dry, although a little overcast at times. They ran every day, walked, laughed, ate fish and chips sitting on the wall looking out to sea, played cards and drank the best wine they could find from the local supermarket. It was a blissful open space, and they had loved every minute of it.

"I don't want to go home," Laura said quietly, as she rested her head on Mike's shoulder. They were sitting on a bench with Grace overlooking a restless sea, and the tide had come in.

"Don't worry girls, we will definitely be back. It's been magnificent. Shall we come for Christmas? We'll need a bigger holiday home though if your mum and dad want to join us."

Laura and Grace squealed in delight and excitement.

By the time they had packed up, ready to go home, their return was cast in stone. A phone call to Carol and Ron confirmed that Christmas in Llandudno would certainly be something to look forward to.

CHAPTER FIVE

"Welcome back," cried Pam cheerily, when she entered the staff room the following week. "Have a good time?"

Mike sighed. "The best, Pam. The best. How's the training coming along?"

She stopped for a moment, and looked at him very proudly. "Really well!" she announced. "Do you know," she said, talking in a low voice and moving closer to him, "I can run 5k now without having to stop for a wee." She nodded triumphantly.

"Fantastic!" he whispered, and put a thumbs up. This sounded promising for when they did the actual race. Poor Pam, she was a slave to her bladder.

Suddenly, the door burst open, and Sue, one of the other nurses hurried in. She was a thin girl in her mid-twenties with mousy hair, which was always piled messily in an excuse for a bun on top of her head.

"Guys, Agnes in Bay 3, the phlebotomist came to take her bloods, thinks she's gone in her sleep," she said breathlessly.

Mike and Pam leapt to their feet, and went out onto the ward, heading for Bay 3. Over in the far corner, lay Agnes. She was a sweet old lady who had only recently been admitted. Pam quickly drew the curtains around the bed. She lay seemingly motionless, her skin was sallow and stretched across her face. Her mouth wide, and toothless. No breath seemed to be present. They tried to find a pulse.

"Is she for resus?" he asked.

Pam checked quickly but shook her head.

Mike put his face closer to the old lady's. He held his breath, looking for signs of life. Even her hair seemed lifeless, it was pure white and dull. Her eyes were sunken in their sockets.

Pam shook her head in sadness.

"Agnes?" Mike whispered softly to her, and touched her arm gently.

Nothing happened. He watched her closely.

"Yes!!" she shouted suddenly, sending, Mike, Pam, Sue and the phlebotomist into so much shock the four of them shouted with fright and jumped back from the bed.

The previously lifeless woman was now very much awake, and sat up blinking at the startled crowd around her bed. Mike's heart was thumping in his chest as he tried to calm his breathing.

"You gave us a bit of a fright there, Agnes. Are you ok?" he asked laughing.

"Yes, absolutely fine dear, thank you. Having a lovely sleep, I was dreaming about all sorts of nice things," she gave him a gummy smile.

"That's lovely, just so long as you're ok," he said.

"Christ," said the phlebotomist under her breath. "Sorry, I was convinced she was a gonner." The poor woman was clearly in a state of shock, her hand covered her mouth and she looked pale.

"It's ok, don't worry. Easy mistake to make. She had us all convinced, to be fair," Pam reassured her.

Moving away from the bed and drawing back the curtains, the nurses dispersed, their hearts beating a little faster, nerves in tatters.

"Oh, Nurse!" cried the newly resurrected patient. "Could I ask you a favour?"

Mike turned around and smiled. "Yes, of course, what can I do for you?"

The old lady winked and gave him another enigmatic gummy grin.

"I don't suppose you would be a love and just give my dentures a swill under the tap, would you? It was meat pie for tea last night, and it always gets stuck."

Pam touched his arm lightly. "As I said earlier, welcome back."

* * *

'Surprising how sobering it is to return to work, after an idyllic holiday,' Mike thought, as he grabbed a quick cup of tea on his break. He consoled himself with the fact that it was Laura's birthday the following weekend, and happily, it fell on a Saturday. It was his day off, and they had all sorts of great things planned.

Of course, Shrewsbury Park Run was on the cards, followed by a spot of shopping in the town, and then a party early evening with the usual crowd.

He had bought her an eternity ring as a main present, a simple band of white gold with five white stones in it, which complemented her engagement and wedding rings. He often sat and looked at his own band of gold these days, and smiled. He thought himself so very fortunate. Mike Snow, single man of many years, with only his rather fat feline as companion was now a married man with a step-daughter and blissfully happy. He was exactly where he wanted to be in life, at the very summit in fact.

'*Snow at the summit,*' he said quietly to himself and smiled at the analogy, twisting his wedding ring around a couple of times, before heading out to the ward again.

* * *

The day of Laura's birthday was a bright one. Despite the chill of Autumn, the sun shone. The park run was well attended, and the three of them completed it in 33 minutes, guaranteeing a great start to the day.

Mike was true to his word, and spoilt his little family with a combination of shopping and lunch. On their return home that afternoon, a bouquet of flowers arrived for Laura. The card said, 'For my wife, on her birthday'. The rest of the message was private, just between the two of them, written in his own hand.

"Mum's coming early, and she's going to make a punch!" Laura announced. "Not had one of those for years!"

"Wasn't that a 70's thing?" Mike recalled. "I vaguely remember a big bowl of something highly potent and little glass cups hanging off the side. Can't recollect anything else though, all a bit hazy," he laughed.

"Dad bought her a trendy new punch bowl and glasses. She wants to try it out. Be rude not to," Laura added as she busied herself around the kitchen preparing food.

"So, how many exactly have we got coming?" asked Mike.

"Nine, plus us three," she confirmed.

"Excellent. I'll get a couple more chairs out then, so everyone has got somewhere to park."

The house became a hive of activity then, as Grace started to help her mum lay the buffet out. Carol and Ron arrived carrying a large box.

"Wow, Mum, that's got to be the biggest punch bowl ever," exclaimed Laura, and her eyes lit up.

"I know, bloody awesome, isn't it? I said to your father there's fun to be had with that, Ronald." Carol placed it down in the kitchen, and took out her cigarette case. "Just nipping out for a swift one darling, and I'll be back in to help. Where's my favourite son-in-law?"

"Sorting out extra chairs," Laura shouted. "You all right Dad?"

"I'm fine, how are you, love? Happy Birthday," he smiled and gave his daughter a warm kiss. "Did you try out your new running kit this morning?"

Carol and Ron had bought their daughter a complete set of new gear. Trainers, tights, running top, and waterproof jacket.

"Yes, thanks so much Dad, it was really comfortable, loved it. We did a PB of 33 minutes this morning!" she smiled.

"Well done. I'm so proud of you. Look how far you've come in such a short space of time, and now training for a half marathon. Who would have thought it?"

"I know," she replied thoughtfully. "So much has

changed for the better. I'm a very lucky girl," she kissed his cheek. "Now you go and sit down, the others will be here soon, and Mum and I have a punch to make."

Carol appeared a few moments later, bringing a familiar smell of cigarettes with her, mixed with perfume.

"Have you invited Mel?" she asked.

"Yes, but he can't make it. Sent me a very nice card and present though," Laura replied.

"Hmmm, that's nice of him. Shame he isn't coming. I was looking forward to a good old chat, catch up, see if he's gone back to being an arsehole, or whether he's changed into a nice person permanently." Carol tossed her hair aside with a beautifully manicured hand. She wore red nail varnish today, a vibrant warm colour and she oozed classic charm and charisma. At almost 72, she was still beautiful.

She laughed that deep, throaty smokers' laugh, and rubbed her hands together. "Now then! Let's make punch!"

Mike came in at that point, carrying two bottles of champagne, and a large bottle of lemonade.

Carol smiled at him, and gave one of her firm hugs. God, she hugged tight.

"What's that?" she said pointing to the lemonade.

"Don't you put it in the punch, to dilute it slightly?"

Carol threw him a look which could have turned milk to yoghurt.

"DILUTE???" she echoed. "Jesus Christ man, we don't dilute in this family. Thought you'd learnt that by now. Take it in the other room, it's for kids and lightweights, that stuff." She flicked him and his weak excuse for a drink away from her like an annoying fly, being careful to wink at him and blow a kiss, to show she still loved him, despite his faux pas.

He grinned. He must have the most incredible mother-in-law. Ever.

"I do love you, Carol" he laughed, disappearing out the door.

Finally, their creation was ready. The two women stood back and admired it. The square bowl held two full bottles of champagne, an entire litre bottle of vodka, and a bottle of sherry. It tasted divine, so they decided to go traditional, adding slices of fruit and mint leaves.

"Perfect," exclaimed Carol, clapping her hands together. "Let's take it in."

The table was so full of food that they had to improvise, and quickly placed the very full bowl on a smaller table at the side of the sofa. Their guests could still help themselves easily enough to the potent mixture.

It grew dark quickly, and friends started to arrive. Sidney decided he had had enough of being petted and admired, so he took himself off to Angela's next door, for a bit of peace and quiet. There was only so much a cat could take when the conversation consisted mainly of remarks about his weight. Humphrey however, was enjoying himself very much indeed, and decided to stick around. There would of course be food dropped accidentally, and if it was on the floor, there was an unwritten rule that it belonged to him.

The humans seemed to have a great time. They laughed, joked and talked about all sorts of things. He managed to snaffle a fair bit from the carpet too, a few crisps, a cocktail sausage and a mini sausage roll. Grace fed him a few more sausages until her mother said that was enough. He was by now, rather thirsty. The humans had started getting a bit louder than normal, and dispersed into the kitchen to cut the birthday cake.

He was left alone then, his tummy was full. His eyes suddenly settled on the glass bowl in the corner of the room, and there seemed to be a little bit of liquid left in it. Certainly, enough for him to have a good drink out of it, anyway. He looked towards the door, no one was coming, the coast was clear.

He hopped up onto the sofa and made his way confidently over. It smelled good, if a little strange, but certainly better than just plain old water.

He drank thirstily, drinking every drop that was left, and even licked the sides for good measure.

Sitting back on the sofa, he sighed, broke wind, and licked his lips. My, life was good, the little dog thought. He began to feel happy and emotional at the same time. The room started to sway slightly, and he felt sleepy.

* * *

"Mr Snow, please, with Humphrey Bogart," called the vet in the waiting room. It was late Sunday morning, and Mike sat alone cradling a snoring dog on his lap, his tongue hanging sideways out of his mouth.

"Come on in," added the vet.

It was, by unhappy coincidence, the very same vet he had seen when Sidney Greenstreet had his unfortunate accident with the cat flap.

"Thanks very much for seeing us," Mike said quietly.

"Oh, absolutely no problem," he replied. "So, how can I help?"

"Well, last night we had a party for my wife's

216

birthday. Humph was left alone in the lounge for about half an hour, and when we came back in the room, he was lying on his back with his legs in the air, snoring. We've not been able to wake him up properly since, and he's been sick a couple of times."

The vet nodded. "Hmmm, ok." He then proceeded to check the little dog over, who was still completely oblivious to his surroundings.

"Right, well," said the vet after giving Humphrey a thorough examination, and clearing his throat, "I'm fairly certain I know what's wrong with him, Mr Snow."

"Oh good, is he going to be ok? I mean we were worried, you know, that's why we asked for an emergency appointment."

The vet sniffed, and held his hand over his mouth for a moment. He placed the other hand on his hip and took a deep breath.

"Has he had any access to alcohol, at all in the last 24 hours, because I can smell it on him, to be honest."

Mike coloured slightly and felt uncomfortable. "Well, as I said, we had a party for my wife, and they made a punch, which he could easily have had a drink of, yes." He scratched his eyebrow nervously.

The vet thought for a moment. "Yes, well, that just confirms my diagnosis. He's pissed, Mr Snow. Your dog is pissed. Very likely he will have the hangover from hell, when he wakes up. But he just needs to sleep it off."

Mike could tell that the vet was desperately trying to stay professional, and keep his composure, but the corners of his mouth were curling up, and he continually cleared his throat, and blinked hard. He avoided eye contact with Mike, too and kept putting his hand over his mouth.

"Right," Mike said surprised. "Will he be ok? We don't need to do anything?"

"No, no I've given him a really good check over, his heart is doing fine, and everything else seems good, so as I say, he needs to sleep it off. Clear fluids when he wakes up, but just take it steady, he might be sick again, that's to be expected."

"Right. Well, thank you very much, really appreciate it." He managed a weak but embarrassed smile.

"No problem. So, how's your cat? Sidney isn't it?" said the vet changing the subject and regaining his composure.

"Oh yes, he's doing very well, thank you. Lost a fair bit of weight since we saw you last."

"Great!" said the vet awkwardly. "That's good to hear. Not going around wearing cat flaps now, then!" He laughed nervously, and a little too loudly, Mike thought.

"Erm, no," he smiled.

The vet seemed to lose his composure slightly, and was laughing virtually uncontrollably.

Mike wasn't seeing the funny side. This was maybe due to the fact that he himself was nursing the mother of all hangovers, and now he had the added humiliation of the fact that his dog was as pissed as a rat.

He stood for a moment, contemplating his next move. Just then, the vet returned, having calmed himself down.

"Sorry about that, Mr Snow. It's been a long night, you know. A few emergencies in," he said sheepishly.

"No, no problem at all. Thank you very much for your time."

"Obviously, any problems, just bring him straight back," he added.

Mike picked his very drunk dog up in his arms, and headed out of the room, not looking back. He could hear the door close, and the sound of hysterical laughter filled the otherwise quiet surgery. Raindrops started to fall on them both, so he placed Humphrey on the passenger seat next to him and headed home.

CHAPTER SIX

"Seriously? Did your dog get hammered?" Matt asked at their next training session. "We left quite early, so I didn't notice. He did seem very tired."

"He did, yes... bit of a sore subject really. Anyway, he's fine now, thank you for asking."

"Blimey, sorry Mike," the younger man apologised.

"It's ok, really. Just a bit embarrassing at the vets, that's all." Mike coloured slightly. "Anyway, how's training going? I can appreciate that at this time of year, it can get tough."

"Yeah, it's going ok, thanks. I've joined the gym though, and I've been doing some more core work, so I can probably manage a 10k each time I go out. Do the odd taper, you know if I feel a bit sluggish. I always think that a small run is better than no run at all."

Mike smiled. "My goodness, you're absolutely right there. Laura's been struggling a little bit with the weather closing in, so she's been swimming with Gracie a fair bit."

Matt nodded in agreement. Training could be hard in the winter time, as they all knew. He asked tentatively how things were with Gracie's dad, whilst they were on the subject.

Mike's face seemed to darken slightly, and Matt wondered whether he had asked an unwelcome question. Surprisingly, he spoke freely on the subject. It seemed he wanted to talk about it to someone who wasn't directly connected, to get their viewpoint.

"To be perfectly honest Matt, it's quite hard being a step-dad. Even with a lovely little girl like Grace. I mean, she's an absolute dream of a kid, polite, well-mannered, kind. But there's always the problem when the ex has different views to you. Different parenting skills. Luckily Laura and I are reading off the same set of rules, which is a blessing, but Grace's dad…well, I don't know. We used to be best friends, did you know?"

Matt nodded. They talked some more as they ran, which passed the time. It was just the two of them today, out for an extra training session, and Mike was fond of his younger companion. He was a nice, genuine sort of lad, respectful.

"Do you know," Mike admitted after they had completed 10k out of their 15. "I'm embarrassed to say I don't know what you do for a living, Matt. How bad is that? I feel terrible, so sorry."

"No that's ok Mike, don't worry. I'm not in the habit of telling many people to be fair. It can put them on edge a bit."

"Oh? Why is that? What do you do exactly? Now you're going to tell me it's some random job like a male stripper aren't you?" Mike laughed heartily.

Matt's face dropped. "Bloody hell, how did you

know?" he said stopping suddenly.

Mike looked stunned and slowed down. He also ground to a halt and looked at his friend.

"Really?" he gasped, out of breath. "Seriously? You're a male stripper?"

"Yeah. I do parties, you know. Birthdays. Baby oil, and…..stuff."

Mike paused his sports watch for a moment. He blinked hard, taking in what Matt had just said.

"Oh. Ok." There was a long awkward silence, mainly led by Mike, who was struggling for something to say.

"Shall we carry on? Only another 5k to go."

Matt nodded, and they ran on, not speaking for a while.

"So, do you enjoy your job?" the elder of the two men asked, trying to make light of the situation.

"Yeah, actually I do. Look, Mike I know it sounds weird, stripping for a living, but it's what I do, and the money isn't bad either. My girlfriend is cool with it." He shrugged his shoulders.

"Well, if you're happy, then that's fine," Mike replied, relaxing somewhat. "Sorry, it took me a bit by surprise," he laughed nervously.

The two men ran on, laughing, joking and talking all the way home.

This was certainly something to tell Carol and Laura over a glass of something this evening, Mike thought.

* * *

"He's a WHAT?!" Laura asked that night, her hand around a large glass of white wine, and an Irish Cream truffle in her mouth. She was lying on the sofa watching TV after Grace had gone to bed.

"Jesus! Can I tell Mum?!" she said excitedly.

"Well, I suppose so," Mike replied. "But just don't, you know, go telling everyone. He said it makes some people feel awkward."

"Does he enjoy it?"

"Says so, yes. Money isn't bad either."

Laura sat thinking for a moment. "Can you imagine Keith doing a job like that, in his younger days?"

"Erm, no darling, I can't. In fact I don't even want to think about it. Seeing him in his running tights is enough for me, to be honest." Mike poured himself a whisky.

He went to join her on the sofa.

"So, what are we watching?" he asked putting his arm around her.

"YouTube on training for a half marathon," she said popping yet another truffle into her mouth.

"Lovely. Here we are lying on the sofa, drinking booze and eating chocolates, watching fitness videos. Now there's a thing." He chuckled and squeezed her tight.

CHAPTER SEVEN

It never ceased to amaze Laura, just how fast Christmas came along, after her birthday in October. Quickly they were into November, and the countdown started.

It was true, she did always love this time of year, and it was their first one as a married couple. The holiday house had been booked, and they were to drive over to Llandudno the day before Christmas Eve, to spend the festive season by the sea. Four and a half blissful days, running along the beach if the weather allowed, presents, food, great company and a little bit of strength training in between.

She thought a moment, whilst at work, about what the new year would bring. She was into her early forties now, and apart from the half marathon looming ahead of them, she wondered what else life had in store. For the first time in many years she felt settled, at ease. Gone were the days when she felt anxious all the time, on edge, constantly trying to please Jim and his narcissistic ways; always treading on egg shells.

Ducking and diving around his moods, and the stupid excuses he had for them. Wondering, always how long he would be in one, and how long it would be before he returned to the normal Jim, or normal as he could be. She felt that it was always her fault, to some extent. Did she wind him up? Annoy him? Or was it simply the fact that he just plain old didn't love her anyway. She was but a commodity to him, a glorified housekeeper. Someone to keep their home clean and tidy, cook for him, wash, iron and tidy up, care for their child.

Life with Mike was completely different. He was kind and generous to a fault. A mood never crossed his brow, ever, and he worked hard. He was kind to Grace and made time for her. They played board games and read books to each other. In her private moments she wished Grace was his child, because he was the better father, by far. He was a good listener, a caring and thoughtful husband, and the most important thing was, that he loved her. She was not just a commodity to him, she was his equal, his partner, and above all, his soulmate.

"You guys going away for Christmas this year then?" Trudy asked, passing her friend a steaming mug of coffee.

Laura's face lit up, and she snapped herself into the present again. "Yeah, can't wait Trudes, it's going to be epic. What are you guys going to be doing?"

"Helene's dad is coming over, and my mum. Other than that, pretty quiet really. How's training coming along for the half?" She looked magnificent today, Laura thought. Her hair was pale blue, her make-up strong, heels defiant. Her smile displayed a row of perfectly white even teeth. Great looking woman, and nice with it.

"Not bad actually. I've been planking a lot this week, doing the world of good to my core."

"Sorry, didn't understand a bloody word of that, you've been doing what?" Trudy blinked hard and looked puzzled.

"Planking," Laura repeated.

Trudy screwed her face up and made a little noise. "Show me, no idea what you're on about."

"Oh, bloody hell," Laura laughed and checked that no customers were about to come into the shop and disturb them.

"Right, you do it with me, ok?" By now, both women were laughing. Trudy put down the handful of flowers she was holding, and got down on all fours.

"This is totally ridiculous, and only something you would contemplate doing at Christmas time in the middle of your florist shop," Trudy said cheerfully.

The two of them assumed the plank position, and on Laura's instruction had a competition to see how long they could hold it.

"Now there's something you don't see every day," a voice appeared above them. "Would this be the wrong time to ask if you could do me a wreath for next week?"

"Oh my God, I'm so sorry," Trudy apologised as she staggered to her feet. In front of her stood an elderly gentleman, in need of some flowers for a funeral.

"My friend and I were just planking. Good for the core," she patted her tummy and winked at him.

"I'll take your word for it," he replied politely and smiled.

After he left, they planked three more times. Trudy surprisingly held it for 40 seconds, proving that she was probably fitter than Laura realised.

* * *

The thing about core work, and planking in particular, Laura found quite addictive. Many a time Mike had come home from work to find his wife assuming the position, counting the seconds, her abdominals shaking until she could stand it no more.

Three days before they were due to go to Llandudno, he returned from his shift to hear her calling him from the lounge.

"Mike!" she sounded desperate and in some discomfort. "Mike! Can you come and help me please?"

He rushed into the room, and stopped in his tracks.

Half way between the television and the coffee table, was Laura, in a collapsed plank. But sitting in the small of her back, was Sidney Greenstreet. He turned to look at his owner, but made no attempt to move. An expression of accomplishment sat defiantly on his face, and did not alter. Sniffing the air, he turned away and proceeded to stick his claws into Laura's skin, pawing her and purring. He settled himself down with a satisfied thump, planning on going to sleep.

"Get him off me Mike, I can't bloody move. I think he needs to go back on the diet again. Weighs a freaking ton!"

"How long have you been there?" her husband asked rushing over to remove his pet.

"Ten minutes. I held the position for 2 minutes with him on me, how good is that? But then he just wouldn't shift. Grace is at Mum's and there was no one to help me. Thank God you came home when you did."

Sidney was not at all happy that he had been moved, and took a disgruntled swipe at Mike, a scowl forming across his furry brow.

He certainly did feel heavier. When the cat was in a better mood, they decided to weigh him.

"Right," said Mike. "I can't understand this at all. He's been on the revised diet for how long? A fair while now, and he weighs in at just over a stone!"

The couple stood looking at him. They assured each other that he was categorically not having any treats, and Gracie was under strict instructions not to feed him any extra titbits.

"You don't suppose he's getting food from somewhere else, do you?" Laura asked after a while.

Mike turned to his wife, and the same thought came into both their minds at the same time.

"Angela," they said out loud.

The following day, it was Mike's enviable task, not only to investigate Sidney's mysterious weight gain, but also to ask his neighbour if she was still happy to look after him whilst they were away. He wasn't sure which subject to start on first. Should be mention the dramatic weight gain at all, even?

Angela welcomed him into her home. She looked exactly the same as she always did, the cardigan perfectly positioned, almost part of her anatomy.

She offered him a cup of tea, which he gratefully accepted.

It was only the second time he had seen the interior of her house, and it reflected her personality typically.

The lounge décor was uncomplicated with varying shades of brown, her sofa and the carpet plain and the wallpaper simple and soothing. No photographs, only paintings adorned the walls. A clock stood on the mantelpiece, and it dominated the room with its tick tock, tick tock. He noticed the absence of a Christmas tree, but a few bland cards sat next to the timepiece.

Mike stood and looked at it, in his hand was a present for her. He tapped it with his finger. There was the distant sound of his neighbour in the kitchen, kettle boiling, the familiar clink of teaspoon on china, and all the time the clock ticked, ticked, ticked loudly. He wondered how she could stand that noise, day in day out, sitting here as no doubt she did, staring at the wall, listening to the clock and her life passing with every minute…tick, tick, tick. His hypnosis was broken by Angela walking quietly in to the room in her slippers, a smile on her face, hand outstretched, a fine bone china mug in her hand. Her eyes fluttered shut, and he smiled back, taking the tea.

"Do have a seat, Michael," she said with her usual nervous delivery.

"Thanks, Angela," he perched on the edge of the sofa, and she positioned herself at the other end, her back ramrod straight, cardigan perfectly placed.

He cleared his throat nervously. "Erm, just wondered if it's still ok for you to feed Sidney for us, whilst we're in Llandudno? We're back the day after Boxing day. Doing anything nice over Christmas?" He suspected not, but thought it only polite to ask.

Her hands were folded neatly in her lap. "No, no. I don't really bother with the festive season, what with being on my own. I'm quite happy to look after Sidney for you, he can be a bit of company for me."

"Lovely thanks, Angela. We do appreciate it," he smiled weakly, and hurried to finish his tea. They sat in silence for what seemed like an eternity, and the clock dominated the room once again.

She asked him eventually what their plans were, and if they were taking Humphrey, what Grace was having for Christmas, and how training was going for the half marathon. He was wondering whether to mention Sidney's expanding waist line, and a thought came to him.

"Sidney's got to lose a bit more weight Angela, the vet said when I took him for his check-up. Still not at his target, so he's given us a revised amount per feed. Don't want him getting diabetes, you see. I'll get Laura to write it down for you, is that ok?"

She blushed noticeably.

"Oh yes, absolutely fine. I did think he was a little underweight when I fed him last time, and he seemed so hungry, so I hope you don't mind but I gave him half my bacon sandwich each morning. Liked it so much, he comes every morning now."

Bingo. Mystery solved, and she's even admitted it.

"Ah......well, he's quite crafty you see, when it comes to food. He may look totally emaciated, but in fact isn't. If we cut the treats out, the vet will be much happier."

"Of course, of course. My mistake. My apologies Michael."

He spent the next ten minutes assuring her it was absolutely fine, and she had been hoodwinked by a consummate actor on four legs.

They laughed about it, and the atmosphere in the room became more relaxed.

"Oh, before I forget, we have a little gift for you." He passed over a shoebox sized present, wrapped and adorned with a silver bow.

Her face softened and her eyes opened wider than usual.

"Thank you, Michael, that's so very kind of you all." She placed it on the coffee table. "I have a little something for you all, too." She walked over to the sideboard, and took out a box, unwrapped.

"Here, for you to share, after Christmas lunch." She proudly handed him a box of mandarin and lemon segments.

"Lovely, thanks Angela." He stood up to leave, and formally shook her hand.

"Merry Christmas, to you and yours," she said through closed eyes.

Mike was keen to get out of the confines of Angela's time capsule of a life, and once out of the door, breathed a big sigh.

He hurried home, with the box of jellied fruits clasped firmly in his hand.

CHAPTER EIGHT

It occurred to Mike and Laura, that going away for Christmas, although a wonderful idea, was also quite stressful to organise. By the time they had packed the car, they could barely see through the rear window for presents. Grace sat in the back seat with Humphrey on her knee, and a suitcase at her side. She was only too grateful that her grandparents were travelling separately in their car, and there was no more luggage.

"Will Sidney be ok, Mum? When we come back he might be the size of a tiger." Grace was concerned that her feline friend would be totally indulged over the holidays, and take even more bed-space from her upon their return.

"He'll be just fine love. Mike had a really good chat with Angela about it. Surreal, but a good chat all the same." Laura was mentally checking and double checking they hadn't left anything behind. She would be able to relax once they arrived in their holiday cottage, and if they had forgotten anything, there were plenty of shops nearby.

It was a bleak misty drive to the Welsh coast, and it failed to get properly light all day. As usual, Grace dozed most of the journey, and Humphrey gave a deep sigh every half an hour. It was his way of saying, "are we nearly there?"

"Not long now, Humph," Mike assured him after sigh number six. "And no alcohol for you this Christmas, my lad."

Laura giggled. Despite the fact he had been sick twice, she had found it rather funny.

They arrived in a dull grey Llandudno, but the west shore was still as dramatic and beautiful as they remembered it. Carol and Ron had arrived an hour earlier, and were busy unpacking.

"Darlings look!" Carol rushed out to greet them and virtually pulled them into the house "they've only gone and put a bloody Christmas tree up for us, how marvellous is that? And a bottle of champagne in the fridge! Hot tub is nice and warm…place is amazing!" She lit a cigarette and flicked back her hair, Joan Crawford style. Mike noticed she had newly manicured nails, and was wearing her charity shop fur coat. He looked at her in awe.

They settled into their temporary home quickly, and the following day, which was Christmas Eve, went into the town to do some last minute shopping.

Carol had disappeared into the local supermarket, and came out half an hour later, carrying a large bag of sprouts in one hand and an enormous fresh turkey in the other. A cigarette hung out of her mouth.

"Take this for me, Michael," she muttered, slinging the bird at him like a carrion missile. "Heavy bugger," she added, taking the cigarette out of her mouth and blowing a cloud of smoke into the cold air.

"Are we all going to midnight Mass or anything later?" he asked her.

"Shit, no," she replied confrontationally. "Can't be bothered with all that, especially if there's champagne and some amazing food on offer. You can go if you like, with Laura."

"No," he said after a moment. "The champagne and great food sounds much more interesting."

He wasn't about to argue, as it was pretty much a foregone conclusion that they were up for a boozy Christmas Eve, which didn't sound half bad. As long as they weren't planning on making another punch.

Before darkness descended on them, Mike and Laura decided to have a long run. The tide was out, and although it was a dull moody day, here and there a little winter sunshine peaked through the clouds, reminding them that it was in fact, still there.

They left Carol, Ron and Grace back at the house and took Humphrey onto the beach. It seemed to stretch out for eternity, and the three of them stopped briefly to take in the view. The wind had died down somewhat, replaced by a gentle breeze, which whispered in their ears, and played with Laura's hair, flicking it playfully around her face. She took a deep breath, and they set off then, the firm sand crunching gently beneath their feet. The clouds were grey, but high, chasing the three runners along the shore. Humphrey was loving every minute of it, stopping occasionally to sniff the sea weed or drink from a rock pool, then running back to his owners when they whistled or called him.

They ran on, all the time watching the tide. After an hour or so, it was showing signs of coming in, so they completed their return journey along the path which ran adjacent to the beach.

Mike had noticed that they had already run four and a half miles, so by the time they got back, they would have done a very impressive, nine. He was extremely proud of his wife, as it had probably been the furthest she had run in one session. He noticed she was starting to tire a little into their 6 mile, and he instantly thought of something to take her mind off it.

"Nice running jacket, love. Waterproof?"

"Yes, bought it last week when I was in town. First time I've worn it."

"Great colour. Good price too. Fifty percent off?"

There was a period of silence whilst Laura's mind computed what he was saying, but she ran on in front of him.

"Yes."

"Not bad. You did well to get it for £12.99."

She stopped suddenly, a questioning look on her face. "What? How do you know all this?"

He reached over her shoulder with his right hand, and gently pulled the collar of the jacket.

"Left the bloody labels on haven't you? Been flapping around in front of me for the past few miles!"

Laura laughed so hard, she bent over double, already out of breath from running, and her cheeks were red and rosy.

She punched him playfully in the chest, motioning him to remove the labels.

"You could have said!" she shouted when they had both composed themselves.

"I was having too much fun." Mike removed the offending articles with his teeth, and put them in his pocket.

"Spending too much time with my mother, that's

your trouble. Pair of you are mischief! Come on, let's get back before it goes dark. There's a bottle of Prosecco on ice with our name on it, and I'm ready to eat the contents of the American-style fridge".

They both laughed and ran home, if a little slower. The cold December air was bracing, and invigorating at the same time, but nine miles was a long way, and they would both be asleep on the sofa before 10pm.

* * *

The next few days were a happy mixture of smaller taper runs, walks and festive cheer. It had been certainly the best Christmas for many a year, and the day they all left, was a sad one. It had gone too quickly, as great times always do. The trip home was conducted in some silence, but some happy memories had been made, never to be forgotten. One thing was certain, they were set to return the following year, and hopefully for a little longer.

It was nice to be home, and Sidney showed no signs of any dramatic weight gain. He was however, a little disgruntled that the family had left him for almost a week, and proceeded to sulk in the garden, with his back to the house, for 12 hours, only to be coaxed in by a little turkey.

CHAPTER NINE

Grace had managed between Christmas and New Year to go and see her father and Julia, but didn't want to stop overnight. Instead, Mike had said he would take her, go off for a couple of hours to walk the dog on the beach and come and pick her up when she was done.

Their journey to the coast that cold December day, Mike thought, would be etched on his memory forever. It was one of those simple but momentous journeys that you sometimes have in life.

Laura had to work, so Mike, Grace and Humphrey got in the car on that very cold frosty morning, and headed over to Aberdovey. They chatted most of the way, sang a few songs, and Grace dozed off for half an hour.

Not long before they arrived, she woke up, bleary eyed. Her young face bathed in winter sunshine. She blinked and smiled at him.

"Looking forward to today?" he asked.

"Sort of," she shrugged.

"Well, don't worry. You don't have to stay over. Just a few hours with your dad and then we can go home, ok?" Mike reassured her as best he could, because his gut told him that she was nervous.

Grace nodded. "It's really dark in their house."

"Is it?" Mike wanted to know more, to try and get a better picture of how his old friend was living.

"It's on three floors, but it's so dark. I don't like it, scares me. The lounge is downstairs, kitchen on the middle and then the bedrooms are at the top. I get left on my own a lot, and it smells. Julia is always in a bad mood and doesn't talk to me much. I hate going there."

"What does it smell of?" Mike asked her gently.

"Like….damp. You know when you can smell the ground, outside, but on the inside? The garden is a right tip as well. The place just gives me the creeps. As soon as I walk through the door, I get this horrible feeling in my tummy."

That's your gut, telling you that things aren't right,' he thought to himself.

"Look, if you feel unhappy whilst you're there, just phone me and I'll come and get you, ok?"

She nodded and gave him a weak smile. It struck him just how young she looked, the childish innocence in her face seemed to plead with him, and he felt overwhelmingly protective of this little girl. A tear stung his eye, but he blinked it away.

"Your dad loves you, you know. He's maybe just going through some stuff right now he needs to deal with."

"Yeah, I guess." She was silent for some moments. "Mike?"

"Yes, darling?"

"Don't be mad at me for saying this…but I wish you were my dad."

He felt a lump rise in his throat, and that old familiar tear pricked the back of his eye again, threatening to force its way out and trickle unapologetically down his cheek.

Fighting it, he croaked, "As far as I'm concerned, you're my special little girl, and you always will be." He stared at the road ahead.

Suddenly, they were there, and the moment was broken, but he just managed to swipe away the escaping tear from his face before they got out of the car.

The cold sea air took his breath away, and the lump in his throat disappeared.

"Now listen, I won't be far away, if you need me, either text or call me. You can text me throughout the day anyway, if it makes you feel better. Same goes for your mum." He held her face in his hands, then gave her a big reassuring hug. "Love you."

"I love you, Dad," she whispered in his ear, and he held her a little bit tighter.

Jim then opened the door with a grissly Noah in his arms, and Grace's face darkened a little.

Mike and his old friend nodded to each other, but the atmosphere between them was filled with sadness and regret.

"I'll pick her up again at four." Mike turned and waved.

"Ok," was all Jim gave in return.

How things had changed for these two former best friends. Now, not enemies, but certainly the bridge between them was rapidly in decay, possibly never to be repaired.

Mike took a deep breath once back in the warmth of the car, and allowed himself a little weep. It had been the first time he had cried since the death of his mother, and that had been many years ago.

Humphrey of course put a whole new spin on things by jumping onto the front seat and unceremoniously washing his privates, and Mike laughed, rubbing the little dog's head.

"Come on, you old scruff bag, shall we go for a nice long walkies?"

Humphrey yawned and wagged his tail. He looked back at the now closed door of Jim's house and whined.

"Don't worry, we'll be picking her up again in no time," Mike reassured him.

He dropped Laura a quick text to assure her all was well. Winter sun shone brightly now, and the tide was out. The beach beckoned them.

"Come on then, let's see how far we can go." He looked down at his furry companion, and they headed off into the distance with only the seagulls and their thoughts for company.

* * *

Darkness crept over the sky mid-afternoon, and after a long but enjoyable walk, Mike and Humphrey headed off to the local shops. They had an hour to kill. Grace had texted him three times over the day, and from what he could gather, things were going ok.

He called in at a small gift shop, purchasing a couple of presents for his girls to take home, and he then sat in the car waiting for the clock to confirm it was 4pm.

Laura answered the phone within two rings.

"Everything all right, love?" she asked wearily.

"Absolutely fine. She'll be out in ten minutes," Mike assured her. "What time did you finish work?"

"Two. I've just been for a swim, and then I walked home. Did 40 lengths at the baths."

"That's brilliant. Still planking?"

She laughed "Yes, done three today. Do you think I'm doing enough training? Should I be doing any more?"

"To be honest darling, I think you are right on track for the half in September. Keep up what you're doing now, maybe step up your core work, but I think you're doing just fine. Mileage wise, keep to the eight or nine mile mark, maybe increase it to ten in the early summer."

She sighed. "Ok. Has Grace texted you today?"

"Three times. What about you?"

"Three. Bless her. She says she's hungry Mike, can you get her something on the way home?"

He gave a big angry sigh and muttered something under his breath. "Absolutely no problem, I'll take her for tea somewhere. Love you, see you later."

He hung up just as Grace appeared at the window; she waved at him with her gloved hand and opened the door, jumping inside.

"Hi Dad" she said excitedly. "Can we go and get something to eat? I'm starving."

"Sure thing," Mike smiled back at her, as she planted a kiss on his cheek, and they set off for home.

Relationships, he realised, are such complex things. There was a time when he felt like he and Jim would be friends forever, and now Mike thought the man was a comparative stranger. Maybe Jim had been putting on an act all these years, because the man Mike saw now, was a dark, hollow shadow of his former self. He wore an expression of guilt and regret on his weary face that afternoon, a screaming child in his arms, and two days' worth of stubble on his chin. Had the gamble of leaving Laura, and running off with his daughter's teacher, backfired? He wondered long and hard about it. But times had moved on, Laura was his, and Grace too, for the most part, most certainly in her heart she was. Mike prided himself on his loyalty to the family, promising it would always be that way.

The Trotters, Carol and Ron spent New Year's Eve together, in their now traditional style and even Trudy and Helene had stopped by earlier on in the evening, on the way to a party at the local wine bar.

The only member of the club who was absent, was Matt. He had a prior engagement which involved baby oil and easily removable clothes, so made his apologies, promising to drop by later on, if he could.

Carol had indeed insisted on making a punch, but it sat safely on the cupboard top in the kitchen, out of Humphrey's way. He seemed somewhat disgruntled by this, but Mike assured him it was for the best.

Laura and Pam spent most of the evening talking about their training, and Beige Keith and his wife were deep in conversation with Ron about the wonders of Ebay and the amazing array of running gear available to purchase on it.

Mike flitted from one conversation to another, finally settling next to his mother-in-law at the kitchen table.

Slightly mellow from the punch, he put his hand on her shoulder and sat down.

"I'm just off for a fag, actually darling. Fancy a whisky when I come back in?" She went to put on her coat.

"You know what? I'll come with you," Mike quickly wrapped Laura's scarf around his neck, and to his surprise, Carol passed him her coat.

"Put that on," she barked. "Bloody freezing out there. I'll get Ron's coat."

He wasn't about to argue, A) because he thought it was quite funny, and B) because you never argued with Carol.

So there the two of them stood, on a freezing cold patio, Mike in a pink glittery scarf and white fur coat. Carol had thought it so funny that to complete the look had stuck a Santa hat on his head.

"Beautiful darling.....just.....beautiful." She took her silver cigarette case out of her pocket and lit it.

Mike smiled and winked at her.

"Suits you," she added pointing a slightly pissed finger in his direction. "Do you know something. She should have married you years ago, before that other arsehole." She took a deep long drag and blew it out over the garden.

"Well, at least we've got each other now Carol, better late than never."

"Too bloody right. Jim's full of regrets, it sounds like. Too late now. Reap what you sow in this life Mike. End of," she snapped.

She was right of course.

She finished her cigarette and they went back inside, to find Laura and Pam in the kitchen, laughing hysterically at the sight of him in a ladies' fur coat.

CHAPTER TEN

It had been a particularly hard winter, but it gave way to a fresh and colourful spring. Training had been reasonably tough throughout the colder months, and they had met at the local nature reserve for long runs when it was icy underfoot. Snow had been plentiful, but illness had evaded them all to a large extent, apart from the odd cough and cold. As individuals they were physically and mentally stronger to stand up to the challenges of half marathon training, and felt better for it. Pam was noticeably slimmer and more toned, choosing to lay off the ginger biscuits until the end of September. Beige Keith was still his slim, lithe self, and had cheered their winter runs with his colourful attire. They were well on target.

It was late April, and they met at Trentham Gardens for what would be their longest run yet. Mike had called them all together, as the day promised to be cloudy and dry, but with a cool light breeze. Perfect conditions.

The five friends met at the entrance, ready for the task ahead. A wire fairy sculpture hovered over them, and Laura fancied it was listening to their plans.

"Right," said Mike, clapping his hands together. "Today, we are attempting our longest yet, and I thought here would be the best place for it," he checked his sports watch. "Ten miles is our target. Is everybody ok and ready to go? Any problems, just shout. Remember your training, pace yourselves, run the mile you're in, stay hydrated, and don't forget to keep popping those glucose sweets just before you need them."

His audience nodded nervously, but seemed determined and up for the challenge. If they could nail this, Lake Vrynwy 'half' was in their grasp.

The breeze increased slightly, promising to keep them cool when things got tougher. Pam and Laura looked serious but focused, and Keith was sporting shorts again, assured that April was not the time for wasps. Matt and Mike set off in front, looking back regularly to make sure all was well.

Happily, they covered the first four miles with relative ease; Laura and Pam stayed together as always, Mike and Matt ahead, with Keith in the middle. On their second lap of the lake, Pam seemed to be flagging slightly, so she and Laura speed-walked a short while, whilst the men slowed their pace to accommodate. It was important, Mike felt, that they all stuck together on this one.

After a drink and a couple of sweets, Pam found another burst of energy, and they entered into mile six and seven. The end was fairly near, and the girls started talking about a trip to the café afterwards for a flavoured latte, and possibly a sneaky doughnut. Mike couldn't help wonder why these two always talked about food on their runs.

He looked at his watch, nearly mile nine. The sweat was now pouring off them, their faces red and strained.

"Is everyone still ok?" he shouted.

"Just keep going, can't stop now. Nearly there," Laura sounded exhausted.

It was true, but the last mile seemed to drag on forever. Mike checked his watch more frequently, but the sweat was blinding him, and he wiped his forehead.

Laura and Pam were quiet now, concentrating on the task ahead of them.

"Hurry up and tell me we're nearly bloody finished because I can't last much longer," gasped Pam, who was noticeably struggling.

"My hips are killing," complained Keith, his face the colour of a fine merlot.

"Half a mile to go," Mike shouted to anyone that happened to be listening. Matt, although the youngest and probably the strongest physically in the group, carried a pained but determined expression on his face, and Mike could see the sweat running down his back. This was a mental and physical test for them all.

After what seemed like an eternity, Mike held up his hand and motioned them to stop. They had indeed ran ten whole miles without stopping.

"Stretch now, everyone," he gasped.

The tired but happy runners relieved their muscles as best they could. Hearts raced still, and blood pumped fast around their bodies; joints ached in a way that only runners now how. It is an unusually happy place to be.

Hugging each other, Mike gave them all a pep talk, and promised that the coffee and doughnuts were all on him. He was so very proud of these people. His mind flashed forward in time to September, and he could foresee the five of them triumphant again, after completing their first half marathon.

"Let's go and get something totally delicious, from Totally Delicious," Laura beamed, happy with herself and those around her, and they headed off in the direction of the café.

Coffee and doughnuts ended up being coffee and bacon sandwiches, which were devoured quickly. Pam decided to hell with the 'no biscuit rule' and had four with another coffee. Laura, Keith and Mike then polished off large pieces of cake.

"Well done, everyone, that was pretty amazing," Keith beamed. He was very proud of his friends. "So, what now, Boss?"

They all looked towards Mike for guidance.

"Right, then. Well, we've all proved to ourselves that we can do it, haven't we? We can run 10 miles. So, a half, as we know is 13.1. We have five months now to keep on top of things. Carry on with your core work, keep cross training, get plenty of rest, obviously, as it's just as important as your training. I think some 8 or 9 milers mixed with a few taper runs over the summer should do it. Maintain your fitness levels. We'll be just fine. Watch out for over-doing it though, we don't want any injuries. If you feel anything hurting, get yourselves off to the sports physio." He stopped suddenly. Here he was giving advice to a group of people; but he was no expert. The realisation that they were hanging on his every word hit him like a brick. He took a deep breath as his confidence dropped out of him. Laura saw it immediately and put her hand on his.

"Listen, folks. I'm not an expert in this, but I have been running for a long time. I'm giving you the best advice to my knowledge, it worked for me, and I just hope it's going to work for you. Sorry."

"Mike, you've got us this far. Look where we were in the beginning. Five-k and I thought I'd climbed bloody Everest. Look at us now. We value your experience, whatever it may be. We can all do this, whatever plan we follow, we can do it. We're with you all the way." Pam's face was serious but full of admiration.

Matt and Keith agreed.

Despite the fact that their leader wasn't as he said, an expert, they had indeed come a very long way, not only as individuals, but as a team, and it was largely due to the fact that Mike Snow believed in them, and had never let go of that. Through thick and thin, bad weather, family crisis, wasp stings, illness and injury, he had always been there. Now here he was, having a wobble. It was their turn to support him, in his time of need, and so they did.

"Thanks guys. I just want to do right by you, that's all."

"You do Boss, every day." Keith put a hand on his friend's shoulder. "We can do this."

CHAPTER ELEVEN

It is true, that as we get older, the seasons go faster, and Spring gave way to the most beautiful Summer in what seemed like a heartbeat.

Soon, Laura thought, it would be her birthday again, and she watched as her daughter started to blossom into a young lady, and her husband began to grey slightly at the temples. In some ways, the passing of time was a good thing, but for the most part, it saddened her greatly, because it went too quickly. She was in her early forties now, and rapidly approaching the time in her life where her body would start to change, and she was conscious of this. Grace was soon to embark on something similar, her whole life ahead.

She tried to focus on what was wonderful and positive in her life, and busied herself with training and preparation for the half marathon which was fast approaching. They had literally six weeks to go, and Laura felt her heart beat faster at the very thought of it. She was proud of herself and of the group for what they had already achieved. Her husband, the driving

force behind the Trentham Trotters, who was normally a strong leader, had wobbled, temporarily. The fact that everyone had held him up, metaphorically speaking, during this time was testament to the fact that he was well loved, and admired. Not once, even in her head had she ever thought they couldn't do it, the half marathon. They trained hard, stayed focused and dedicated even during the cold winter months when it was a test of mental strength as much as physical.

Six weeks was all they had left.

Six weeks until they ran 13.1 miles.

Bloody hell.

She tried to push it out of her mind, and busied herself at work. She and Trudy had three weddings to do, one after the other, and it was hectic, but Laura was glad of it. Every time she thought about the race now, her stomach lurched.

She guessed that the weather would be good, due to the fact that they had enjoyed a lovely summer, but secretly she wished for a cooler 14 degrees, high cloud and a good breeze. If it decided to drizzle slightly, then that would be fine too.

Catching sight of herself in the large silver framed mirror, she stopped and looked.

'Early forties now, Laura. Time is ticking away.'

* * *

Mike thought it a very good idea to do a long run in that six week period running up to the event. One more 10 miler, he decided would be good, then some taper runs of six to eight miles should just about clinch it.

He was sitting in the staff room at work, alone with his thoughts. A coffee sat steaming on the table next to him. Wisps of the hot liquid swirled up into the air, and disappeared. It smelled divine, and he couldn't wait for it to cool slightly so he could drink it. He found it comforting and uplifting, both at the same time.

He sighed deeply. The nerves were starting to kick in. In six weeks' time, he would be taking his friends to North Wales to run a half marathon, and he was terrified. Had he trained them properly? Were they ready? Would he feel dreadfully responsible if one of them had to drop out? And what if they got injured? Was a ten mile run this week too much? Should they taper instead?

He muttered a mild expletive under his breath and drank half his coffee. It was hot and sweet – comforting. He breathed in the aroma and smiled to himself.

'We're all going to do just fine,' he thought to himself.

* * *

One particularly dull Friday evening in late August, Mike assembled the Trotters for their last long run.

"Now then, is everyone ok?" he asked, checking there were no illnesses or injuries lurking in the background.

Everyone nodded.

"How do you all feel about tonight, are you happy to do it?"

Pam and Laura looked at each other, but the general feeling was positive. They nodded again.

"Listen. If any one of you, at any time, feels like

they can't or don't want to do this, then you must say so. I don't want to force anybody to do what they don't want to. I won't be offended, nor will the others. The most important thing is your health. As long as you are happy, mentally and physically to carry this through, then that's great, but if not, please say."

Laura was conscious of the fact that Mike was rambling and repeating himself, but she could see where he was coming from, and smiled at him.

It was a bit like standing at the altar and asking if anyone had a reason why the bride and groom should not be married. Mike waited and looked at them all in turn. He nodded and smiled.

"Ok everyone. Let's do this. Then it's tapering all the way until the big day. Happy with that?"

The mood picked up then, and they braced themselves for the journey ahead. It was street running tonight, and Pam enjoyed it because she could look into people's houses and get tips on interior design. She was in the process of redecorating her lounge, so to keep her mind off the mileage, she busied herself with bagging the neighbours. By the time they had covered six miles, she had picked throws, cushions and a rather nice sofa, not to mention the colour of her walls.

As the group ran comfortably into mile seven, Laura dropped back, noticeably struggling. They slowed down to accommodate her and Mike ran over, offering a couple of energy sweets.

"You all right love? What's wrong?"

"Yeah, no, honestly I'm absolutely fine. I'm just really hungry all of a sudden and my energy dropped through my boots."

He offered her a drink, which seemed to bring

everything back up to acceptable levels. They agreed that she must have been dehydrated, and soldiered on.

Pam looked concerned, and put her hand on Laura's arm as they ran together again.

"It's ok Pam, honestly. My sugar levels just went south, feel fine now," she smiled.

She felt herself blush as Pam's stare seemed to scan her brain to see what was going on inside it.

Mile eight, and nine felt reasonably comfortable to the group, or as comfortable as it could do when you have pounded the streets for nearly two hours, but the last mile was always the hardest. When Mike put up his hand to say that their target had been reached, Matt, Keith, Laura and Pam breathed a sigh of relief.

"Bloody hell mate, found that hard…has to be said," Matt said bending over, his hands on his knees.

It was on the tip of Pam's tongue to say, "I bet all your customers say that," but she bit her lip, so as to not embarrass him. He was blissfully unaware that she knew what he did for a living. Mike and Beige Keith exchanged a knowing glance and a wry smile.

Laura tried desperately to keep a straight face and turned away. It occurred to her that it was a bad choice of words on Matt's part. Visions popped into her head that she was keen to dismiss.

"Pint anyone?" she asked cheerily, changing the subject.

A general murmur of agreement went round, so after a good few stretches they piled into the local watering hole for a well-earned drink.

The men chose three pints of the best beer, but Pam and Laura opted for lime and soda. "Plenty of ice!" Pam requested, and drank it thirstily, going swiftly back for a second, returning to the table with ten bags of crisps.

"So, how did that feel?" asked Mike after downing half of his beer.

"Apart from the usual aches, I'm bearing up pretty well," said Pam industriously working her way through her second packet of crisps. "Never been so fit in my life!" she added stuffing another smoky bacon snack into her mouth.

"That's great, Pam," smiled Mike. "Everyone else?"

Each of them in turn confirmed that despite the fact that it was hard, and they were tired, the only thing they had to complain about was aching hips and feet.

'What a very long way they had come in twelve months or so,' he thought to himself. How much fitter, and slimmer they were too. He was proud.

"Laura, how are you coping with the training?" Matt asked. He was referring to the dip in her energy levels a couple of hours before.

She shuffled in her seat slightly, and scratched her eyebrow. Mike knew her well enough by now that this was something she did when she was nervous.

"Yeah, good," she replied quietly. "Looking forward to the actual race now. Bit nervous about it to be honest."

"We are going to be just fine," Beige Keith reassured her. "We Trotters are made of tough stuff!" He did a little fist pump, but felt awkward about it, so picked up his pint instead.

"The nerves are bound to get us in the next few weeks, guys. Don't let them ruin the day though. Once we start the race, we will be ok. Remember, just run the mile you're in." Mike tried to lighten the mood around the table, but it was evident that tensions were bubbling under the surface.

"We've come this far…come a long way, in fact, all of us. Can't give up now," Laura said.

Mike smiled at her. He stood up and stretched, his legs were feeling sore. "Another drink anyone?"

CHAPTER TWELVE

The following weeks seemed to drag, but then race packs arrived, and it was at this time excitement took over the nerves. *'Always the same,'* Mike thought. As soon as the package landed on your doorstep was when it felt real, and he was once again like a kid in a sweetshop. Text messages flew between the Trotters that day in an upbeat and positive way.

Pam had her bag packed three weeks before, but couldn't make her mind up what she was going to wear.

"I'm thinking shorts, but then it might be a bit nippy, so I don't know, what do you think about capri tights? Do you reckon full length tights would be too hot?" She talked quickly and excitedly to Mike as they made a patient's bed one morning.

The doctors were doing their rounds, and the ward was busy.

"Shorts," Mike confirmed. "You'll get too hot otherwise. I tried doing Shrewsbury half in full running tights once, regretted it five miles in. Always race in shorts now."

Pam thought this was a great idea. Their patient listened eagerly to the conversation between the two nurses.

"You doing a running race are you?" he asked.

"Yes Cyril, Lake Vyrnwy Half Marathon," Mike replied proudly. "Only a matter of weeks now."

"Hmmm," the man screwed up his face in distaste. "Want to be careful of that running lark, bad for your knees, you know. And I've heard of people dropping dead from heart attacks on them as well. You want to watch out."

Pam and Mike stopped and looked at each other. "Thanks for that vote of confidence Cyril, that's really filled us full of positive energy and good vibes," Pam replied, trying her hardest to be diplomatic.

"Just saying." The old man pulled his dressing gown tighter around him and sniffed.

Mike forced a broad grin "Time for your meds Cyril. Then you're booked in for a colonoscopy at four."

'There was something very satisfying about that last line,' Mike thought. Very satisfying indeed.

The old man looked nervously at him and shuffled in his seat.

* * *

"Can we come and watch you on this one?" asked Trudy two weeks before the big day.

"Oh yes I think so, if you want to, there are plenty of spectators at the start and finish line, and a few pockets of people around the course," Laura confirmed. She was holding three pink roses in her hand, ready to start a bouquet.

"We'll be there then. Be a nice day out. Sure there's a tea room where we can get something to eat while we wait for you."

"Oh there is, and they lay on cake and sandwiches in the village hall apparently, so we won't go hungry!" Laura's mind yet again was firmly on food. It had been that way for some time now, and she had put on a little weight.

"We ok to come on the mini bus with you?" Trudy asked hopefully.

"Yes of course, plenty of room. But we aren't letting Beigey drive it," they both laughed. "He's like Toad of Toad Hall when he gets behind the wheel!" Laura cast her mind back to their first trip to Vyrnwy and she shuddered.

"We'd all like to arrive there alive and in one piece," she added and headed into the office to make tea for them both.

* * *

Their last run before the half marathon was a quiet one. A general air of positivity and determination settled quietly between them, and on the Wednesday evening, they set off together with only one member missing. Pam had to work, but would do her final training run on her own the following day.

It was decided beforehand that seven miles would be adequate. These days, Mike was taking a bit of a back seat with the decision making, leaving it up to the group as a whole to make their own minds up about distance and training. They were seasoned runners now, quietly confident and no longer always looking to him for advice. This secretly pleased Mike, it was like watching birds fly the nest. His mind wandered and he thought of them all running the London Marathon in years to come. They were capable of great things, the Trentham Trotters, a group united by strength, determination, friendship and a steadfast love of running.

The adrenalin finally kicked in and they disappeared off into the distance together, the sun just starting to set over the hill.

They were ready.

RACE DAY

Laura was thankful that the race did not start until 1pm that afternoon. She had woken at 6am feeling so very nervous that nausea had kicked in. Mike brought her some toast and a cup of tea in bed, which she ate cautiously.

"What time is Matt coming with the bus?" she asked her husband.

"Not until 10.30. We've got plenty of time. Still raining here though. Don't know what it's going to be like weather wise over there. Just hope not too wet." He sat on the bed next to her.

The toast and tea had settled her stomach and she felt better. The previous night had been their usual carb fest, consisting of large amounts of pasta, which thankfully the whole family loved.

Humphrey jumped onto the bed, and looked longingly at Laura's now-empty plate. She apologised to him for not leaving any, and got up, heading for the shower.

Mike made the bed and laid out their running kits,

side by side, a ritual he liked to keep. The bag was packed ready, and he went in to wake Grace.

He was feeding Sidney and Hump their breakfast when a shout came from upstairs.

"Oh no, bugger! I don't bloody believe it!" Laura stood at the top of the stairs in her running kit.

"What's the matter?" Mike called up to her.

"I've ran out of bloody fake tan! Done one leg, and it ran out! Look at me! I'm not running a half marathon with one brown leg and one the colour of a church candle, it just isn't happening," she shouted.

"Look, don't worry, I'll get you some from somewhere, just calm down, it's ok."

Laura looked like she was going to cry.

Grace came into the hallway and laughed. "Oh my God Mum, that looks really funny."

"You are not helping, Grace Eddison. Not one little bit," Laura snapped at her daughter through gritted teeth.

"Maybe Angela has some! Shall I go and see?" Grace had composed herself enough to realise it was a good idea to try and be helpful.

"NO!" Mike and Laura replied in unison.

"I honestly don't think Angela knows what fake tan is, darling let alone have any in her bathroom," Mike said thoughtfully.

"She calls blusher 'rouge' and perfume 'scent' for goodness sake; the woman is stuck in the fifties. You'd shock her too much by asking for something as modern as fake tan," Laura snapped again.

"I'll phone your mother!" Mike had the bright idea that he could be at Carol's in minutes and have the tan on his wife's white leg in no time.

Laura agreed and disappeared back into the bathroom.

* * *

"Luckily, yes I do, Michael," drawled Carol on the other end of the phone. "Don't come over darling, we're setting off soon, be with you a bit early, give Laura a chance to stain her other leg."

Mike thanked his mother-in-law from the bottom of his heart for solving the fake tan crisis and hung up.

"Your mother's coming over in ten minutes; she'll bring some with her," he shouted up the stairs.

"Oh, thank the Lord for that. Thanks love," Laura's muffled voice replied from the other side of the bathroom door.

'Minor crisis sorted,' he muttered to himself and went to finish feeding the pets.

* * *

A little way across town saw Pam in her own bedroom. She had been awake since 4am and had tried on three different running tops and two pairs of tights, opting in the end for shorts, just as Mike had suggested.

Two streets down lived Beige Keith. He now had a wardrobe full of running gear, most of it brightly coloured. He intended today to be lit up like a Christmas tree, and the Union Jack tights came out, because he was feeling particularly patriotic that morning. His wife quickly reminded him though, that he was running in Wales, so he disappeared back upstairs to swap them for the yellow ones.

Four streets away from him, was Matt, still in bed.

His alarm went off noisily and unapologetically at 8am, and threatened to pester him unless he got up and switched it off. He sat up sleepily, swung his legs round, perching on the edge of the bed. His girlfriend stirred sleepily and put the pillow over her head.

He headed for the shower, stumbling and stubbing his toe on the way. He swore under his breath. That was all he needed today of all days, a sore bloody toe whilst running a half marathon.

Ten-thirty am came all too soon, and Matt busied himself picking everyone up. Trudy was there, minus Helene, who had stopped at home to prepare a roast dinner for everyone on their return. Carol and Ron stepped regally onto the bus, the former enjoying a quick cigarette before Laura reminded her mother that they needed to go. Mike, Beige Keith and his wife, Pam, Grace and Humphrey crammed themselves excitedly onto the coach, waving goodbye to their home.

The atmosphere in the bus was jovial and light-hearted, and it wasn't long before they had crossed the Welsh border. The scenery changed subtly, and it had finally stopped raining. Autumn was fast approaching, and as she looked out of the window, Laura could see the odd leaf here and there gently swaying in the breeze, only to drop to the ground with a light crisp 'tap'. All too soon, it would be joined by thousands more, leaving the trees bare against the skyline.

"We're here!" shouted Matt.

Pam's stomach lurched, and she shivered with anticipation and fear; Laura took hold of her hand and squeezed it. "Stick with me, we're gonna be ok," she whispered. In a strange sort of way, Pam's nerves made her feel stronger, protective. They would run together today, as they always did.

There then followed the usual race day ritual, the pinning on of bib numbers, chips inserted carefully into shoes, warming up and a bit of last minute refuelling. Mike looked at his watch, it was quarter to one. His stomach did a huge flip, and he took a deep breath. Only a week before, Laura had said to him not to wait for her, their pace was different, and Mike was physically the better, more seasoned runner. She and Pam would do their normal thing and stay together, he was to run his own race today, see if he could get a PB if everything went in his favour. He was happy with this arrangement only for the fact that she was not running alone. He would have gladly sacrificed a personal best time for her sake.

Beige Keith jogged towards them in his yellow tights and orange top. He looked like a stick of rock. "Group hug! Only ten minutes to go!" They held each other tight, wished one another all the luck in the world. Mike saved the biggest hug for Laura, and he held onto her longer than he realised.

"Just do your best, run the mile you're in. I love you and I'm proud of you," he whispered in her ear.

Tears stung the back of her eyes, and she whispered back. Getting into place, she looked over at the crowd near the start line. She could see her mother and father, Grace, who was holding Humphrey and making him wag his paw at them, and Trudy. To the left of them stood Keith's wife and Matt's girlfriend, their arms folded, a look of trepidation on their faces.

The clock struck one, and they were off. The usual surge of emotion coursed through Laura as she stood waiting to cross the start line on the narrow village lane, and she wiped a familiar tear away from her cheek. It was quickly followed by another one, which she allowed to roll down her face and drop onto the ground. Pam reached over and took her by the hand, and they were off.

There was no sign of the lake at this stage, but it would soon come into view. The weather threatened to be changeable, but they didn't mind. A strong breeze got up as they took a turning left. Mike and Matt disappeared from view, but Keith was clear to see up ahead of them. Laura felt comfortable, her tanned legs were carrying her slowly but steadily. She never warmed up properly until she was three miles in, settling then into a steady rhythm with her trusty friend at her side.

Pam seemed to be doing fine; she popped a cube of jelly-sweet into her mouth and offered Laura one. She took it, despite the fact that she didn't feel the need at this stage. They had 13.1 miles to run, and it was going to get a whole lot tougher than this, so any extra fuel on board would be most welcome.

The scenery was indeed just as stunning as they remembered it. The lake was clear, still and serene. To the side of them was the mountainside, and here and there springs and waterfalls babbled away gently. Laura looked up at the trees, they were so very tall, some of them, towering up high into the sky, looking for all the world like beanstalks, melting into the clouds, only to be met by a big angry giant.

The two women were thankful that the route was fairly flat. It had been a little up and down to start with but nothing they couldn't handle. Laura wondered when Pam would tap her on the arm, and motion to her that it was wee time. A little while yet, she hoped.

The road ahead stretched out long, and Laura couldn't see the end. Mike's mantra was going around in her head, 'run the mile you're in. If it helps, switch your brain off and listen to some music'. So, she did. Her headphones were already plugged into the phone which was strapped to her arm. Quickly selecting her playlist, she stopped thinking about how far they still had to go, and relaxed into the music.

Running steadily into mile five, she felt the familiar tap of Pam's hand. She was glad of it, because she needed to go herself, and a couple of minutes rest would be welcome.

The two women walked up the bank away from the road in search of a private spot. Laura was on look-out first, talking to her friend all the time.

"You feeling ok, Pammy? Going all right?" she asked, feeling the adrenalin still coursing through her veins, excitement in her voice.

Pam let out a long sigh, "Actually fine! Might be a point up ahead where I retract that statement, but at the moment, it's A-OK!"

Great, Laura thought. She was actually starting to get into it seriously now. Her body was warm and raring to go. The sweet had kicked in, and she was already planning another one very soon. She took a swig of her orange drink from the sports bottle, and Pam did the same.

"Ready to go?"

"Yep, let's do it!" and with that the two of them walked back onto the road to join the other runners.

At mile 8, Laura started to notice a subtle change in her body. It was a familiar one on longer runs. She began to feel queasy. Another sweet did not seem at all tempting to her, instead she took a good drink of cordial. Initially, it did not help the sickness in the pit of her stomach, and she panicked slightly. Taking a few deep breaths, she asked Pam if they could walk a little, and her friend was only too keen to comply.

"I just need to get past Mile 8. It's always where I find I hit the wall." She was visibly struggling, but Pam knew her friend very well by now, and saw the determination in her face. She was not going to give up.

Sweat poured down her neck and she could taste the salt as she licked her dry lips. Taking another drink, the sickness subsided, and she was thankful. They were coming into Mile 9, which meant only four more to go. They kept telling each other that they had more road behind them than there was in front. Laura switched off her music, and they talked for a while, in-between brief periods of silence to catch their breath. They were tired. More tired than they had ever been in their lives. Pam's left hip started to ache, and her feet were sore. Laura looked at her sports watch, they were approaching Mile 10.

"Shit," she said suddenly. "Sorry. I'm just so knackered, and every damn thing hurts." She let the tears flow freely down her face, but did not stop running.

"Let's walk a bit then. Have another drink," Pam suggested.

"Ok," Laura replied, sobbing. "You got a tissue?"

"Here. Sorry, it's used." She handed a crumpled excuse for a tissue her way, but Laura was past caring.

Wiping her face with it she started running again. "Pam?"

The older woman nodded, too exhausted and out of breath to answer.

"I've got something to tell you. Only don't say anything to anyone else at the moment, promise?"

Pam nodded again. But she did not look surprised.

* * *

Mike and Matt had finished in 2:32:10, running wearily over the finish line virtually together. The two men hugged, collected their medals from the local Cubs and Beavers who stood patiently handing out the race bling. Beige Keith came over the finish line fifteen minutes later, running an impressive half in 2:47:06. His face was so red he now resembled one of those striped ice lollies that Grace was so very fond of.

Their attention soon diverted as to where the girls were, and after congratulating each other on finishing the race, they looked in earnest at the steady stream of runners still coming over the finish line, but neither Laura nor Pam were among them.

Three hours had passed, and still no sign.

Mike started to panic. It was now 4.15 in the afternoon, and there was no sign of his wife and friend.

"Look, hold my stuff for me, I'm going to look for them. If there's a problem, I'll give you a ring," he said quickly to Keith. Grabbing his phone and putting it in the back pocket of his running shorts, he set off.

Keith, Trudy and Carol stood together, waiting. Carol's face darkened.

"There's something wrong. What's bloody wrong?" she shouted.

"It's ok Carol, honestly, everything's fine. Mike's just gone up to see if they're nearly finished." Trudy tried her best to console her, but failed miserably.

"Jeezus," muttered Carol under breath. "I need a bloody fag."

Keith stood patiently by the finish line, waiting. His wife came to stand with him, bringing a change of clothes. He did not take his eyes away from the road ahead. It was now 4.25pm. He shuffled his tired feet, and felt a chill in his bones. Reaching into his sports bag he took out a pair of track suit bottoms and a hoody to wear, all the time staring into the distance. A lump formed in his stomach. It was a feeling of dread.

"Come on, come on girls. Come on!" he whispered under his breath. He was starting to get agitated.

Suddenly, his heart leapt, and Trudy and Carol let out a scream.

"They're coming!!" They're bloody coming!! Look!!" Carol dropped her cigarette on the floor, still lit and ran towards the finish line, her arms outstretched, coat flapping in the air.

"Mum!!" Grace shouted, and burst into tears, running behind her grandmother.

Sure enough, in the distance, the figures of Laura, Mike and Pam could clearly be seen. Barely yards away from the finish line, they looked ready to drop. But they had done it. Mike stepped back and allowed them their moment of glory as the two women held hands and crossed the finish line of Lake Vyrnwy Half Marathon in 3:30:02.

* * *

The atmosphere in the mini bus was significantly lighter on their return home. Laura beamed from ear to ear, and seldom took her eyes off her medal. The striped ribbon hung around her neck and she held the shiny metal disc in her hand. It read 'RanVyrnwy' on the front of it. Well, they certainly had. She put her arm around Grace, snuggled up to Mike and fell asleep for the rest of the journey.

"I don't know about anyone else, but I hope Helene has made a lorry load of Yorkshire puddings. I feel like I could eat that many," said Pam quietly. A ripple of laughter circled the bus.

"Don't worry Pam, we have plenty to go around," Trudy assured her.

Mike relaxed back in his seat, his wife's head on his shoulder. He thought back to the very beginning, when Jim had made his announcement in the pub, and how his heart had secretly leapt with joy.

Mike stared at the road ahead as Matt drove them home.

'I take immense pride in how far we have all come,' he thought, *'and have faith in how far we still have to go.'*

EPILOGUE

FIFTEEN YEARS LATER

An icy cold wind blew on a bright December day. It was a cloudless sky, and a crisp glittering frost had settled on Trentham Gardens like a silver veil.

Mike and Laura looked out together over the lake, the winter sunshine casting a deep yellow hue onto the water.

Laura took a deep breath in. "You ready then?"

"Yes, ready! Can we do just two laps? I've got football training this afternoon."

Mike and Laura's son, Daniel stood in front of them, tall for his age, but strong and muscular. He was the image of his father, only with more hair, but the twinkle in his eyes was most certainly all from his mother.

Grace, now in her twenties, got up from the bench she was sitting on.

"Come on, little brother!" she teased. "Beat you to the café! Last one buys the coffees!"

271

Mike smiled. Never a day went by that he didn't look at his family and be thankful for all that he had. From the very beginning, from the moment he first set out to win her heart.

He was always going to be in it for the long run.

THE END

ACKNOWLEDGEMENTS

Without the help, love and support from the following people, this book would never have been possible.

To my dearest friends Karen and Alastair Shakeshaft, Emma Collins, Vickie Guthrie, Lauren Ellerton, James and Kirsty Partington, Lesley Hall, Hilary Venables, Laura Turner, Joey Jordan, Elkie Brooks and the wonderful team at Jordan Joseph. Helen Nuttall, Rachel Clegg, Rose Hall, Lorna Sowry, Angie and Malcolm Waugh, Anne McCarrol, Brad Fitt and the lovely Mr Stewart Bint.

Gratitude also to Grant Mantle, my new friend at Trentham Gardens, also Lizzie Thompson, Emma Batkin and Antonia Gentile. Grateful thanks to my friend Matt Bowman for the advice on half marathon training, and to Mike McSharry for his invaluable insight into the Lake Vrynwy Half.

To my new, but already great friend and screenwriter Vikki Thomas, for her support, trust and belief that between us, we can make great things happen. Here's to some wonderful times ahead.

Thanks as always to my Drama Wine Club girls, Ali, Kitty, Becky and Michelle, I love you all.

To Sue Miller, Alan Jones, and John Evans from Team Author, thank you guys, what would I do without you; thank you so much for putting up with me.

My gratitude also to two wonderful actors who inspired this book in the first place. Jason Watkins, probably one of the best actors this country has. The character of Mike Snow was written for you. To Haydn Gwynne, who not only had me in fits of hysterics with her characterisation of Camilla in "The Windsors" but inspired the character of Carol in the story.

To my amazing dad Harry, who never stops believing in me. My best friend and my rock.

To my husband Richard and daughter Freya, with my love always, and thank you so much for your patience and understanding.

Finally, to Lola my dog, for being extra patient waiting for walkies whilst I finished another chapter, and one of the coolest cats ever to grace this planet, Shackleton, for inspiring the character of Sidney Greenstreet.

ABOUT THE AUTHOR

AV Turner was born and raised in Nottingham. Shortly after she moved to Shropshire in 2002, she gave up her 26 year career as a stage actor to concentrate on having a family. She now divides her time between being a busy mum, housewife and writer.

A keen runner since 2012, she regularly enjoys 10k and 5k races, and plans to run her first half marathon before she is 55.

Follow AV Turner for updates on her books:

Facebook: AVTurnerAuthor
Instagram: AVTurnerAuthor
Twitter: @AVTurnerAuthor